P9-CLB-588

SEEKERS
GREAT BEAR LAKE

Explore the World of ERIN HUNTER

SEEKERS

Book One: The Quest Begins

WARRIORS

Book One: Into the Wild
Book Two: Fire and Ice
Book Three: Forest of Secrets
Book Four: Rising Storm
Book Five: A Dangerous Path
Book Six: The Darkest Hour

WARRIORS: THE NEW PROPHECY

Book One: Midnight
Book Two: Moonrise
Book Three: Dawn
Book Four: Starlight
Book Five: Twilight
Book Six: Sunset

WARRIORS: POWER OF THREE

Book One: The Sight
Book Two: Dark River
Book Three: Outcast
Book Four: Eclipse
Book Five: Long Shadows

WARRIORS MANGA

The Lost Warrior
Warrior's Refuge
Warrior's Return
The Rise of Scourge
Tigerstar and Sasha #1: Into the Woods
Tigerstar and Sasha #2: Escape from the Forest

WARRIORS SPECIALS

Warriors Super Edition: Firestar's Quest
Warriors Field Guide: Secrets of the Clans
Warriors: Cats of the Clans

SEEKERS

GREAT BEAR LAKE

ERIN
HUNTER

HARPERCOLLINS*PUBLISHERS*

Great Bear Lake

Series created by Working Partners Limited

 For information address HarperCollins Children's Books, a division of HarperCollins Publishers, 1350 Avenue of the Americas, New York, NY 10019.
www.harpercollinschildrens.com

Library of Congress Cataloging-in-Publication Data

Hunter, Erin.

Great Bear Lake / Erin Hunter. — 1st ed.

p. cm. — (Seekers ; [bk. 2])

Summary: Three bear cubs of different species are united for the first time as they begin their long journey in search of destiny, hope, and what it truly means to be a bear in the wild.

ISBN 978-0-06-087125-3 (trade bdg.)

ISBN 978-0-06-087126-0 (lib. bdg.)

[1. Bears—Fiction. 2. Fantasy.] I. Title.

PZ7.H916625Gr 2009 2008045067

[Fic]—dc22 CIP

AC

Typography by Hilary Zarycky

1 2 3 4 5 6 7 8 9 10

❖

First Edition

Special thanks to Cherith Baldry

Seal Rock
Walrus Rock
Place of the Caribou Flat-faces
Place of Everlasting Ice
LAST GREAT WILDERNESS
BLACKWATER MOUNTAINS
Place of Fishing Flat-faces
Ice Break River
Snowgoose Island
Caribou Valley
Bear Rock
Great Bear Lake
Paw Print Island
SMOKE MOUNTAINS
Big River
The Claw Path
Place o
Metal Bir
SKY RIDGE
TOKLO'S BIRTHDEN
Bear Snout Mountain
Three Lakes
SilverPath
LUSA'S BEAR BOWL
Great Salmon River

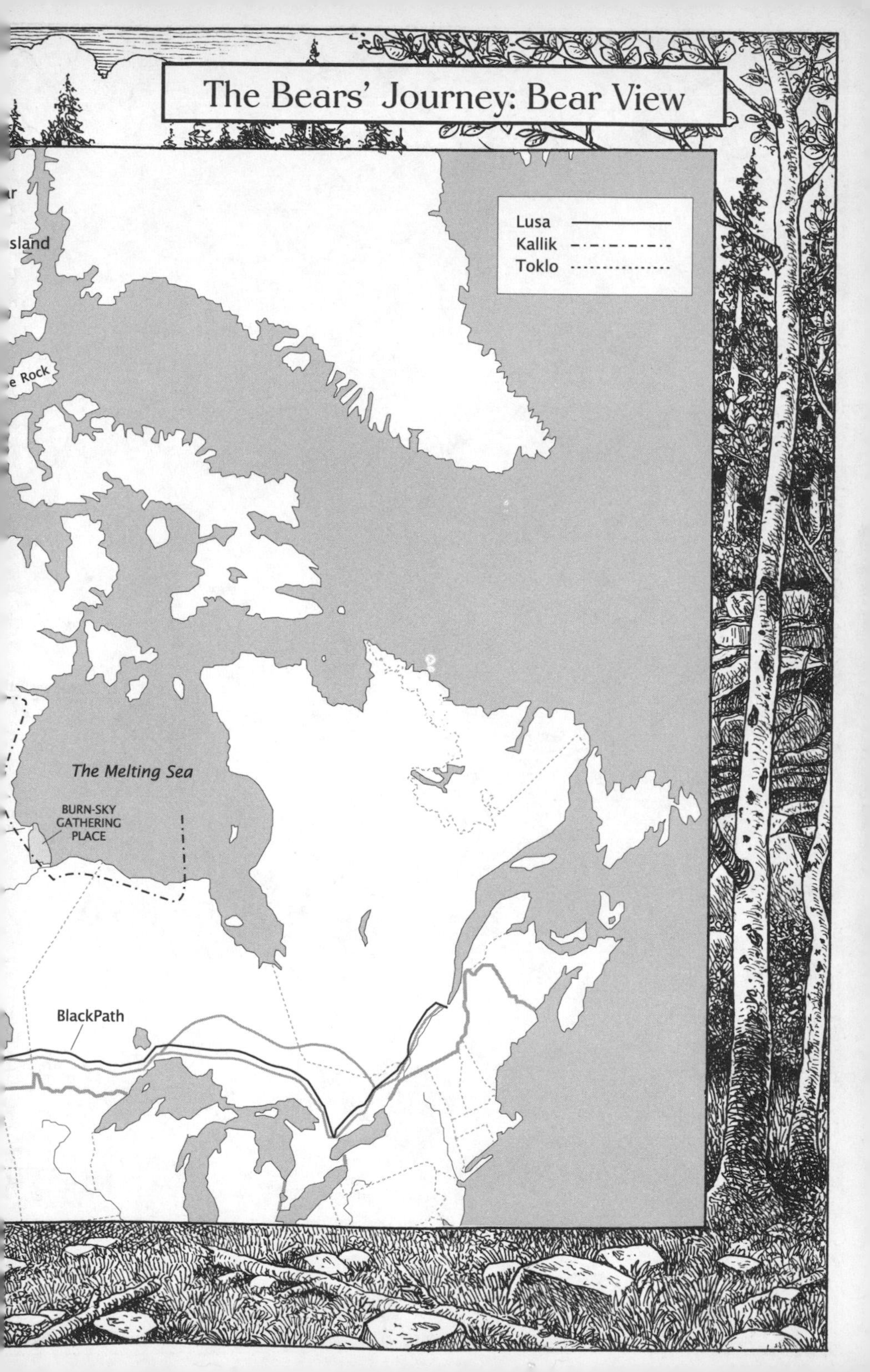
The Bears' Journey: Bear View
Lusa
Kallik
Toklo
The Melting Sea
BURN-SKY GATHERING PLACE
BlackPath

0
800 mi
0
1200 km
Arctic Sea
QUEEN ELIZABETH ISLANDS
Arctic Village
Beaufort Sea
BROOKS RANGE
ARCTIC NATIONAL WILDLIFE REFUGE
Kaktovik
Parry Channel
BANKS ISLAND
Atigun Pass
Alaska
VICTORIA ISLAND
Fairbanks
Yukon River
MACKENZIE MOUNTAINS
Mackenzie River
Superstition Island
Anchorage
Great Bear Lake
Gulf of Alaska
Whitehorse
Yellowknife
Great Slave Lake
Juneau
ROCKY MOUNTAINS
Prince Rupert
CANADA
Pacific Ocean
REVELSTOKE NATIONAL PARK
Edmonton
Calgary
VANCOUVER ZOO
Vancouver
Regina
Canadian Pacific Railw
Seattle
Helena
Portland
Columbia River
UNITED

The Bears' Journey: Human View
GREENLAND
Godthab
BAFFIN ISLAND
Iqaluit
Atlantic
Ocean
Hudson Bay
St. John's
WAPUSK
NATIONAL
PARK
Quebec
Montreal
Trans-Canada
Highway
Ottawa
Boston
Toronto
St. Paul
Minneapolis
New York

CHAPTER ONE

Lusa

Lusa stared at the grizzly cub. He was twice her size; in the struggle when she was trapped under his weight, she had thought he would kill her for sure. But she wasn't scared of him now, as she watched him crouched in front of her with his flanks heaving. Red light from the setting sun trickled through the leaves, speckling Toklo's brown pelt with spots of burning russet.

She had found Oka's missing cub.

I could have searched for him all my life and never found him. Did the spirits guide me?

Toklo glared at her. "How do you know my name?"

"I—I've been looking for you," Lusa stammered. "I've come all the way from the Bear Bowl—"

"The Bear Bowl?" Toklo curled his lip. "What's that?"

"It's a place where bears live," Lusa explained, on more confident territory now. "Black bears like me, and grizzlies, and huge white bears. Flat-faces feed us and mend us when we get sick, and other flat-faces come and look at us. There are other animals, too," she added. "Tigers, and flamingos, and animals with long, dangly noses."

Toklo interrupted her with a huff of contempt. "You lived with other animals?" he growled disbelievingly. "Flat-faces fed you? Proper bears don't do that. What sort of bear *are* you?"

Lusa felt her belly go tight; he looked really angry, and she knew she wouldn't be able to fight him off a second time. But she had promised Oka that she would pass on her message to her only surviving cub. "The flat-faces brought your mother to the Bear Bowl. She . . . she died there." She decided there was no point making Toklo even angrier by telling him how Oka had been crazed with grief for her lost cubs, so deranged that she had attacked a flat-face. "Before she died she gave me a message for you. She said—"

Toklo turned away. "I don't want to hear it!"

Startled, Lusa took a pace toward him. "But I promised—"

"I said, I don't want to hear it! I don't want to hear anything about that bear. She abandoned me. She is *not* my mother." He stalked away, his paws crunching through the dried leaves until he stopped under a twisted fir tree.

"She was sorry," Lusa murmured.

She didn't think Toklo had heard her. Without looking at her, he snarled, "Go back to the Bear Bowl!"

Lusa blinked, puzzled. She had risked her life to find him, and to tell him what Oka had wanted him to know. She had expected that Toklo would be grateful to her. Maybe he would even become her friend, so she wouldn't be on her own anymore. What had she done to make him so hostile?

She couldn't go back to the Bear Bowl. The wild was bigger

than she had ever imagined, scary and confusing. But it was exciting, too. After the freedom she had known in the last moons, she couldn't think of returning to the little space where two or three trees made a forest. But what would Toklo do if she didn't leave? She clamped her jaws shut to stop a whimper from coming out. There was no way she'd show Toklo how scared she was.

Lusa turned to look at the other brown bear cub, who was sitting watching her with bright interest. She tipped her head on one side, remembering what she had seen just before her struggle with Toklo. She had been chasing a hare, hadn't she? A growl from her belly reminded her that she was hungrier than she'd ever been in her life. She'd been chasing a hare *and it had turned into this cub.*

Her mother hadn't said anything about hares that turned into bears, or any other animal for that matter. Was this a bear, or a hare? Would it change again? Lusa stared at it suspiciously, looking for long ears suddenly shooting up.

The brown cub stood up and padded over to her. He was smaller than Toklo, and his eyes were warm and curious. "My name's Ujurak. You're Lusa, right?"

Lusa nodded. "Are . . . are you a bear or a hare?" she burst out.

Ujurak lifted his shoulder in a shrug, rippling his shiny brown fur. "I don't know," he admitted. "I can be lots of other creatures, too. A salmon, an eagle . . . sometimes I'm a flat-face cub."

Lusa stiffened. Would Ujurak be a kind flat-face like the

feeders in the Bear Bowl, or one of the dangerous ones who shouted and shot their metal sticks? "Why would you want to be a flat-face?"

"I don't exactly want to be anything," Ujurak replied. "Except a bear, of course. It just happens." He glanced at Toklo. "I'm trying to control it, but I'm not very good yet."

"So you're really a bear?" Lusa stretched her head up and checked. His ears were definitely small and round right now, nothing like a hare's.

"I think so." Ujurak blinked. "I hope so."

Lusa looked around. The trees grew close together here, with little room for berry bushes underneath, but there was no scent of flat-faces or dogs. "Is this Toklo's territory?" The big grizzly cub looked quite strong enough to score his claw-marks on the trees and defend his feeding ground from other bears.

"No, we're on a journey." An amber glow lit deep in Ujurak's eyes. "We're going to the place where the bear spirits dance in the sky."

"Where's that?"

Ujurak looked at his paws. *Definitely bear's paws,* Lusa thought. "We don't know exactly," he confessed. "We're following the stars." He looked up again. "But I *have* to get there. However long it takes."

Something in Lusa prompted her to reach up and touch her nose to the cub's furry ear. "You'll find the place, I know you will."

Ujurak turned his head to stare at her. "You understand,

don't you?" he said softly. "Because you kept going until you found Toklo."

Lusa nodded. "I promised Oka that I'd find him, and I did."

"Are you going to come with us?" Ujurak asked. "To the place where the bear spirits dance?"

Lusa wondered if Oka's spirit would be there, and if Oka would tell Toklo herself how much she loved him. Lusa wanted to see that happen more than anything. And she didn't have anywhere else to go. Besides, she'd been good at finding Toklo, hadn't she? Perhaps Ujurak would need her help to find the place he was looking for.

"Yes, I'll come," she announced.

"Great!" yelped Ujurak, bouncing on his front paws. Even though he was younger than Lusa, he was bigger than her, and she took a step back to avoid getting bounced on.

"Do you think Toklo will mind?" she asked, looking at the brown bear standing under the fir tree with his back to them. "He doesn't seem to like me very much."

Ujurak followed her gaze. "Toklo doesn't like anyone very much. Including himself," he commented quietly.

Lusa glanced at him in surprise, but before she could say anything Toklo had swung around and pushed his way out from under the spindly branches. He glared at Lusa. "You can't slow us down," he warned.

Lusa bit back a growl. It wasn't Toklo's journey, it was Ujurak's, so he shouldn't be bossing her around. But she just shook her head. "I'll keep up," she promised. Though she hoped they'd stop to eat soon, because her legs were feeling wobbly underneath her grumbling belly.

Toklo swung his head from side to side. "Why are we standing around here? We need to find shelter for the night." Without another word he headed into the shadows under the trees. Ujurak trotted after him, his stumpy tail twitching.

Lusa stood still for a moment. Was this really what she wanted? Being a wild bear didn't mean traveling who-knew-where with two brown bears, did it? But the only other choice was staying here without them, and she had had enough of being on her own. *Even wild bears have company,* she reminded herself.

"Wait for me!" she called, and bounded off to catch up to her new companions.

Lusa shifted into a more comfortable position and parted her jaws in a huge yawn. Moonlight filtering through the leaves turned her paws to silver. She was curled up in a tree, where two thick branches met the trunk and made a bowl shape just big enough for a small bear.

She knew she ought to go to sleep, but her pelt prickled with curiosity and every time she closed her eyes, excitement made them fly open again. She had found Toklo, but now she was on another journey—and none of them knew exactly where it would lead.

Toklo and Ujurak had squeezed themselves into a hollow beneath the roots of the tree. They weren't asleep, either; Lusa could hear them shifting about and snuffling below her. She caught the deep growl of Toklo's voice, and craned her neck to hear him more clearly.

"This is ridiculous," he was saying. "She can't stay with us."

Lusa's belly clenched with fear. Was Toklo going to leave her behind after all?

I don't care! If they won't let me travel with them, I'll just follow them.

"You said she could come," Ujurak reminded Toklo.

"No I didn't!"

"Well, you didn't say she couldn't."

"I'm saying it now," Toklo replied irritably. "Why should we want a stupid black bear with us? You heard her. She comes from a place where she didn't have to catch her own prey. Flat-faces fed her, and *watched* her. What kind of a bear is that?"

"I think she's interesting," Ujurak replied.

Toklo huffed. "She's only a black bear. She'll just slow us down."

Lusa wanted to jump out of the tree and confront Toklo. She might not have been born in the wild, but she had managed just fine for moons and moons. She *wanted* to be a wild bear, even if it meant never going back to the Bear Bowl, and her family. And black bears were better than grizzlies any day! Her father had said that they were the kings of the forest.

She was bunching her muscles to leap down when Ujurak spoke. His voice was soft, and he sounded older than before.

"I think I was meant to find Lusa. I think she is meant to come with us."

A scoffing noise came from Toklo.

"If she can't keep up, she won't want to stay with us

anyway," Ujurak went on. "But I think the spirits of the bears are waiting for her, just as much as they are waiting for you and me."

Above them, Lusa shivered as she crouched on the edge of her sleeping place, staring down into the bear-scented darkness. Was Ujurak right? Were there bear spirits waiting for her?

But whose—and why?

CHAPTER TWO

Toklo

Toklo shifted restlessly beside Ujurak. The cub was asleep now, letting out gentle snores that fluttered a dead leaf close to his nose. But Toklo's belly churned as if he had eaten rotfood, and he couldn't sleep.

It was all the fault of that black bear! *I don't want her traveling with us.* Envy tore at him like a claw. *Ujurak is* my *friend! Why does she have to come and spoil everything?* He drew his lips back in the beginnings of a growl. If Ujurak and Lusa liked each other so much, they could travel by themselves. He could be free again to take care of himself.

Toklo blew out a gusty sigh. It wasn't as easy as that. Ujurak, curled up in a splash of moonlight, looked small and defenseless; Toklo knew the cub was crazy enough to run into danger without a second thought, let alone what could happen if he turned into the wrong sort of animal. If he continued alone with Lusa, they wouldn't survive more than a couple of sunrises. He needed someone stronger to help him.

Why does it have to be me*?* Toklo shifted again, as if the question was a hard pinecone digging into him. *It doesn't,* said a tiny voice inside him. If he stayed with Ujurak, it would be his decision, no one else's. Toklo looked at Ujurak again. A leaf had drifted down to lie on his shoulder, casting a tiny shadow on his moonlit fur. Toklo remembered another cub covered with leaves—and dirt and sticks as well. His breathing had been soft as moonlight before it faded away, leaving a cold, empty shape beside Toklo.

"I'm sorry, Tobi," Toklo whispered. He had watched his brother die, and left him where their mother buried him. He had abandoned one cub that had needed him; he wasn't going to let that happen again.

But there was still the problem of Lusa. Peering up into the tree, Toklo could just make out the black cub's shape, balanced in a crook between two branches with her nose tucked under her paws. Black bears were weak; everyone knew that. They were always scurrying up trees because they were too scared to sleep on the ground. Lusa was as soft as any of them—softer, probably, because she had let flat-faces take care of her.

Uneasiness stirred in Toklo's mind. Lusa had come all the way from her Bear Bowl to find him; that had taken courage, he admitted grudgingly. *And she knew my mother.*

When he looked at Lusa, Toklo sensed the huge shadow of Oka looming over her. He couldn't see it, but he knew it was there, like the dark part of the moon. *Why did she abandon me? Why couldn't she look after me, like she looked after Tobi?* Toklo dug his claws into the ground. He didn't want to think about

Oka. If Lusa hadn't come, he would have been able to forget all about her.

I wish she would go away and leave us in peace! And I'm not going to listen to her stupid message!

Toklo closed his eyes and scuffled deeper into the dried leaves. But it was a long time before sleep came.

Toklo heaved himself out of the hollow and shook leaves and pine needles out of his fur. Taking a deep breath, he reveled in all the different scents of the forest: leaves, damp earth, a raccoon that had shuffled past during the night. The air was moist, but the threat of rain had passed, and long claws of sunlight pierced the leaves above his head.

"It's a great day for traveling!" Ujurak scrambled out from the shelter of the roots to stand beside Toklo. "Let's go!"

For a heartbeat Toklo hoped that Ujurak had forgotten about Lusa. They could sneak off and leave her asleep in the tree. He huffed in disappointment when Ujurak turned back, rearing up to rest his front paws on the tree trunk.

"Lusa! Hey, Lusa, wake up!"

"Wha . . . ?" The black cub raised her head and peered sleepily at the ground. Her gaze brightened when she spotted Ujurak. "Is it time to go?"

She slithered down the tree and stood beside Ujurak. For a fleeting moment Toklo wished that he could climb as skillfully as Lusa, but he pushed the thought away. Brown bears were strong; they didn't *need* to climb trees.

"Come on," he growled.

He led the way through the forest, padding along softly as he sniffed the air in the hope of prey. The scents of living things—green, furred, and glossy, like berries—flowed around him, drawn up from the ground or wafting down from the trees. He pricked his ears, but the sounds of any small scufflings were drowned out by Ujurak and Lusa bumbling along behind him.

"Quiet!" he snapped, glancing over one shoulder.

A flicker of movement in the corner of his eye alerted him; he swung around to spot a ground squirrel streaking across an open patch of grass. Toklo let out a snarl and took off after it. His outstretched claws brushed its tail just as the squirrel dived into its burrow. Roaring, Toklo dug into the ground with his claws. Soil and scraps of grass flew up around him and stung his eyes.

Then Toklo felt his claws sink into flesh. He snapped the squirrel's neck with a twist of one paw, and dragged it out of the earth. He dropped the limp body at Ujurak's paws. "Let's eat," he said.

As he sank his teeth into the warm body he noticed that Lusa was standing a bearlength away, looking longingly at the food but not moving to take any.

"Come on," Toklo huffed. "You can share."

"Thank you!" Lusa trotted up and crouched down beside Ujurak, tearing off a mouthful of the prey.

With three of them sharing the squirrel, no bear had quite enough. *But that doesn't matter,* Toklo thought. *I can find more.* He licked the warm blood from his snout and padded away to the shade of a tree, leaving his companions to finish the meal he had provided. He sat contented, sniffing the air. He could trace the musky smell of fox on the bark of the tree. It was stale—the fox would be far away by now. He lifted his snout and sniffed deeper, drawing a new and richer scent into the back of his mouth. It was deer: A deer had passed this way less than a sunrise ago. Toklo stood up, drawing in the scent of deer, letting it show him the way to go. He was proud of the senses that told him where to find food or water, or where there might be danger from flat-faces or other bears. Every bend in the way, every hilltop or valley was filled with meaning, like a voice whispering to him without words. Toklo dipped his shoulders.

"Time to move," he said.

"Follow me," Ujurak called. He turned off the trail and bounded up a steep slope, away from the scent of deer.

"Ujurak!" Toklo called. "You're going the wrong way!"

But the little brown cub continued up the slope, kicking up stones and mud behind him.

Toklo looked at Lusa. "Come on!" He didn't want her to think that he disagreed with Ujurak about which way they should go. She needed to understand that he and Ujurak were on the same journey—*their* journey, not Lusa's—and she was just tagging along. Besides, there'd be other deer to catch.

He ran after Ujurak, with Lusa following a short distance behind. As they climbed, the trees gradually gave way to bushes and scrub, and then to a bare mountain slope of broken rocks. Thin grass and an occasional twisted shrub grew in the cracks between the rocks. A stiff breeze drove clouds across the sky; the rocks cast long shadows as the sun dipped toward the horizon.

"Wait for me!" Lusa called.

Ujurak stopped at the top of the slope. He was gazing ahead with the wind buffeting his fur. Toklo climbed up beside him. In front of him, he could see mountain after mountain, like ripples of long grass stretching away into the misty distance. Their rocky peaks formed an unbroken ridge high in the sky. On either side, bare slopes fell away to sunlit lowlands, the shadows of clouds scudding across green woods and fields.

There was a scuffling sound and a patter of small stones as Lusa scrambled up to join them. "We can see the whole world!" she gasped.

She was gazing around her with a mixture of wonder and fear, as if the vastness of the view were going to swallow her up. Toklo almost felt the same—compared with the sweep of ground in front of them, they were just tiny fleabites—but he pushed the thought away. Brown bears weren't scared of mountains!

"Are we heading down there?" he asked Ujurak.

The smaller cub shook his head. "Our way lies along the Sky Ridge."

"What?" Toklo gazed along the line of rocky peaks that stretched into the distance as far as he could see. "But there's no prey up here. There's nowhere to shelter—"

"We still have to go this way," Ujurak insisted.

"How do you know?" Lusa asked curiously.

"I don't *know*," Ujurak replied. "I'm not even sure exactly where we're going. But there are signs I can read, and they tell me that up here we're on the right path."

Toklo rolled his eyes. Bears looked for places where they would be safe, and where there was plenty to eat. Anything else was just cobwebs and moonshine. *So why are you following him?* a small voice inside him asked; Toklo did his best to ignore it.

"What sort of signs?" Lusa persisted.

Ujurak's eyes were puzzled. "They could be anything . . . a tree, the scent of water, the way moss grows on a rock . . . I don't really know how I know, but I understand what I have to do. And most of all, I follow the Pathway Star."

"The Pathway Star!" Lusa started as if a snake had reared up in front of her. "Do you mean the Bear Watcher? He helped me when I was looking for Toklo."

Toklo stifled a snort of contempt.

Ujurak turned to face the Sky Ridge. "Even when the star is hidden in the sky, I can feel it there, tugging at my fur. . . ." His voice died away.

"I've felt that, too, exactly the same!" Lusa responded with an excited little bounce. "Maybe we were following the same star! Maybe I was meant to come on this journey, and that's why I was able to find Toklo."

"And maybe both of you have bees in your brain," Toklo interrupted. His fur felt hot with resentment at the way the two cubs were digging up things in common—things that he knew were nonsense. The only thing they had in common was that they spent too much time dreaming. He knew which star they were talking about, but it wasn't leading them anywhere. It lived alone, circled by hostile stars that wouldn't let it rest. He knew how that felt, too.

"Are we going to stand here until we start to grow moss?"

Ujurak gave him an affectionate poke with his snout. "No, we're going now." He began to lead the way along the ridge.

Though Toklo had been uneasy about Ujurak's choice of path, in the days that followed he grew more used to the vast stretches of land spread out on either side of their mountain trail, and the feeling of wind buffeting his fur with nothing but the wide sky overhead. His big worry was the shortage of prey; they lived on roots and insects grubbed up from the scant soil between the boulders, or now and again berries from thornbushes rooted in cracks. Pangs of hunger gripped Toklo's belly from morning to night. At least the black bear didn't complain, but then she was smaller than he was, so she didn't need to eat as much anyway.

Several sunrises into their journey, when the moon had swelled to twice the size it had been when they left the forest behind, the path led them onto a narrow ledge; sheer, spiky rocks stretched upward on one side, while the ground fell away in a dizzying precipice on the other. Toklo led the way. Glancing behind to check on the others, he noticed that Lusa had dropped back a few paces. She was staring up at the sky.

"What's that bird up there?" she called, tilting her muzzle

toward the small dark brown shape hovering far above.

"A golden eagle," Ujurak replied. "I turned into one once, when we were hunting a goat. I caught it, too."

"You mean that bird's big enough to catch a goat?" Lusa gasped, still gazing up at the distant shape of the eagle. "It looks so tiny!"

"That's because it's a long way away, butterfly-brain," Toklo cut in. "Up close, it's big enough to catch nosy, chattering black bear cubs."

Lusa stared at him, her eyes huge, as if she weren't sure if he meant what he said. Then she relaxed. "You would be racing for cover if there was any danger," she pointed out. "If it's big enough to catch me, it's big enough to hurt you. We're all safe as long as the eagle stays up in the sky."

"It's okay," Ujurak said, brushing her pelt reassuringly. "When I was being the eagle, I could tell what they think, what kind of animals they like to hunt. They don't mess with bears unless they're really tiny."

"If you're quite ready, can we keep going?" Toklo chafed. The sun was going down in a blaze of fire that stretched right across the sky. He wanted to get off the ledge and find a place to shelter before it was completely dark.

But almost as soon as they set off again, Toklo's paw scuffed against a loose stone at the edge of the path. It fell over the precipice; at once a harsh cry came from below, and the strong beating of wings. A second eagle rose into the sky.

Toklo risked a glance over the edge. A bearlength below was a narrow ledge where three large eggs lay in a twiggy nest.

One each, he thought, his belly rumbling as he imagined the warm tasty stickiness sliding down his throat. It didn't look too hard to climb down; there were pawholds and—

"Toklo!" Ujurak squealed.

Another harsh squawk sounded close above his head. The mother eagle had gained height and was swooping down on him, talons extended; Toklo jumped back from the edge just as he felt the wind of her wings in his fur. Looking up, he saw that the other eagle, the one Lusa had spotted, was plummeting down to join his mate. Toklo huffed in alarm when he realized how big they were close-up.

"Get back!" he ordered the others.

Ujurak shoved Lusa into a cleft between two rocks, and squashed himself in after her. Toklo stood in front of them, rearing up on his hindpaws to swipe at the second eagle. The bird veered off with a furious screech. His wings split the air like thunder and a long brown feather floated down the side of the mountain.

Toklo glanced back at Ujurak. He was huddled in the cleft with Lusa peering over his shoulder, her eyes full of terror.

"Come on, run," he barked. "Before they come back."

He waited until the two cubs were scurrying along the ledge ahead of him before he followed, ears alert for the sound of beating wings and shoulders braced for talons digging into his pelt. But the eagles' cries grew fainter. As the ledge widened out and became a gully among rocks, Toklo looked back to see both eagles hovering above their nest. The mother bird settled again on the untidy pile of sticks, while her mate soared into the sky, keeping beady watch over his family.

"That was close," Toklo muttered.

"You were terrific!" Lusa's eyes shone in admiration.

Embarrassed by her praise—after all, he had been scared by the eagles, too—Toklo shrugged. "I wish we could have gotten the eggs."

Ujurak gave him a friendly nudge. "I'm glad you didn't try. They weren't worth being pushed off the ledge."

By now the sun was gone and only a few red streaks remained in the sky. Toklo led his companions a little farther, until it was too dark to travel safely. There was nowhere to shelter so they huddled together in the gully with the wind whining among the rocks above.

Toklo felt as if he had hardly closed his eyes before the rays of the sun woke him the next morning. On they trekked, keeping to the Sky Ridge, looking down on forests and streams glinting in the sunshine. Up here, the clouds were almost close enough to touch. Sometimes they settled on the Sky Ridge and everything went misty and cold.

"Is this what flying is like?" Lusa asked Ujurak.

Ujurak shook his head. "I never flew into any clouds. I flew when the sky was clear. It's like plunging into a river of air, full of currents, warm in some places, cold in others. You have to swim from one current to the next, scooping the air with your wings until it lifts you up."

His eyes glazed as if he could feel the currents of air all around him once again. Lusa was staring at him in fascination, her paws twitching on the rock as if she wanted to scoop the air, too. Toklo sighed. Cobwebs and moonshine, that was what filled these cubs' heads. *And cobwebs catch no prey.*

Every day, Toklo saw the sun rise in the sky on one side of the mountains and slide slowly down on the other. The days of burn-sky were growing longer and warmer, and although Toklo would have been grateful for the fuller days of hunting down in the forest, up here on the Sky Ridge there was little prey to catch.

Soon they began to rest in the middle of the day, finding a patch of shade to drowse and lick pads that were sore from traveling over the jagged rocks. Ujurak was always the first to jump up and make them keep going.

"It's as if there's something waiting for us," he explained with a puzzled look in his eyes. "I don't know what it is, but I know we shouldn't be late."

Lusa seemed willing to be caught up in his urgency and Toklo went along with them, even though he didn't understand. Arguing with Ujurak wouldn't do any good. Besides, though he would never have admitted as much to the others, he liked being the one who was big and strong enough to haul them up the steepest rocks, or let them clamber onto his back to climb over huge boulders. He liked being the best hunter; once he brought down a skinny grouse as it tried to fly off, and felt as if he was giving the others a feast.

At one point the Sky Ridge became so spiky that the bears had to leave it and follow a path a few bearlengths down the mountainside.

Ujurak's paws dragged. "I don't like this," he complained. "We should stay at the top."

"We'll go back when the path gets smoother," Toklo promised. "You might want your pads bleeding, but I don't."

Even so, as he led the way along the new path, Toklo realized that he didn't like it, either. Something was wrong; he kept glancing around for any sign of danger, his ears pricked and his nose quivering. All he could sense was rock and water and the thin scent of sparse mountain plants, but something close to fear made his fur stand on end. His paws tingled, and he jumped when several loose stones rattled past them.

"What was that?" Lusa whimpered.

Toklo was furious with himself for letting Lusa see that he was startled. He shrugged. "Nothing. Come on."

"We should climb a tree," she said.

Toklo swept a glance across the rugged mountainside. "Do you see any trees?" he demanded. "Bee-brain."

Lusa flinched. "I just thought—"

She stopped as howling broke out behind and above them. Toklo saw four lean shapes crest the ridge and stand outlined for a moment against the reddening sky.

"Wolves!" he snarled. For a heartbeat he wanted to turn and fight, but there were too many of them—more than he could count on his paws. They were thin and savage with hunger. And after so many days of near-starvation, Toklo knew he wasn't strong enough to fight them off. "Head for the valley!"

"But it's the wrong way!" Ujurak protested.

"Run!" Toklo barked. He shoved Ujurak in front of him

as he launched himself down the slope, not waiting to see if Lusa was following. Silently he cursed the wind; it was blowing away from them, carrying their scent to the wolves.

Beside him, Ujurak stretched out his neck and ran, leaping from rock to rock with his stubby tail bouncing on his flanks. Toklo glanced back to see that Lusa was keeping pace just behind him, her legs a dusty black blur.

The wolves streaked down the mountain, silent now, fast as floodwater. Beside Toklo, Lusa stumbled. *Perhaps she'll fall back,* he thought. *Then Ujurak and I can outrun the wolves.* But something inside him wouldn't let him abandon the black cub to be torn apart. With a fierce growl he dropped back until he was behind her and gave her a shove. Lusa lost her footing and skidded headlong for several bearlengths, scattering grit and pebbles. She crashed to a halt against a rock, then scrambled to her paws and pelted on. There were streaks of red on the rocks behind her; her pads were bleeding, leaving a scarlet, meat-smelling trail.

The valley with its covering of trees was growing closer. But the wolves' howling was closer still. Toklo didn't dare look back again, but he could imagine their hot breath ruffling his fur. He gazed around frantically for somewhere to hide, and spotted where the stream plunged into deep undergrowth.

"Over here!" he gasped to Ujurak. "The water will hide our scent."

Ujurak didn't reply. Without slackening his pace, his legs began to stretch and his fur seemed to melt away until it was a sleek pelt of chestnut-brown hair covering a slender, agile body. Small buds appeared on his head and sprouted into branching antlers. In the shape of a mule deer Ujurak swung around and faced the oncoming wolves.

"Ujurak!" Toklo yelled. A young mule deer, plump and grass fed, would be even tastier prey for the pack.

The Ujurak-deer hesitated for no more than a moment. Then he sprang away, heading along the slope above the tree line.

Lusa skidded to a halt and stood with her mouth hanging open. "He changed again!"

Toklo slammed into her and pushed her into the stream. "Get under the bank!"

She toppled in with a noisy splash, spluttering and shaking her head. The water came up to her belly fur. She scrambled for a foothold on the pebbles and clawed her way to the edge of the stream, where the bank hung over the water, casting a thick, cold shadow onto the ripples.

Toklo slithered down the bank and thrust himself beneath the overhang behind her, flinching at the icy bite of the water, and held his breath to listen even though his chest felt like it was on fire. For a few moments he could hear the patter of the deer's hooves on the rock, and the wolves racing after it, howling, their belly fur brushing the ground as they gave chase. Then the sounds died away until all Toklo could hear was the gurgling of the stream and the rasping of his own breath and Lusa's.

They were standing in the stream with water swirling close to their bellies. The current had scoured out a hollow at the side; grasses trailed down from the bank above and branches dipped down to the surface of the stream. For now they were safe.

But instead of relief, Toklo felt rage building in his chest. He let out a low growl.

"What's the matter?" Lusa asked.

"Ujurak." The word came out as a furious snarl. "Why won't he listen? I *told* him what to do. . . ."

The wolves will tear him in pieces. A mule deer couldn't possibly outrun a pack of wolves.

"He'll be okay," Lusa reassured him.

"You don't know that," Toklo snapped.

"I'm sure he'll be—"

"Quiet!" Toklo snarled.

In the shadows under the bushes Toklo could just make out the small black bear next to him, frightened and confused. He turned away, clamping his jaws shut. A dark place opened up inside him when he thought of the wolves springing on Ujurak, bringing him down, ripping at him with claws and fangs. . . . *And I'm stuck here where I can't help him. He'll never make it on his own.*

His belly churning, Toklo forced himself to stay alert, his ears pricked as he tried to peer through the grasses that screened them. He could see and hear nothing but the gradually darkening woods and the splashing of the stream. *Ujurak, where are you?*

Beside him he could feel Lusa shivering and hear her teeth chattering. He watched her from the corner of his eye and saw her eyes roll upward as if she was about to lose consciousness. Was the silly creature going to collapse, as if they didn't have enough problems?

Toklo reached out with all his senses, but there was no sign of any threats nearby. "Okay," he growled, giving Lusa a shove. "We can get out now."

Lusa scrabbled at the bank, but Toklo had to give her another hard shove from behind before she hauled herself out of the stream and crouched shivering on the grass.

"You can't stay there," Toklo told her. "We need to take cover." He padded over to a clump of thornbushes near the bank. "Over here."

Lusa raised her head and peered blearily at him, then struggled to her paws and stumbled across the grass until she could creep under the lowest branches. "I'm hungry," she whimpered.

"So am I." Toklo's belly was howling, but he knew he had to ignore it. "It's not safe to hunt yet. The wolves might still be around."

Night had fallen and moonlight trickled through the branches above. Toklo struggled to stay awake; Lusa had long ago closed her eyes, and some bear had to keep watch. He tried to think of what they ought to do next, but the shock of losing Ujurak seemed to fill his mind with thick, choking earth.

Toklo jerked fully awake when he heard the sound of another animal pushing its way through the undergrowth.

Lusa's head shot up, her eyes stretched wide with alarm. "What's that?"

"I don't know. Keep quiet."

Toklo took a few deep sniffs. The animal approaching was another bear. He braced himself for a fight, sinking his claws into the damp earth. Had they strayed past the clawmarks of an adult grizzly who would attack them for trespassing on his territory?

The rustling stopped; tensing his muscles, Toklo prepared to leap out. *But I'll never beat a full-grown grizzly. I can't keep myself safe, let alone Lusa.*

Then a voice came out of the darkness. "Toklo? Lusa? Are you there?"

Lusa jumped up with a happy squeal and wriggled underneath the lowest branches. "Ujurak, over here!"

A wave of relief crashed over Toklo. He pushed through the thorns to see Ujurak, back in his bear's shape, standing a couple of bearlengths away along the bank of the stream. Lusa was pressing her muzzle against Ujurak's. "Thank you for saving us."

Toklo's relief was blotted out by anger, like storm clouds covering the sun. "I thought you were dead!" he roared. He paced forward until he could look Ujurak in the eye. "Didn't you hear me telling you to hide in the stream?" he growled.

"Yes, I know, but . . ." The cub sounded confused. "I wanted to be something fast enough to lead the wolves away. And then I felt myself changing."

"It was a stupid thing to do!" Toklo wasn't sure if Ujurak had changed on purpose, and he guessed that Ujurak didn't know, either. "A mule deer isn't faster than wolves."

"I know. But mule deer are *clever*, Toklo. In that shape I could jump over logs and boulders and flat-face fences. I could leap up onto high rocks. Sometimes the wolves had to go around, and I could dodge when they were out of sight, and confuse the scent. In the end I lost them."

Toklo could imagine the furious chase, and couldn't help being impressed by his friend's courage. "You took your time getting back," he grumbled.

"I know, but . . ." Ujurak shifted his paws uneasily. His eyes were full of sadness. "In that shape I could feel what the deer felt. I followed their trail as far as a wide stone path with silver beasts roaring on it, and I saw flat-face dens where the deer used to live. They miss their home, Toklo. There isn't enough room for them and the wolves on this side of the ridge."

"Who cares what mule deer feel?" Toklo huffed, but Ujurak went on, the fur above his eyes wrinkling with concern.

"I thought every sound in the woods was a flat-face hunter coming after me. When I drank from a pool the water tasted sour, as if it was dying. The deer's world is getting smaller and sicker, Toklo."

"Are we going to get sick?" Lusa whimpered, her black eyes round and shiny in the half-light.

Toklo shrugged. "Not if we do what we always do, and fight to survive. Life is hard. It always has been."

Ujurak sighed, and Lusa touched his shoulder with her muzzle, ruffling his fur with her warm breath. A sharp pang of jealousy stabbed through Toklo. He realized that his mouth was dust dry from fear and thirst, and turned away, padding back to the stream to drink.

"No!" Ujurak exclaimed. "You can't drink from there. I told you the water's sick!"

"But I'm thirsty!" Toklo retorted. He dipped his muzzle into the cold, fur-soft current, aware all the time of his two companions standing silently behind him. The water tasted fine to him.

CHAPTER THREE

Kallik

The white bear cub Kallik crouched at the top of the slope, taking a last look at the burning metal bird and the body of Nanuk slumped beside it. She knew that she had to find the place where the spirits danced on the ice, but it was hard to tear herself away from the stubborn, lonely she-bear who had protected her. Nanuk's fur had been so cold when Kallik woke up, still curled in the curve of the older bear's belly, after the metal bird fell out of the sky.

Too dazed to wonder which direction she should take, Kallik began to scramble down the slope on the far side of the ridge. Stinging sleet buffeted her face, making her screw up her eyes; ice-cold mud soaked between her paws and into her pelt. Her whole body ached and pain stabbed through one foreleg whenever she put that paw to the ground.

At the bottom of the slope rocks poked through the muddy ground, where clumps of tall grasses were bent almost flat by the sweeping wind. Kallik staggered forward for a few more bearlengths, until she stumbled over a slanting rock and rolled into a hollow. She knew she ought to pull herself to her paws and struggle on, but even raising her head felt like trying to lift an ice floe. Sparkling darkness flooded her eyes; she collapsed on the ground and lay still.

Kallik was floating, her body and legs as soft as snowflakes drifting through a night without stars or wind or the scent of water.

Kallik! Kallik!

What is it, Mother? Kallik looked all around, but nothing broke the darkness: not Nisa's white pelt, or the twinkling of her mother's spirit-star. *Where are you?*

I am with you, little one, her mother's voice replied. *I am always with you.*

Then why can't I see you?

One day you will, her mother told her gently. *But not yet.*

Why not? Kallik longed to curl against the warmth of her mother's belly and listen to her stories again.

Because there is something you must do. I cannot travel with you, my precious child. You must go on alone.

I can't. . . .

You can. You are strong, little one. You have survived.

The wind rose, drowning Nisa's voice.

No! Kallik cried. *Mother, don't leave me!*

You are strong, Nisa repeated in a sighing breath that was lost in the sound of the wind.

Kallik's mind drifted until she thought she was swinging in the net again, far above the ground with the wings of the metal bird clattering overhead. There was fire, she remembered, and a dreadful screeching as the bird fell from the sky. She seemed to hear the screeching all around her now, filling the whole world. . . .

Her eyes flew open to see a firebeast bearing down on her, roaring as if she were its prey. Instinctively Kallik rolled to one side. The firebeast swept on, roaring and flattening her fur with the wind of its passing.

Kallik lay without moving, without even breathing, until the firebeast had vanished into the distance and its growling died away. She realized that she was lying beside one of the flat-faces' stone paths, which she hadn't noticed in the dark and sleet the night before. Now the gray light of morning showed her the stone path stretching out of sight in both directions, through a sea of mud broken up by clumps of grass and stunted bushes. Clouds covered the sky, but Kallik guessed the sun was barely above the horizon.

When she tried to get up, every one of her muscles shrieked in protest. The fur on her injured foreleg was matted with blood. Kallik dragged herself a few bearlengths from the stone path and crouched to lick her leg until the fur was clean and she could see the jagged gash beneath. A little more fresh blood oozed out of it, but the pain had ebbed.

At least I'm alive, she reminded herself. *Not like Nanuk.* She hunched her back against a fresh pang of grief, feeling dust under her eyelids when she screwed up her eyes. Opening them again, she blinked to make them water.

She was gathering her strength to stand up when she heard a high-pitched barking coming from the other side of the stone path. She heaved herself to her paws and took cover behind a bush, then peered out through the twisted branches. The long, pale grass on the opposite side of the path parted and a reddish brown Arctic fox emerged. It was thin, with all its ribs showing, and one of its ears was torn as if it had been in a fight. It hesitated for a heartbeat, then ran across the path and passed within a couple of bearlengths of Kallik's hiding place. Its muzzle was close to the ground, as if it was tracking prey.

At the thought of food Kallik's empty belly seemed to roar as loudly as the firebeast. Setting her paws down lightly, she emerged from the bush and began to follow the fox.

The creature twisted and turned among the clumps of grass, too intent on its prey to notice it was being followed. The wind helped Kallik, blowing the fox's scent toward her. Sometimes its brown pelt blended into the muddy ground so that Kallik lost sight of it, but she could still smell it, and never lost the trail.

At last the fox skirted a thorn thicket and disappeared on the other side. Kallik heard a scuffling sound, followed by a shrill squeal that was abruptly cut off. She pressed herself close to the ground, and crept around the thicket to see the fox standing over the body of a hare. The scent of the freshly killed prey tore into Kallik's belly like a claw. Roaring, she rose up from the cover of the grasses and bore down on the fox. The animal shot one terrified glance at her and fled.

Kallik crouched over the hare's body. All her instincts were telling her to swallow it in two or three famished gulps.

Not so fast, little one. She heard her mother's voice, teaching her and Taqqiq, back on the ice. *Gulp your food like that, and you'll give yourself bellyache.*

Kallik sank her teeth into the body of the hare and tore off a mouthful, giving herself time to savor the rich juices before she swallowed it and dipped her muzzle to take another bite.

A rustling sound alerted her and she whipped her head around. The fox was glaring at her from underneath a prickly bush. Kallik planted one paw on the hare and bared her teeth in a snarl. "It's mine!"

The fox backed off, but as she ate Kallik could sense that it was still around. *Tough luck; this is my kill now. You'll have to catch another.*

With her belly comfortably full, Kallik retreated into the nearby thicket and curled up at the foot of a tree to sleep. When she woke, mist had crept over the landscape, and the dim light told her evening was approaching. Her jaws parted in a huge yawn and she swiped her tongue a few times over the wound in her leg. The bleeding had stopped, and when she stood up and put weight on her paw she felt no more than a dull ache.

Shaking scraps of leaf from her pelt, Kallik sniffed the air. Her spirits rose as she detected the scent of water on the wind. Perhaps she wasn't far from the place where the ice returned, where the bears were gathering.

"Maybe Taqqiq will be waiting for me," she said aloud.

She set out, facing into the wind, following the scent of the water. The dim light faded until she was walking in darkness, but the smell still guided her pawsteps.

She was tiring as she plodded up an endless slope, with no trees to shelter her from the wind, and scratchy grass under her paws. Her legs felt too heavy to lift, and there was an ache between her shoulders. Hunger had begun to gnaw at her belly again. But she kept going, sure that the water she was seeking was not far away.

At last she reached the crest of the hill and looked down. In front of her paws, the ground fell away steeply; a few bear-lengths below her lay a dark stretch of water.

But this was not the place Kallik had been hoping to find. There was no sign of ice, no sign of other bears. The only sound was the water lapping gently among the reeds that fringed it. And she could just make out the shore on the other side of the water. It was as if the bay had reached a paw into the land. She remembered the vast stretches of glittering ice where she had been born, and thought that her heart would break in two from longing to be back there.

"Where am I?" Kallik cried, but there was no bear to answer her. "What's happening to me?"

She looked up into the night sky, hoping to see the Pathway Star hanging in the darkness to guide her. But all she could see was the mist. Terror and confusion swept over her again; she felt as helpless as a fish flapping out of the sea. She could smell salt and seaweed, but no trace of the ice she craved. She would have to struggle on even farther before she found it, and she didn't know which way to go.

Stumbling with weariness, she made her way down the slope, weaving among scrubby plants and rocks until she reached the water's edge. She climbed onto a dark rock that poked out over the water and crouched there, gazing into the indigo depths.

The wind picked up, shaking the reeds and rippling the surface of the water. Her mother had told her that all water was melted ice, but Kallik felt no sense of familiarity with this strange place. Instead, the darkness seemed to beckon to her, and she remembered how her mother, Nisa, had slipped away, saving Kallik from the orca. Kallik fought the temptation to slide into the water like her mother, to let it close over her head and cover her. Then she wouldn't have to struggle anymore, and maybe she would find her mother's spirit somewhere below the restless surface.

Kallik stretched out her paw, reaching down to touch the ripples.

Taaaaa . . . qqiiiiq.

She snatched back her paw and pricked her ears.

She could hear the lapping of water against the rocks, and the wind stirring the reeds. It sounded like the whispering of the ice spirits.

Taaaa . . . qqiiiiq, it came again.

Hot shame swept over Kallik. She had been within heartbeats of giving up. In her dream her mother had told her that she was strong, and Nanuk had said the same. Kallik didn't feel strong, but she knew she had to keep going. The sound of her brother's name on the wind made her realize that she couldn't leave this life without knowing what had happened to him.

"Ice spirits, where should I go?"

She looked up. The night sky was muddy looking and starless, and offered no guidance. She closed her eyes and tried to picture the Pathway Star. Her memories of the harsh sound of the metal bird and the roaring flames clouded her thoughts. She opened her eyes, but there was still no sign of the star.

"Where are you?" Kallik called. "I need you."

She dropped her head and stared at the water as the wind shook the reeds. As she stared, a tiny speck of light appeared on the water. *The Pathway Star.* She didn't dare to look up, but she knew it was shining above her, beyond the spur of water, guiding her paws along the edge of the bay.

"Ice spirits, is this my way?" she whispered.

Suddenly, the mist cleared and moonlight shone on the water, obliterating the Pathway Star in a dazzling strip of light that reached away from her paws.

Kallik stood up and opened her eyes wide in astonishment.

The ice-path rippled brightly, but it did not lead along the edge of the bay toward the Pathway Star, which Kallik expected it to do. Instead, it stretched along the part of the lake which led *away* from the sea, away from her birth lands, into unknown places.

"Ice spirits," she whispered. "Bears belong by the sea. Are you telling me to leave and go inland?"

Taaa-qqqiiiiq, the spirits murmured.

Kallik watched as the ice-path rippled and gleamed along the narrow spur of water, pointing away from the sea. She had lost her mother; she could not lose her brother, too, not if there was the tiniest snowflake of a chance that she might find him.

"All right, Taqqiq," Kallik whispered. "I will turn my back on the Pathway Star. I will go where I have to. And I will find you."

CHAPTER FOUR

Lusa

Lusa stood beside Ujurak on a flat rock jutting out from the ridge. After they escaped from the wolves, the shape-shifting grizzly cub had led them back into the mountains, where they trudged on for days with little food or water, and no shelter from the relentless, claw-sharp wind. Lusa jumped at every unexpected noise. Sometimes she thought she could pick up the distant scent of wolves, but to her relief they never caught sight of any slinking over the rocks.

Toklo padded up to join them. "How long do we have to stay up here?" he huffed. "There isn't a sniff of prey."

The air was full of the scent of freshwater; a few bearlengths below where the cubs were standing a stream gushed out from a gap among the stones and leaped from rock to rock down the mountainside until it vanished into the trees far below. Instead of replying to Toklo, Ujurak slid down and drank from the spring.

"Do you *want* to starve?" Toklo snapped. "If you ask me, we should never have left the forest."

Ujurak looked up; glittering drops of water sparkled on his muzzle. "Our path has divided," he replied. "Our way is out of the mountains now, following the water. My mind is full of the sound and scents of water."

"Well, of course it is!" Toklo muttered. "You're standing with your paws in a stream!"

He scrambled down the slope until he stood next to Ujurak. Lusa followed and dipped her nose in the stream. The water was cold and delicious; she couldn't remember when she'd last enjoyed a drink so much.

I'm sure this water isn't sick, she thought, remembering Ujurak's unhappiness on the night they escaped from the wolves. *Maybe Ujurak is worrying about nothing.*

Toklo dipped his head to drink, too; while his snout was plunged in the stream, Lusa checked him over, giving him a good sniff. His eyes were clear and his scent was just the same; he was bad tempered, but no more than usual. Drinking from the stream didn't seem to have done him any harm, even though Ujurak-deer had been convinced the water was sick.

Ujurak padded a few paces farther down from the ridge and waited for the others to finish drinking. His eyes were bright and eager.

"This stream is a sign, right?" Lusa said, as she and Toklo scrambled down to join him. "I wish I could understand them like you do. Will you show me how?"

Toklo let out a snort. "One bear seeing invisible signs is quite enough. You'd be of more use, Lusa, if you learned to hunt properly."

Lusa puffed huffily. "You're just jealous because Ujurak can change into all kinds of creatures and receive messages from the spirits."

"Ujurak has fluff in his ears, that's all," Toklo replied.

Lusa glanced at Ujurak. She wondered if he would be hurt by the older cub's scorn, but the look Ujurak gave Toklo was warm and friendly. *He understands Toklo's moods a lot better than I do,* Lusa told herself.

"I'll show you the next sign," Ujurak said to her. "Then maybe you'll understand."

Lusa couldn't restrain a little bounce of excitement. "Thank you!" *And maybe Toklo will understand, too.*

"For now, I know we have to leave the mountains," Ujurak said, gazing at Toklo. "Isn't that what you wanted?"

Toklo sighed. "Okay. Lead on."

Ujurak set off confidently downward, along the edge of the stream.

The sun felt warm on Lusa's back as she followed Toklo and Ujurak down a grassy slope, weaving their way among scattered pine trees. They were leaving the mountains behind now; the foothills looked gentle and welcoming, with softer ground underpaw. Lusa sniffed the warm air. *There must be* something *good to eat here!*

In the far distance were more mountains, blue and mysterious, with snow-tipped peaks. The sky was blue, too, arching overhead; even after moons of traveling, Lusa had never imagined it could look so huge, until she felt like a tiny black beetle crawling across the grass.

"Hurry up! You're slower than a snail!" Toklo growled.

She broke into a run to catch up with her companions. They were a strange pair to be traveling together, Lusa thought: one so friendly and the other one angry all the time, even grouchier than the grizzlies in the Bear Bowl.

"I'm going ahead to check for danger." The big grizzly cub jerked his head in the direction of a thorn thicket. "You two hide in there until I get back."

"Okay," Ujurak said. "Be careful."

Lusa watched Toklo pad away. He might be grouchy but he was brave, too. She crept underneath the bushes beside Ujurak, feeling her fur snagged by the thorns on the low-growing branches. Once under cover she flopped down, grateful for the chance to rest and rasp her tongue over her sore pads.

"Is it much farther to the place where the spirits dance?" she asked.

Ujurak shook his head, confusion in his bright brown eyes. "I don't know. I just know which way we have to go."

"If you've never been there before, how will we know when we get there?" Lusa persisted. "Will we see the spirits?"

"I don't know that, either," Ujurak confessed. "But there will be a path of fire waiting for us in the sky. When I go to sleep, that's what I dream of."

A shiver of anticipation made Lusa's fur stand on end. She wanted so much to see the fire in the sky, and the spirits dancing—though how could they dance when every bear knew that their spirits went into trees when they died?

"What will we do when we get there?" she asked.

"The spirits will show us," Ujurak replied solemnly.

Lusa fell silent. She wished she could be as close to the spirits as Ujurak was, but she sensed that it didn't really matter. She trusted Ujurak to get them where they were going.

"Come on!" Toklo's voice interrupted her dreaming. "Let's get a move on. It's safe for now—there isn't even a butterfly stirring around here."

Lusa pulled herself out from the thicket to see the big cub already several bearlengths away. Ujurak padded beside her as they followed in Toklo's pawsteps. Lusa snuffed up the scents of green growing things, enjoying the feel of the cool grass that brushed her paws. All the world seemed deserted in the heat of sunhigh, just as Toklo had said. The only movement Lusa could see was the tiny dot of an eagle, hovering high above.

"I wish *I* could be an eagle," she said wistfully, as she watched the bird's outstretched wings slicing through the air. "Flying looks like fun. Can you teach me how, Ujurak?"

Ujurak shook his head. "I don't know how to fly when I'm a bear. Besides . . ." He turned his head away and his voice grew sad and quiet. "In other shapes, you learn too much. I think I'd be happier just being an ordinary bear."

"Learn too much?" Lusa didn't understand how any bear could *not* want to know more about everything. Then she remembered the night when Ujurak had led the wolves away. "You mean what you said after you changed into the deer? About the water being sick?"

The brown cub nodded. "Every time I change into another creature, I realize that a bit more of the world is dying. Sickness is spreading everywhere—in the air and water, and deep inside the earth. There's too much of it to fight! What am I supposed to do?"

By the time he finished speaking he was shaking uncontrollably, his eyes staring into the distance as if he could see something dreadful ahead. Lusa pressed herself against his flank.

"You don't have to do anything," she told him. "It's not your fault. Even if the world is sick, it's not your responsibility to put it right."

"Then whose is it?" Ujurak turned that horrified gaze on her. "Remember the dead forest? What if everywhere was like that?"

"It won't happen," Lusa said. "And even if it does, I'll be here to look after you. Toklo will, too."

Instead of replying, Ujurak jerked his head up, startled, as pawsteps thudded toward them. While they talked, Toklo had drawn ahead; now Lusa saw him doubling back, his muscular legs propelling him up the grassy slope.

"Ujurak, is something the matter?" he panted when he halted beside them.

"No, I'm fine," Ujurak replied. He cast a quick, anxious glance at Lusa, as if he didn't want Toklo to know what they had been talking about. Lusa didn't intend to tell him. Toklo would probably say it was nonsense.

Toklo looked closer at the little brown bear. "Then why

have you stopped? I looked behind me and . . . and you weren't there!"

Ujurak shook his shoulders, rolling his baggy pelt from side to side. "I'm still here, aren't I? We're coming now. Lusa?"

She followed the two brown bears as they padded side by side down the slope. Toklo's shadow fell across Ujurak's back so that there was just one shadow on the ground, with eight legs. Her own shadow looked small and fuzzy, flitting over the grass beside her. For a moment she wished she were walking between Toklo and Ujurak so that Toklo's shadow covered them all, keeping them safe, moving them forward on many tireless legs.

At the foot of the slope they came to a rocky outcrop where water trickled between moss-covered stones and fell into a pool below. Toklo plunged his muzzle into the water without hesitating. Lusa waited for him to finish drinking, wondering if this water was sick like the stream under the trees two nights ago.

When Toklo backed away, Lusa padded up to the pool and took a deep sniff; all she could sense was water, moss, and rock. She glanced at Ujurak, but the brown cub said nothing; he was gazing into the distance, and his eyes looked full of clouds. Lusa dipped her snout and drank. The water was cool and clear, and she felt energy pouring through her as she swallowed. *The spring on the ridge was good water,* she thought. *Maybe this is, too.*

Ujurak drank, too, but reluctantly, and only a few mouthfuls. Being convinced that the world was dying must be a huge burden, like trying to carry a full-grown grizzly on his back.

Perhaps he'd stop worrying when they got to the place where the bear spirits danced.

When they had all drunk as much as they wanted, Ujurak stood still for several heartbeats and stared at the sky with his head cocked on one side, before leading the way along a narrow track at the bottom of a valley. Green hills swelled gently on either side, speckled with thick, leafy bushes. A warm breeze blew into Lusa's face, carrying the scent of beetles and worms and other tasty things, but she didn't want to ask to stop in case Ujurak lost his fragile trail.

They followed the track as it curved around the foot of the hill. On the other side the ground fell away until they could look down across wooded slopes, fading into the distance. Way below, Lusa spotted the gleam of a river running through the trees, and beyond it a stone path, with tiny glittering specks that she knew were firebeasts racing up and down. They were so far away that she couldn't hear their roaring.

The sun had begun to slide down the sky by the time the cubs rounded a shoulder of the hill and came face-to-face with a tumble of rocks and earth, shaggy with ferns and grasses. The path forked; one part led back toward the mountains, while the other zigzagged across the downward slope and into the forest. Toklo, who had taken the lead, came to a halt, growling softly in his throat. He stretched out his neck, sniffing the air as if trying to decide which way to go.

Lusa turned to Ujurak. "Is there a sign?"

Ujurak trotted forward until he stood at the exact point where the track forked. He stood still and tense, his eyes flickering back and forth. Lusa clamped her jaws shut and forced herself to be quiet.

At last Ujurak relaxed and tipped his head, inviting Lusa to join him. "Is there a sign? Can you read it?" she demanded as she bounded up to him.

Ujurak ignored a heavy sigh from Toklo. "Yes, look." He faced the direction that led into the mountains, pointing with one paw at a huge boulder right in the middle of the track, halfway to the top. "That's blocking the way," he explained. "But the other path"—he swiveled around to face the forest—"is clear, as if it's telling us to go that way."

Lusa thought about that. The boulder wasn't really stopping them from taking the upward path if they wanted to; all they would have to do was squeeze around it. But the lines gouged into its surface gave it a forbidding look, like a huge bear with an angry face. She shivered, deciding that she didn't want to go that way anyway.

"It's as if the spirits are warning us," she whispered, hoping Toklo didn't hear.

Toklo let out a snarl. "Not you as well! Why am I stuck with *two* squirrel-brains?"

But he swung around and headed along the downward track without any more argument.

Ujurak set off after Toklo and Lusa had to run to keep up. Soon they reached the first pine trees; Lusa relaxed when she heard bear spirits murmuring in the branches above her head. Leaf-shadows dappled the ground and she felt the crackle of pine needles under her paws. Looking up, she saw crisscrossing branches outlined against the sky. Peace flowed into her like rain filling a hollow, and she felt a sense of familiarity that she had missed up in the mountains. Already she could scent water and make out in the distance the rush of the river she had seen from the upper slopes.

"Toklo, do you think there will be salmon in the river?" Ujurak asked.

"Might be." Toklo still sounded grumpy. "If there are, just stay out of the way till I catch one."

Lusa's belly rumbled at the mention of salmon. The last proper meal they had eaten had been a muskrat Toklo had caught in the mountains. Apart from that, on the bleak mountain ridge, they had survived on berries and insects grubbed up from the ground. Lusa had never tasted salmon, but Oka had told her how delicious it was, back in the Bear Bowl. Even better than blueberries, the grizzly had said.

The sun was sinking, casting long shadows across the water, when they came to the river. Curiosity attacked Lusa like a tormenting fly as she realized that the path divided again, going along the bank in both directions.

"Ujurak, can I try reading the signs?" she begged. "Please!"

Toklo shook his head and padded off to stand at the very edge of the river and peer down into the eddying water. Ujurak touched his muzzle to Lusa's. "Try."

Lusa paced forward to stand where the track divided. She stood, still and alert, looking up and down the stream. Upstream the track looked boggy and overgrown. Here and there the bank had crumbled into the river, and bushes stretched out their thorny branches, barring the way.

Downstream was no better. The track was firm and dry, but there was little undergrowth to provide cover. Lusa remembered how terrified she had been when the wolves were chasing her and there were no trees to climb. Now that they were off the mountain, they should be safer, but this path still looked too open.

Lusa couldn't see anything that suggested to her that one way was better than another. *What am I supposed to be looking for?* she wondered, with an uncertain glance at Ujurak.

The brown cub nodded encouragingly. "The answers are there. Just look."

Briefly Lusa closed her eyes, imagining that she could see the Bear Watcher shining down on her. *Arcturus,* she prayed, *please show me.*

When she opened her eyes again the forest looked brighter, the colors more intense. The muddy patches upstream seemed wider and deeper, and the bushes seemed to stretch out twiggy paws to trap her. But her pelt prickled with apprehension as she imagined trying to find cover in the scanty undergrowth downstream.

I have to choose one, she thought desperately.

Then she realized that she had a third choice. The river in front of her looked cool and inviting, and according to Toklo it might be full of tempting salmon. Her paws tingling, she turned to Ujurak.

"We cross the river," she announced.

She winced as Toklo let out a scornful snort, but she ignored him. It was Ujurak who would tell her whether she was right.

The small brown cub nodded and pride filled her from her nose to the tips of her claws. "That is our way."

"What?" Toklo's voice was outraged. "Bears don't swim."

"Of course we do!" Lusa was shocked that there was something she knew that Toklo didn't. Grunting with delight, she flung herself into the river, rejoicing in the surge of water around her. She ducked her head and came up again, then dived deeper until she could scrabble her paws among the pebbles on the riverbed.

When she resurfaced she looked back at the bank to see Toklo and Ujurak standing side by side, watching her. Ujurak looked fascinated, but Toklo's expression was fierce.

"Come back!" he ordered.

Lusa ignored the command. "Come on in, it's lovely!" she invited.

Ujurak took a step toward the water's edge, but Toklo stayed where he was. "Come back *now*," he repeated. "We can't cross here. I told you, I don't swim."

"All bears swim," Lusa argued, batting at the water with her paws so that drops splashed up and glittered in the sunlight. Why was Toklo making such a fuss, when any bear could see he was wrong? "Try—like this." She demonstrated how she moved her paws through the water. "You'll love it."

Ujurak teetered on the edge for a moment, then plunged into the river and paddled over to Lusa. His brown eyes sparkled. "I feel like a fish!"

"Come *on*, Toklo," Lusa repeated. Satisfaction surged up in her, as strong as the current, to think that for once she wasn't the weak black bear who didn't know how to live in the wild. This was something she could do better than Toklo. "What's the matter?" she added. "Why won't you try?"

The big grizzly cub began pacing up and down the bank, pausing every now and then as if he were about to dive in, then starting to pace again. "I . . . I don't get along with water," he muttered.

Lusa didn't understand what he meant. After all, he had to get into the river to catch salmon, didn't he? She'd never seen a grizzly catch fish but she was pretty sure the fish didn't leap onto the bank to be eaten. "Just jump in," she said. "Your paws will know what to do."

"Come on!" Ujurak called. "It's easy! You'll be fine."

With an impatient growl, Toklo crouched on the riverbank, his muscles bunched with tension, and threw himself into the water. His head went under; when he reappeared he was flailing his paws frantically, using far more energy than he needed, but making slow progress toward the opposite bank. Lusa swam over to keep pace with him, and saw that his eyes were wide with terror.

"It's okay," she said. "You're doing great."

Toklo's head whipped around to face her. "Leave me alone!" he snarled, swiping a paw at her.

Alarmed, Lusa backed off. But Toklo's attempt to smack her had broken the rhythm of his strokes. He took in a great gulp of water and sank.

Lusa gave him a couple of heartbeats to resurface, but the grizzly didn't appear. Icy fear, colder than the current, crept through her fur. Maybe he really couldn't swim! What if Toklo drowned, after she had persuaded him to jump into the river?

Lusa dove deep into the water, keeping her eyes as wide open as she could; swinging her head from side to side, she spotted a dark, bulky shape a short way downstream. It was Toklo being swept along by the current. He was floundering helplessly, his eyes and mouth wide open in alarm, bubbles of air streaming up to the surface from his jaws.

Lusa's stomach lurched. They couldn't lose Toklo! All three of them belonged together, on the journey to see the spirits dance. *One shadow, many legs.*

Swimming toward Toklo, Lusa gave him a hearty shove upward. As their heads broke the surface, she felt a stinging blow on her shoulder. Toklo had lashed out at her with his claws. She wasn't sure if he was still trying to attack her, or just thrashing around in panic because he thought he was drowning.

"Stop it!" she gasped. "Swim, like I showed you."

Ujurak's head bobbed beside her in the water. His snout was pointing upward, his neck crooked back to keep his nose in the air, and his legs paddled so hard he was making waves of his own.

"Can I help?" he spluttered.

"No—keep back!" Lusa couldn't imagine how she would cope with both of them in trouble. "Toklo, *swim*! Move your paws like this!"

Toklo coughed up a mouthful of water. "Don't let me drown!" he begged.

"You won't drown," Lusa promised, shoving her shoulder underneath him to support his bulk in the water. To her relief, he started paddling again, though panic still glittered in his eyes. "I can manage now," he gasped.

"Okay." Lusa wasn't sure he could, but she let him go ahead, staying close and keeping an eye on him. He was tiring himself out with those clumsy strokes, and the far bank was still a long way away.

"Over here!" Ujurak called.

Lusa thanked the spirits when she saw a narrow spit of pebbles in the middle of the river. Ujurak was standing at the very edge of the little island with river water washing around his paws.

"That way!" Lusa summoned all her energy and thrust Toklo across the current, propelling him through the water with very little help from the grizzly's feeble flailing paws.

Ujurak had found a dead branch lying on the pebbles; he grabbed one end in his jaws and rolled it into the water. Gulping and choking, Toklo managed to sink his claws into the branch and drag himself toward Ujurak, while Lusa pushed him into the shallows where they could both touch the bottom and heave themselves out.

Toklo shook himself, sending drops of water flying into the air in an arc around him.

"Are you okay?" Lusa checked.

Toklo coughed up another mouthful of water. "I'm fine. I'd

have figured it out on my own." He paused a moment, then added ungraciously, "Thanks."

"You did well," Lusa said quietly.

Toklo held her gaze for a heartbeat, then hesitated at the water's edge before wading back into the river.

"Where are you going now?" Lusa asked, alarmed. "You need to rest before we head for the other bank."

Toklo turned to look back at her. "I told you, brown bears don't need to swim. I'm going to catch a fish."

Lusa watched him until he stopped with water halfway up his legs. The current tugged at his chestnut-brown belly hair, but he stood without moving, his gaze fixed on the water. Satisfied that he was okay, Lusa let herself sink to the ground. It felt good to rest her aching legs; she loved swimming, but not when she had to push along a much bigger bear who didn't know how to help himself.

"You did great back there!" Ujurak shook the water out of his pelt and flopped down beside her on the pebbles. "You swim really well. I changed into a salmon once, but it's more fun swimming as a bear."

Lusa felt a jolt of fear deep in her belly. "You changed into a *salmon*? What if a bear had eaten you?"

"Toklo made sure they didn't," Ujurak replied.

Lusa glanced at Toklo's hunched shape in the river, and wondered if she would trust the grizzly as much as that. He was so determined to do things on his own, she sometimes thought he didn't want companions.

"You *can* trust him, you know," Ujurak insisted, as if he had guessed her thoughts. "He's angry, but not with us."

No, he's angry with his mother. But if he'd just listen to what Oka wanted me to tell him, he wouldn't need to be so angry anymore.

She stretched out beside Ujurak, licking the sore place on her shoulder where Toklo had scratched her, and letting the slanting rays of the sun warm her pelt. She watched impatiently for Toklo to come back with a salmon. But when the grizzly cub finally turned and waded out of the river, his jaws were empty.

"Didn't you catch anything?" she asked, dismayed. Her belly felt emptier than ever.

"There's nothing to catch," Toklo growled. "There are no fish here."

Ujurak's eyes widened in alarm. He scrambled to his paws and led the way across to the other side of the pebbly spit of land. "We have to keep going," he urged.

"I'm not getting back into that river," Toklo stated.

"What?" Lusa stared at him in dismay. He'd proven he could swim, hadn't he? What was wrong now? "We can't stay here. Come on, Toklo. I'll help you."

"No." For once Toklo wasn't getting angry, but his voice held a quiet determination that Lusa sensed she couldn't argue with. "I'm not swimming again, and that's that."

Lusa exchanged a glance with Ujurak. "What are we going to do?"

"We have to stay together," Ujurak said decidedly. "Let's follow this bank of pebbles and see where it leads."

They crunched their way along the narrow spit in the middle of the river, first heading downstream, in the direction of the current. Just around a curve in the river, the pebbles sloped down until they sank beneath the surface of the water. Toklo didn't say anything, but Ujurak turned around and headed back the way they had come. They passed the place where they had come ashore and continued upstream with Ujurak in the lead. Sunlight bouncing off the water dazzled Lusa's eyes, so she could hardly see where she was putting her paws. Anxiety nagged at her like a bear gnawing its prey. What would they do if they couldn't get to the other side of the river without getting wet? Would she and Ujurak be strong enough to push Toklo into the river and force him to swim?

As they padded on, Lusa noticed that Ujurak kept casting uneasy glances across the river, and sometimes back over his shoulder. She picked up her pace to catch up to him.

"What's the matter?"

Ujurak shook his head frustratedly. "We should be going the other way."

"Well, it's okay," Lusa reassured him. "We haven't lost the path. Once we get across, we'll go the right way again."

Ujurak didn't argue, but he still looked uncertain, and his pawsteps dragged as if a current like the river was trying to pull him back. Lusa padded beside him, brushing his pelt with hers in an effort to encourage him. After a while the pebbly spit of land grew so narrow that she was afraid it was coming to an end; the bears walked single file, the outsides of their paws touching the water on either side. Toklo, who was in front now, said nothing, just plodded onward with his head down. Just when Lusa was about to point out that they might have to swim anyway, the spit of stones widened out again. It drew closer to the opposite bank, but the channel between was still too wide to leap, and looked too deep to wade.

"There's something up ahead!" Ujurak called. He pushed past Toklo and broke into a trot.

Lusa bounded after him and made out a long, dark shape stretching from the far bank. When she caught up to Ujurak she saw that it was an old fallen tree. The branches and leaves had been washed away, and even the bark was mostly stripped off. Only the bare silvery trunk remained, the root end resting on the bank and the narrower end, where branches had grown, on the pebbles.

"See?" Toklo said, joining them. "I knew we wouldn't have to swim."

Lusa didn't reply. She studied the tree carefully; it made a very narrow bridge across the channel, and she thought they might have trouble keeping their balance. She would much rather swim, but she didn't want to make Toklo angry again. He obviously wasn't going to get back into the river. Although the tree trunk might not give him a choice if it tipped him off. . . .

"I'll go first," she offered, scrambling up to dig her claws into the trunk. She figured that since she was the smallest and lightest, it made sense for her to test the bridge.

Dark green moss grew on the trunk, making the barkless surface slippery. *Are you there, bear spirit?* she asked silently, resting her front paw questioningly against the tree. She didn't know what happened to bear spirits whose trees fell or were cut down. Perhaps that was when they went to dance in the sky. *If you're still here, please help us,* she begged.

Carefully setting one paw in front of another she headed out across the channel. The trunk bounced under her weight, scaring her at first. *But what's going to happen, bee-brain? If you fall in, you can swim!*

Heartened by that thought, she moved faster, and soon got close enough to leap down onto the grassy bank at the far side.

"Come on!" she called to the others. "You'll be fine!"

Ujurak was already climbing onto the trunk, squeezing through the few remaining root stubs. He crossed with quick, neat pawsteps, apparently unworried by the movement of the tree beneath his paws.

He let out a sigh of relief as he joined Lusa on the bank. "Now we can find the right path again!"

Lusa watched Toklo as he clambered onto the trunk and began to make his way unsteadily across. On the island, the end of the trunk sank more deeply into the stones, making a rough grinding sound. Under his heavier weight the trunk bounced harder; Toklo had to drive his claws into the wood at every pawstep to stop himself from toppling off. When he was halfway across, Lusa heard an ominous creaking, as if the trunk was about to break.

Suddenly the tree lurched to one side. Toklo toppled sideways; his hind legs dangled over the surface of the water while he clung on with his forelegs wrapped around the trunk.

"Hang on, Toklo!" Lusa leaped back onto the trunk and began making her way along the wildly bouncing tree.

Toklo scrabbled with his hindpaws, but he couldn't get a grip on the slippery wood. Lusa reached him, sank her teeth into his scruff and hauled upward, digging her claws into the trunk. For a few terrified heartbeats she thought his weight would pull her into the river, but at last he managed to get one hindpaw, then the other, up onto the trunk.

"Okay!" he gasped. "Give me some room."

Lusa let go his scruff. She could see real fear in Toklo's eyes, and wondered why he was so terrified of deep water. It was such a strange thing for grizzlies to be afraid of. Unable to turn around on the narrow trunk, she edged backward and Toklo followed her, breathing hard. Lusa kept her gaze locked with his, as if she could hold him steady and draw him to safety with her eyes. The creaking sound came again, louder now, and she braced herself for the trunk to crack and pitch them both into the river.

"Lusa, you've made it. You can jump down now." Ujurak's voice came from behind her.

Lusa looked down to see the grassy bank beneath her. She leaped off beside Ujurak, stumbling because she had to jump backward. Toklo, still over the water, tottered again and let out a grunt of fear. Ujurak sprang up beside him and steadied him with his shoulder.

The tree trunk rolled underneath them and started to crash down into the river. Water surged up; Ujurak jumped to safety but Toklo slipped, clinging to the crumbling edge of the bank while his hindquarters dangled into the stream.

"I can't hold on!" he yelped.

Lusa reached over and fastened her teeth in the thick fur on his shoulder. Ujurak grabbed him on the other side and they heaved together. Scrabbling with his hindpaws, Toklo pushed himself upward and collapsed ungracefully on the bank.

Lusa padded a few pawsteps up the bank and looked around. She was standing on a narrow strip of grass on the edge of a stone path; as she watched, a red firebeast roared by, filling the air with its noise and harsh smell. The bright glare of its eyes flashed across Lusa and was gone. Beyond the stone path, a grassy bank led up into more trees.

"Which way now?" she asked Ujurak. She felt exhausted; every muscle in her body ached and her belly was bawling with hunger. But she knew that they couldn't stay here, so close to the firebeasts.

Ujurak's eyes were dark and desolate, and he did not reply.

Anxiety clawed at Lusa's belly. "What's the matter?"

"Why were there no fish in the river?" Ujurak whimpered. "Where have they gone?"

CHAPTER FIVE

Toklo

Relief surged through Toklo as he dragged himself away from the river and onto a narrow strip of grass alongside a BlackPath. Beyond the BlackPath, a tree-covered slope led steeply upward. A few bearlengths farther away from the river, Ujurak and Lusa were waiting for him, their fur buffeted by the wind of the flat-faces' firebeasts as they roared past.

Instead of joining them, Toklo shook earth from his pelt, then flopped down again, panting, on the grass. He had hated crossing the hungry river on the fallen tree trunk, but he hated swimming even more. Ujurak liked it, but Ujurak was strange in a lot of ways, and as for Lusa . . . what did she know about being a brown bear? Toklo was furious that Lusa was better at swimming than he was, and more furious still that she had helped him, as if he were a feeble cub who couldn't manage on his own. He wouldn't let her know how scared he had been.

Oka had told him that the spirits of dead bears drifted down the river to a faraway land where they could be forgotten by living bears. But he still remembered his mother and Tobi, so that meant their spirits must still be in the river. Toklo just wanted to forget them, forget what had happened—but how could he, when Lusa kept shoving them in his face?

The thought of plunging into the river with the spirits of his dead mother and brother had filled him with horror. Perhaps they were angry with him because they had died while he was still alive. And when Lusa and Ujurak forced him to swim, he had felt Oka's and Tobi's dead claws hooking into his fur, trying to pull him down to the bottom of the river until the water gushed into his jaws and everything went black. . . .

"Are you okay?" Lusa asked, jolting him back to the present. The concern in her dark eyes reminded Toklo all over again of how scared he had been as the river closed over his head.

"Of course I am," he growled. "At least, I will be when we find some food. I've almost forgotten what meat tastes like."

"So have I." Lusa sighed. "I guess I could find some berries in the forest."

"Berries aren't proper food for a bear," Toklo retorted. "You can eat them if you like, but I want something a lot more satisfying." His jaws watered as he remembered the taste of salmon; what was the good of a river if there weren't any fish in it?

Ujurak gazed longingly downstream. Toklo could see that he just wanted to move on.

"We can't travel if we don't eat," he told the smaller cub. He padded away from the others, his muzzle raised to sniff out prey. Spotting some white smears along the side of the BlackPath, he added, "Look, that's salt. We should lick it up.

It won't fill us, but it's better than nothing."

"Salt?" Lusa remembered the flat-faces hanging up a block of the white stuff for the bears in the Bear Bowl to lick. "Did the flat-faces put it here for us?"

"They put it here, but not for us bears, that's for sure. And don't ask *why*," Toklo snapped as Lusa opened her jaws to speak again. "I don't *know* why flat-faces do what they do. They're crazy—even crazier than black bears."

To his relief, Lusa kept quiet as all three bears stepped warily out onto the BlackPath to lick up the patches of salt. Toklo sniffed in disgust as his tongue swiped over it; the white stuff was cold and dirty—so dirty that in some places he could hardly distinguish it from the BlackPath. *But it's better than nothing.*

He remembered the day Oka had found salt like this, and told him and Tobi that it was good to eat. For once Tobi hadn't complained, and they had all stayed together, eating companionably, until—

"Run!" Ujurak squealed.

Toklo looked up to see a huge blue firebeast bearing down on him. Terror pounded through him; he leaped away and bounded across the BlackPath to the safety of the other side. The firebeast roared past with a high-pitched howling; Toklo didn't dare move until the sound had died away into the distance.

Looking around, he spotted Ujurak still on the other side of the BlackPath, next to the river. "Are you okay?" he called.

"Fine," Ujurak replied, huffing out his breath.

Toklo's belly lurched with relief when he realized that the younger cub wasn't hurt. Lusa had climbed the wooded bank beside the BlackPath and was clinging to a low branch on the nearest tree. She scrambled down as the noise of the firebeast dwindled away, and trotted back to the bank to stand beside Toklo.

"That was close!" she panted. "Was the firebeast hunting us?"

"No," Toklo growled. "But it would have flattened us if we got in its way. They don't care."

Ujurak set a paw on the BlackPath, about to cross, when Toklo heard the rumble of another approaching firebeast. "Keep back!" he barked. Ujurak jumped backward, his eyes full of alarm as the creature roared past.

Toklo waited until the sound had died away. "Okay, come now," he told Ujurak. "It's safe, but run fast."

Ujurak bounded quickly across the BlackPath. "Thanks, Toklo," he said. There was a look of disgust on his face, and he kept passing his tongue over his lips as if he could taste something bad. "Those things stink!"

"Which way should we go now?" Lusa asked. "Up here?" She took a couple of paces up the bank.

Ujurak stood still and closed his eyes.

"Here we go again," Toklo sighed, glancing back at the blue-gray ridge of mountains in the distance, then at the river curling away through woods and hills.

Ujurak opened his eyes. "We must follow the direction of the river," he told them, and padded away.

Toklo huffed and set off after him with Lusa at his side.

Gradually the steep bank beside the BlackPath sank into a gentle slope and then to flat ground covered in trees and bushes. As they padded along, Toklo began to hear something other than the wind in the trees and the roar of firebeasts; his ears pricked as he recognized the sound of flat-face voices.

"Flat-faces!" Lusa exclaimed at the same moment.

"Stay back," Toklo warned her, not sure if she would expect these flat-faces to feed her like the ones in the Bear Bowl. "They won't be friendly to bears."

"They might be," Lusa objected. "Okay, okay," she went on, before Toklo could tell her what a squirrel-brained idea that was. "I wasn't going to let them see me anyway. They might catch me and take me back to the Bear Bowl."

As they drew closer to the flat-faces the strange yelping voices got louder. A delicious scent trickled into Toklo's nostrils. He had never smelled anything quite like it before, but he knew what it was. Food!

Following the scent, he pushed his way into the bushes until he came to the edge of a clearing, and peered out through the branches. Lusa and Ujurak crowded up behind him; Lusa wriggled up to his side so that she could see clearly.

Four flat-faces were in the clearing: two full-grown adults and two cubs. Just beyond them was a kind of den made out of green pelts, and they were all crouched around a squat flat-face thing made out of the same shiny silver stuff as the firebeasts; it gave out a glow of heat.

Lusa looked closely at each of the flat-faces. "I don't

recognize them," she said at last. "I don't think they came to see me when I was in the Bear Bowl."

The mother flat-face lifted a chunk of hot meat out of the object in the middle, and handed pieces to her two cubs. That was what had smelled so good. The older cub took an enormous bite. Toklo's belly rumbled. He scanned the clearing for danger. He couldn't see any metal sticks like the ones that had wounded Ujurak, but they could be hidden. Then he noticed that the smaller flat-face cub had wandered off into the bushes, his food held lightly in his pale pink paw.

Setting his paws down carefully, Toklo began to follow, skirting the clearing until he reached the place where it had entered the bushes. Lusa and Ujurak padded after him, a little way behind. The scent of the food drew Toklo closer, until he spotted the cub squatting down in the shelter of a clump of ferns, staring at a butterfly perched on a grass stem in front of him.

Hunger blurred Toklo's vision until all he could focus on was the chunk of meat in the flat-face cub's paw. He braced himself, ready to pounce, imagining his jaws closing around the delicious-smelling food. In just one heartbeat, the meat would be in his mouth. . . .

Suddenly something barreled into his side, knocking him over with a force that drove the breath out of his body. He let out a yelp as he landed among thorns. Scrambling back to his paws, he saw Ujurak standing in front of him, his brown eyes furious.

"That isn't the way to get food," the cub barked.

At the same moment a sharp call came from one of the full-grown flat-faces in the clearing. The flat-face cub leaped up and ran off, taking the precious food with him.

Toklo took a step forward until he loomed over Ujurak, a low growl coming from deep in his throat. "What do you think you're doing?"

Ujurak stared back at him without flinching. "What you were doing is wrong. There'll be other food."

"But I'm hungry *now,*" Toklo complained. "I nearly had it! We have to eat!"

"I know. But bears must not harm flat-faces."

"Why not? We have to survive somehow," Toklo insisted. He caught a glimpse of Lusa peering nervously around a bush. "It's up to me to make sure of it. Or do you want to see how well you can get on without me?"

"No, Toklo, I know we need you," Ujurak said. "But that doesn't change anything."

"I don't see why." Toklo lifted his muzzle and sniffed the air. He could still smell the flat-face food and, beneath it, another scent. It was warm and milky—the scent of the flat-face cub. Toklo's belly rumbled. "We could hunt the little flat-faces."

Ujurak stepped closer to Toklo, his eyes fierce. "Flat-faces are not prey," he growled.

Toklo reared up on his hind legs. "Who says?"

"Do you think we can fight against the deathsticks, Toklo?"

Toklo remembered the crack of the deathsticks and the blood that blossomed out of Ujurak's shoulder. He dropped to all four paws again, feeling as if the air had been knocked out of him. He stared at Ujurak. "There's nothing more important than survival," he said. "If you haven't learned that, then you're not a real bear."

"I *am*," Ujurak growled. "And that's why I'll only hunt real bear prey."

"And what would you know about that?" Toklo snarled. "You wander around with your head in the clouds, dreaming about stars and spirits. But clouds won't fill our bellies. So don't tell me what to do."

Toklo turned his back, then stomped off a few bearlengths into the trees. He heard rustling behind him and the sound of Lusa and Ujurak whispering together. After a moment, Lusa said pleadingly, "Toklo, the flat-faces have gone."

Toklo turned to see the other cubs behind him, gazing at him with pleading eyes. Without speaking, he swung around and headed back toward the BlackPath and the river. Lusa and Ujurak caught up to him, and all three walked on together in awkward silence.

The daylight was fading at last. The sun was dipping behind the trees. Clouds of gnats hovered in the air and around the cubs' heads; Toklo twitched his ears as he padded through them. His paws felt ready to fall off with tiredness; the days went on forever now, and the time for rest at night was so short. Would the days keep getting longer and longer? *What happens when there's no night anymore?* he wondered. Would they have to learn to stay awake all the time?

Ujurak, who was in the lead, halted in a clump of trees

growing beside the BlackPath. "This might be a good place to spend the night," he suggested.

Toklo paused at the edge of the trees and sniffed the air. There was no scent of flat-faces, apart from the harsh tang of the firebeasts that still passed by a few bearlengths away. There was no scent of other bears, either.

"It's as good as anywhere," he agreed gruffly.

Ujurak gave him an awkward nod, and Lusa scurried up the nearest tree and disappeared among the branches.

Toklo gazed longingly at an inviting hollow among the roots of the tree. A little way away he could hear Ujurak making himself a nest. He was dizzy with weariness, but he knew he couldn't sleep yet. If they didn't eat, they would soon be too weak to go on traveling.

Turning his back on the BlackPath, Toklo padded into the forest. Red light from the setting sun washed over the ground, and the trees cast long black shadows across his path. Sniffing deeply, he picked up the scent of prey and spotted a squirrel scuffling about among the roots of a tree. With a growl of triumph Toklo hurled himself at it and batted it over the head with one huge paw. He swallowed the small body in a few famished gulps. For a few heartbeats he stood still to enjoy the easing of his hunger pangs. Then guilt crept up on him, like ants burrowing into his pelt. What about the others, who had gone to sleep hungry? Did he have to hunt for them, too? Was it really right for bears to journey together? They were supposed to live alone, or at least stick to their own kind. Maybe the journey to find the place where the spirits danced was meant for just Ujurak.

Still confused, Toklo headed back toward the tree where the others were sleeping, but before he reached it, a grouse shot across his path, giving out a raucous alarm call. Almost without thinking, Toklo reared up on his hindpaws and swatted it out of the air. As it fluttered on the ground he grabbed it by the neck and carried the limp body back to his companions.

A sort of faint pink twilight had fallen by the time Toklo arrived back at the tree. Ujurak was curled up in a hollow lined with dead leaves, his paws hooked over his nose. Looking down at him, Toklo felt an unexpected pang of sympathy; the young cub looked so thin and exhausted. He dropped his prey and gave Ujurak a gentle prod in his flank.

"Hey, Ujurak, wake up."

"Wha . . . ?" Ujurak raised his head, blinking sleep out of his eyes. "Is it time to go?"

"No." Toklo edged the grouse toward his friend. "Here . . . eat."

Ujurak scrambled out of the hollow and stared at the bird, his eyes shining. "Toklo, you caught this for us? You're great!" He pelted over to the tree where Lusa had disappeared, and stretched his paws up the trunk. "Lusa! Lusa, come down! Toklo brought us some food."

The branches rustled and Lusa's bottom half appeared as she climbed swiftly to the ground. She padded over to where Toklo was waiting beside his prey. "Thank you, Toklo," she murmured, crouching down and tearing off a mouthful.

Ujurak crouched beside her, but before he took a bite he glanced up at Toklo. "Aren't you coming to share?"

Toklo shook his head. "I've had something."

His belly was nowhere near full, but Lusa and Ujurak were so grateful that he couldn't take any of their meal. He rested his muzzle on his paws and watched them eating. His stomach rumbled but he didn't mind. He closed his eyes and drifted to sleep.

That night, he dreamed his brother Tobi was alive and strong. They hunted together, bringing down a full-grown deer, and afterward they shared the prey that they'd caught as brothers.

CHAPTER SIX

Kallik

Kallik woke in the milky light of dawn and pulled herself to her paws. Her limbs felt stiff and heavy as she set off along the narrow spur of the bay, like she was walking through sticky mud.

"Bears don't belong on the land," she muttered. "What if I was wrong about the silver path? Will my mother be mad at me for going the wrong way?"

At the end of the spur of water, she hesitated, gazing in the direction the moon had shown her. The land in front of her was flat, covered in wiry grass with a thornbush or an outcrop of rock dotted here and there. Shallow silvery pools reflected the growing light in the sky, glittering in the first rays of the sun as it rose above the horizon.

"It's now or never," she told herself. She took a deep breath and padded forward, taking her first steps away from the bay, away from her birthing grounds, away from the place where she knew other bears would gather to go back onto the ice.

As the day grew hotter it was hard to keep her paws moving.

Her fur itched and she longed to find a patch of shade and lie down there, but she made herself keep going.

I wish I was back on the ice, she thought. *I wish I could go home.*

As she trudged, Kallik felt a growing sensation that something was watching her, that silent paws were following her. She glanced around uneasily, but nothing moved or made a sound, except for the reeds beside a nearby pool, brushing together in the breeze.

"Who's there?" she growled, but her voice sounded thin and weak. *It's this weird place,* she thought. *It makes me worry about things that aren't there.*

She padded on but the feeling didn't go away. She did her best to ignore it, but it was hard not to keep glancing over her shoulder.

The sun had begun to slide down toward the horizon when Kallik thought she could hear a strange rumbling in the sky, very faint, but somehow familiar. *Thunder?*

She looked up but the sky was clear, a deep blue streaked with pink. Silhouetted against the setting sun, she could see a dark shape. It was no bigger than a bird but it grew rapidly as it drew closer. Suddenly, her belly lurched and a memory flashed behind her eyes like a seal popping its head out of an ice hole.

The metal bird!

The sound grew louder until it thumped inside her head, hurting her ears. As the metal bird approached her, Kallik could see a web dangling underneath it; inside the web was a huge bundle of white fur, all squashed up. This bird was carrying a white bear—at least one—just as the other bird had tried to carry Kallik and Nanuk back to the ice. Kallik remembered the wind in her fur, and how terrified she had been to find herself flying skylengths above the ground. She had clawed at the web in a panic until Nanuk had soothed her and explained to her what was happening.

But that metal bird had never reached the ice. Kallik shuddered as she relived the moments when its wings had begun to whine and clatter as if it were in pain, until it burst into flames and fell out of the sky. Her heart pounded as she remembered Nanuk's broken body lying amid the wreckage, her eyes closed and her fur already cold against Kallik's muzzle.

The rumbling, chopping sound swelled until it seemed to fill the whole world; Kallik crouched down and put her paws over her ears. Suddenly, the noise changed, becoming more high-pitched and whining. Kallik lifted her head and risked looking up. The bird was sinking closer to the ground, its long metal wings no longer keeping it up in the air.

"No! No!" she yelped, scrambling to her paws and bounding toward it. "Go up! Go up!"

But the metal bird didn't hear her. It went on sinking, lower and lower. Wind from its clattering wings flattened the grass and bent the sparse thornbushes. Kallik hid behind a rock, peering out as she waited for flames to start spouting from its body. She flinched as she heard a high-pitched cry of terror coming from the web. *There must be a cub in there!* She squeezed her eyes shut tight and waited for the earth-shaking crunch of metal and fur amid roaring flames.

Several heartbeats passed; the only thing she could hear was the chopping sound of the wings, throbbing steadily through the air. Daring to open her eyes again, she saw that the metal bird was flying so low, hovering in one place, that the web containing the bears bumped gently on the ground. Kallik pricked her ears hopefully. *No bear could die from a little bump like that!*

She watched from the shelter of her rock as the web fell down around the bears and three furry shapes tumbled out: a she-bear and her two cubs. All three looked bone thin, as if they'd had as much trouble as Kallik finding food on land since the ice melted. Kallik could guess how confused they must feel, dropped here by the bird without anything to tell them where they were. But at least they didn't look as if they were hurt.

The web flopped loosely beside them, amid dust that was spitting into the air from the wind stirred up by the metal bird. The bears rolled sideways, away from the net, and lay still. The noise from the bird's wings grew louder, and it lifted into the sky, clawing its way into the blue air. The wind blew harder beneath it, raising the dust higher and ruffling the bears' fur. Kallik could just make out a flat-face in the bird's belly, looking out at the bears the bird had released. She wondered if there had been a flat-face in the metal bird that had carried her and Nanuk, and what had happened to it when the bird had crashed in flames.

The metal bird's nose dipped down and it flew away. The noise of its wings faded quickly, and the dust settled around the bears. Kallik peered nervously at them. They were very still. Were they still alive? She padded out from the shelter of her rock until she could see the outline of their flanks clearly against the pale brown dirt. They were breathing. *Thank the ice spirits.* Kallik didn't know what she'd have done if she'd seen more dead bears dropped by the metal birds. She remembered how a sharp sting from the flat-face's shiny stick had made her go to sleep before she and Nanuk were carried in the net; perhaps these bears were sleeping, too. She went back to her rock to wait for them to wake up.

The sun had crawled farther across the sky and Kallik was starting to get very thirsty when the first bear moved. A tiny she-cub lifted her head and looked around through half-closed eyes, then rolled onto her stomach and opened her eyes wide in surprise. She was clearly thinking, *Where am I?* She scrambled to her feet and took a few unsteady steps, shaking her head as if it were full of water, before flopping to the ground again. Just then, the other cub, a slightly bigger male, hauled himself up and walked in a circle, gazing at his paws as if he couldn't understand why the ground was so different. He went over to his sister and butted her with his head until she stood up again, still wobbly, and together they stumbled over to the she-bear who was still lying in a heap of fur. They pushed their muzzles into her flank and barked in high-pitched voices until her shoulders twitched and her eyes flickered open. Kallik heard her grunt, long and low as if she were aching after her sleep; then the she-bear propped herself up on her front paws and heaved herself onto her feet with a jerk. She stood still for a moment with her head hanging so low that her snout was almost on the ground, as if she was gathering her strength.

A pang clawed at Kallik's heart, and for a moment she looked away, her eyes stinging. *They look just like Nisa and Taqqiq and me!*

When Kallik looked back, the mother bear had lifted her head and her gaze was sweeping warily across the landscape. Kallik huddled behind the rock, trying to make herself as small as she could. She knew how unfriendly strange bears could be. This mother bear might think she was a threat to her cubs.

But to Kallik's relief the mother bear didn't see or smell her. Kallik guessed that her nose was still full of the smell of the metal bird and the sharp cold wind that sliced through the net when it was flying through the air. Rolling her shoulders from side to side, the she-bear padded over to her cubs. The breeze was blowing toward Kallik—another reason she was able to hide from the mother bear—so that she could hear what they were saying.

"Are you both okay?" the she-bear asked, sniffing each of her cubs from ears to paws.

"My head's spinning," the male cub complained, stumbling forward until he could lean against his mother's shoulder. He had broad shoulders and powerful legs, as if he would be a strong bear when he was full-grown, but Kallik could see that his legs were trembling from the strange journey. "I think I'm going to be sick."

"We'll find some water soon," his mother promised, bending down to touch his shoulder with her nose. "Then you'll feel better."

She raised her head again to scan their surroundings.

A pang of sadness pierced Kallik's heart like a splinter of ice. This mother bear was *so* like Nisa! She was strict with her cubs, but it was obvious how much she loved them. She would do everything she could to protect them and get them back to the ice, where there would be food. Something occurred to Kallik, and she sat up straighter. *The mother bear will know which way the sea is, and where to find the closest ice. I could follow them, and then I'd be back where I belong, with seals to eat.*

"Where are we?" the male cub yelped. "Why did the flat-faces put us to sleep and bring us here?"

"I don't know why flat-faces do anything," the mother bear replied. She paused for a moment, her snout tilted upward as she sniffed the air. "But I think I know where we are. I've been here before."

"Did a metal bird bring you?" the she-cub asked excitedly, her eyes sparkling.

"No, I've never flown with one of those before," the she-bear told her. "I came here on my own paws. I was on my way to the ice. . . ."

"The ice!" The she-cub tried to scramble to her paws, then flopped back down again. "Will there be seals and fish? I'm *starving*!"

The male cub leaned against his mother's shoulder again. "I can only see all this mud and yucky grass."

"But what can you smell?" his mother prompted, looking down at him.

The cub stretched his snout forward and took a couple of deep sniffs. Kallik saw his eyes grow wider. "Salt and fish!"

"That's the sea," his mother told him. "Isn't it wonderful? We'll soon be back there, and it won't be long now before the new ice comes."

Kallik raised her snout to sniff, too, and felt the pull of the sea air drawing her back the way she had come. Uncertainty gripped her again, like the jaws of the orca. *Am I going the wrong way?*

"Come on." The mother bear's eyes gleamed with anticipation as she left the male cub to stand on his own, and nudged the she-cub to her paws. "The sea isn't far away. And then there'll be plenty of fish for all of us. I think I can even make out a trace of ice already."

Ice! Kallik stiffened, sniffing frantically, but she couldn't pick up any ice at all on the air. *I'm not as good at scenting as a grown bear,* she thought sadly. *Maybe I never will be, because I don't have any bear to teach me.*

The mother bear beckoned to her cubs, urging them close to her. "Let's go."

"Can't we ride on you?" the she-cub pleaded, struggling forward shakily.

"Yes, we're tired," her brother added. "And my legs feel as floppy as a fish."

"Walk a bit first," their mother urged, nuzzling each of them encouragingly on the shoulder. "Some exercise will make you feel better."

She gave the male cub a gentle push to get him going. The she-cub tottered after him, and their mother brought up the rear. All three of them headed back the way Kallik had come. Back toward the Pathway Star. Away from the land, toward the sea.

Kallik's muscles tensed. For one desperate moment, she was tempted to plunge out of her hiding place to join them. Maybe they wouldn't attack her. The two cubs could be her friends: She liked the she-cub's bright, inquisitive eyes with their mischievous twinkle, and her brother's strong legs and shoulders would be good for games on the ice.

Most of all, the mother bear was gentle and loving to her cubs; she was taking care of them just as Nisa had taken care of Kallik and Taqqiq. Surely she wouldn't drive away a cub who needed help?

I could go back with them and find the ice!

Claws tore at Kallik's heart as she glanced over her shoulder. The moonlit path had led in the opposite direction. And maybe at the end of the path she would find Taqqiq. *But I'm not sure I'm strong enough to follow the path to the end!*

Looking back, she saw that the mother bear had paused, sniffing the air again.

"What's the matter?" the male cub demanded, swiping his tongue around his jaws. "Can you smell prey? Is it a seal?"

"No," his mother told him, still concentrating on the scent she was picking up. "I think there's another bear nearby."

The little she-cub let out a squeak and flattened herself to the ground. "A big bear? Will it eat us?"

Her brother gave her a scornful glance; he stayed on his paws, but Kallik could see his eyes widen as he glanced around nervously.

"There's nothing to be afraid of. This is a young bear," their mother murmured, half to herself. "I wonder what it's doing here on its own. Maybe I ought to search for it."

Kallik froze. She wasn't sure whether she wanted to be found or not. While she pressed herself deep into the shadow of the boulder, part of her wanted to leap up and squeal, "I'm here! I'm here! Come take care of me!"

"Let's look for it!" The she-cub sprang to her paws and started nosing around in a clump of reeds. "Bear! Are you in there?"

Her brother rolled his eyes and swatted at her with one paw. "Those reeds wouldn't hide a goose, seal-brain!" He scampered off to look behind an outcrop of rocks a few bearlengths away from where Kallik was hidden. Their mother padded off to search a thicket of thornbushes.

Envy stung Kallik like one of the flat-faces' pointy sticks. These bears were so lucky to have one another! She wanted so much to join them and have companions to play with, just as she had played with Taqqiq long ago on the ice. And more than anything she wanted a kind, loving mother to look after her and teach her how to hunt and smell the ice even when it was burn-sky.

Kallik braced herself to come out from behind the boulder. She was wondering what she ought to say to the mother bear when a breeze wafted around her and she heard her own mother's voice whispering along with it.

I will look after you, precious Kallik.

"Nisa?" Kallik breathed. "Is it really you?"

There were no more words, but as the breeze caressed her shoulder fur Kallik felt a sudden sense of safety, as if she could feel her mother's pelt brushing against her. Only for a moment; then the breeze died and Kallik was left alone again.

She took a deep breath and drew back into the shelter of the rock, just poking her snout cautiously around the side so that she could see what was happening. The mother bear had given up the search and gathered her cubs close to her again; she was padding away toward the sea. *If I want to join them, I have to go now or I've lost my chance.*

But Nisa's voice still echoed in her mind: *I will look after you.*

Kallik struggled with a wave of loneliness as she watched the other bears walk away. She waited until they had dwindled into the distance, then rose to her paws and padded off in the opposite direction, along the path that the moon had shown her.

"I'm coming," she promised her mother. "But please let me find Taqqiq soon. And if you can, tell him that I'm on my way."

CHAPTER SEVEN

Kallik

Kallik trudged across marshy ground. An occasional patch of hard gray stone poked through the grass, but all it meant was that her paws were rubbed raw instead of squelching with greenish water. There was no sign of any other animals, not even flat-faces—only a few birds flying overhead and swarms of insects buzzing around her. She paused to swipe a paw in front of her face, trying to drive them off.

Kallik felt as if she were the only bear left in the world. Trying to push down her fear of this empty, unfamiliar landscape, she gazed around for some sign that she was going the right way to find her brother, but she didn't know what to look for. She doubted the ice spirits watched over this place. She could only plod forward and hope that her paws were leading her closer to Taqqiq.

Hunger bawled in her belly, but she couldn't see anything that would make a good meal. Here and there were scrubby bushes that she scoured for berries, finding enough to keep her on her feet but too few to soothe the sharp pangs of emptiness inside her. The sun beat down more and more strongly on her thick white fur and she longed for the cool of the ice. Her paws hurt from the stones and the tough marsh grass; seeds snagged in her pelt and stuck between her claws. She couldn't even smell water anymore, only the endless mud.

Was I really supposed to follow the moon-path? Maybe it was just a trick of the light. Why did I have to leave the Pathway Star? I could have reached the sea by now.

Kallik jumped as a gust of wind rattled the branches of a nearby bush. She spun around, certain once more that something must be creeping up on her, but nothing moved in the empty landscape.

"Who's there?" she barked. Her voice sounded harsh, like stones grinding together. She tried to figure out when she had last spoken aloud, but she couldn't remember. She felt as if she'd been on her own forever.

She strained her ears, then felt foolish for expecting a reply. She realized how much she had been hoping for one; anything to relieve the loneliness of trekking across this endless plain.

When she turned to continue, she blundered straight into a clump of marsh plants, and a cloud of insects rose up around her on tiny wings. They dived into her ears and eyes, sticking to her dry lips and buzzing louder than a firebeast. She halted with her haunches in the mud, while she batted at the swarm with her front paws.

"Ow! Get off!" she squealed.

But the tiny black specks danced away from her flailing paws. They struck her face, crawled around her eyes, and crept into her nose and ears, until she wanted to claw off her fur to get rid of them. She began to run, stumbling through the marsh as she tried to leave the stinging swarm behind, but still the insects kept up with her as if they were hanging on to her pelt.

Kallik felt hard ground ringing beneath her feet. Still surrounded by insects, she stopped and tried to shake the mud off her paws. Somewhere ahead she could pick up the cool scent of a cave. She peered through the cloud of insects and made out a smooth dome of earth, rising up out of the flat tundra. She bounded forward, over the top of the dome; on the other side she spotted a shadowy space underneath a slab of rock. With a gasp of relief, she dove into it.

The insects clung to her fur for a few more heartbeats, then seemed to notice that it was darker and colder than before, and started to buzz away in search of the sun. Kallik kept her eyes shut tight until her pelt stopped tickling, and she was certain the last of them had gone.

Panting, she opened her eyes and looked around her. The cave was small, set neatly under the curved mound. Above her head was one large stone, supported by two uprights. There were carved markings on all the stones, and Kallik gave them a sniff, stiffening when she picked up the faint trace of flat-faces. Had they set up the stones and made the markings? *Why would they build a cave here?* she wondered, then shrugged.

Whatever their reason, they were long gone.

The cloud of insects still buzzed at the entrance to the cave. Kallik let out a long sigh.

"Don't come inside," she pleaded, not daring to take her eyes off them. Her voice still sounded croaky, like the bark of a walrus. "Go away. Find something else to torment." She huffed. "I know you're not listening to me," she added. "I'm just talking to myself."

Hunger clawed at her belly and her mouth was sticky with thirst. But at least the shadowed cave was cool. "I might as well get some rest," she decided out loud.

She pushed farther toward the back of the cave, where her nose twitched at a familiar scent.

"Have bears been here?" Sniffing here and there, she found a scrap of white fur and stared at it, puzzled. She had thought that she was the only white bear for many skylengths; what would others be doing here, instead of heading for the sea?

Kallik's heart pounded. She was afraid that the bears would come back and attack her for invading their cave, but her relief that she wasn't alone anymore was stronger than her fear. This wasn't an empty land after all; it was a place where white bears could live.

Beside the back wall of the cave was an untidy scatter of rabbit bones. There was not much meat left on them, but Kallik gnawed them gratefully, feeling her pangs of hunger ease a little. She wondered if she should leave the cave in case the other bears came back, but she was too tired and hot to keep on walking. Sleep crept over her aching limbs; giving in, she curled up and closed her eyes.

When Kallik woke, the soft pink glow of the early dawn was creeping into the cave. She blinked and rubbed her eyes with her paws; she felt as if she had only just closed them. The nights seemed to be getting shorter and shorter. She yawned and pulled herself to her paws. Peering cautiously out, she saw the gleam of the sun on the horizon. A new day was beginning, and a cool breeze was blowing.

As soon as she padded out into the open, her pelt crawled again with the feeling of being watched. She whirled around, but all she could see was a clump of grass waving in the breeze. Trying to ignore the sensation, she realized that bear scent lingered on the ground outside. Her belly churned; she wasn't sure she wanted to meet other bears.

But they might be friendly, she told herself. *Nanuk was, in the end. Those other bears, the ones from the metal bird, would have been friendly, too. And they'd be company, at least.* Trying not to worry, she padded on into the pale morning light.

Coming to the top of a gentle rise, Kallik spotted pale flecks in the haze, scattered over a wide stretch of mud. A succulent scent drifted into her nostrils.

"Snow geese!" she whispered. "Food!"

The birds were feeding in the mud. Kallik's first instinct was to hurl herself into the middle of the flock and grab the nearest goose, but she realized that would spook the birds long before she could reach them. Instead, she remembered what her mother had taught her. She skirted the flock until the breeze wouldn't carry her scent to the geese before she tried to get any nearer. Their scent blew toward her; when it was strongest she crept forward, keeping low, with her belly fur brushing the ground. She set her paws down so carefully that they didn't make a sound.

Gradually Kallik moved closer to the geese, watching their plump bodies and black-tipped wings. They were so busy feeding that they didn't notice her. She singled out the nearest bird, standing with its back to her and its beak dipped into the mud. Taking a deep breath, Kallik pushed off with her hind legs and stretched out her forepaws in a strong pounce.

The whole flock of geese rose up, flapping and shrieking in their harsh voices. For a moment Kallik's head spun as they whirled around her in a blizzard of wings. But she could feel her claws sinking into her prey, pinning it to the ground. It struggled to free itself, one wing flailing, until Kallik seized its neck in her jaws and killed it quickly.

She blinked, triumphant. The plover she had caught by the shore had been a lucky accident; this time she had spotted her prey, stalked it, and killed it just as Nisa would have done. *I can catch my own prey. I can take care of myself.*

She sank her jaws into the goose, tearing off a mouthful of flesh, crunching the bones in her strong teeth. At that moment nothing, not even seal fat, had ever tasted so delicious. The prey was warm in her belly; she had almost forgotten what it felt like to be full-fed. But before she had finished eating her kill, Kallik's mouth was dry from swallowing feathers; a small one caught in her throat, making her cough. "I need to find a pool," she muttered. She lifted her muzzle and sniffed, picking out a faint trace of water.

She turned aside, then halted and grabbed up the remains of the goose. There was still flesh on the bones, and Kallik didn't know when she might find more prey. Carrying the limp carcass, she padded over the muddy ground toward the tantalizing scent of water. Once again she felt as if she was being followed, but this time she didn't react. She knew that if she swung around to look, she wouldn't see anything.

At last she spotted clumps of reeds surrounding a small pool, its shining surface reflecting the blue sky. Kallik dropped the remains of the goose and plunged her snout into the brackish water, shivering with relief as she drank.

When she wasn't thirsty anymore, Kallik turned back to the goose. But as she was nosing among the feathers for another mouthful of flesh, she caught a flicker of movement in the corner of her eye. She looked up. Eyes gleamed from the middle of a bush, watching her. The branches quivered as the Arctic fox whose prey she had stolen days before crept out into the open; she recognized it by its torn ear.

"You again!" Kallik exclaimed. "You've been following me, haven't you?" Relief fluttered in her belly as she realized that the creature that had tracked her for so many days was no threat to her.

She studied it, tipping her head on one side. It looked as thin as she was, its hip bones jutting out from under its dusty pelt. It was alone, like her. She wondered if it felt as lonely as she did. The fox had its reddish-brown burn-sky pelt at the moment, but Kallik knew it would turn white later. Perhaps the fox was trying to reach the endless ice by then, or else its white pelt would show up too much and it would be harder than ever to stalk prey.

The fox crept a pace or two closer; its eyes were fixed on the remains of the goose. Kallik remembered how frustrated and angry she had felt when bigger bears had driven her away from food, and how her mother Nisa had been prepared to share.

"Maybe I owe you a meal," she muttered.

She backed away from the goose carcass. At first the fox eyed her suspiciously, as if it expected her to pounce if it moved any closer. But its hunger was stronger than its fear. Suddenly it darted forward, snatched the goose, and ran off with it, disappearing into the shelter of the bush.

Kallik's heart ached with a strange sadness when the fox had gone. It was the first company she had had since Nanuk died. She wondered if the fox would still follow her, now that she had repaid its stolen prey. "Travel safely," she murmured. "I hope we both find more prey, even if we can't catch it for each other."

Then she turned away and set out again, feeling lighter than she'd felt in days. She had eaten and drank more than she had in a long time, and she was traveling in the company of another creature, even if she couldn't exactly call the fox a friend. More than that, she was no longer following a hope, or a light in the sky.

She was following the scent of bears.

CHAPTER EIGHT

Lusa

Lusa trotted along beside Ujurak. The sun had risen high in the sky, its light dancing on the surface of the river and turning the bears' brown fur to a glowing russet. They padded in the same direction as the water, weaving their way through undergrowth a couple of bearlengths from the stone path, so as not to draw the attention of the firebeasts.

Lusa stifled a yawn. The night hadn't been nearly long enough to get proper sleep; she was tired and still hungry. For a few heartbeats she longed to be back in the Bear Bowl, but it felt a long, long way away. Too far to ever go back.

Was I right to come? Toklo won't even listen to what I want to tell him. Maybe he's right, and black bears and brown bears shouldn't live together.

"See that herb over there?" Ujurak interrupted her thoughts. He flicked his ears toward a tall plant with long dark leaves and yellow flowers. "It's good for healing wounds and scratches. Toklo found some for me when the flat-faces shot me with their deathsticks."

Lusa trotted over and sniffed the herb; it had a bitter,

pungent smell. "Can you eat it?" she asked hopefully.

Ujurak let out an amused huff. "No, you chew up the leaves and put the paste on the wound. It's not good to eat."

"I wish it was. I'm starving," Lusa complained. "How do you know which plants are good for healing and which are good for eating?" she added curiously.

Ujurak paused, his eyes fixed on something far away. "I don't remember," he said at last with a shrug. "I guess my mother taught me."

"Where did you live with your mother?" Lusa asked, as they padded on after Toklo. "Were there other bears around?"

Ujurak shook his head. "I don't know." He pointed to another plant. "We can eat those, though they're not proper food for bears."

The leaves of these plants had a bluish tinge in the sunlight; they grew thickly, in big clumps. Lusa gave them a cautious sniff, then pulled off a couple of small leaves and chewed them. They crunched pleasantly between her teeth, but the taste was bland.

"Ugh!" She curled her lip. "Berries would be better."

"We should still eat some," Ujurak told her, coming up beside her and tearing off a mouthful of his own. "They'll help keep us going."

Unwillingly Lusa kept on munching; the plants didn't seem to fill her belly at all, and the stringy stems caught in her teeth. *We have to find some better food soon,* she thought.

Toklo ignored the plants completely. Instead, he grubbed among the roots of a nearby tree, and came back to them with earth around his snout. Lusa hoped he had been eating insects and not soil, but she didn't say anything.

"There's another eagle up there." Ujurak pointed upward with his snout as they set off again. "I felt so strong, flying on the eagle's wings," he murmured almost to himself; Lusa had to pad close to his side to hear him. "Its mind was like a claw, reaching out for prey. But there wasn't much worth catching. Flat-faces everywhere. No wild, empty spaces any-more."

"What about the mountains?" Lusa reminded him. "There was lots of space up there."

"But flat-faces still come." Ujurak's voice was faint, as if he was imagining that he soared on eagle's wings. "Once, eagles thought the world belonged to them. Now they struggle for every kill."

While they were talking, Toklo had drawn several bear-lengths ahead; the ground sloped gently downward and thick bushes crowded up to the edge of the stone path. Lusa could barely make out the big cub's brown pelt among the under-growth. Suddenly he stopped and looked back. "Are you coming or not?" he called.

"Yes, wait for us!" Lusa called out, and scampered after him with Ujurak hard on her paws.

Soon after sunhigh, the stone path split into many smaller tracks, and the walls of flat-face dens began to appear among the trees.

"Whoa!" Toklo halted so abruptly that Lusa nearly barged into him. "We can't go this way."

Ujurak padded up beside him, peering curiously at the den walls and giving the air a cautious sniff. "It smells of firebeasts," he murmured.

Lusa's paws tingled with anticipation. The two brown bears had hardly ever been close to flat-faces; they had no idea of the delicious food you could find in their big silver cans. Taking a deep sniff, Lusa thought she could pick up tantalizing hints of something good to eat.

"We should keep going," she declared. "I know where there's food."

Toklo glared at her. "Are you bee-brained? Bears don't go near flat-faces. Do you want them shooting at us with their deathsticks?"

"They won't, not if we're quiet and clever. I'll show you how."

"Like I want a black bear showing me anything," Toklo huffed. "We're going back into the woods. I'll catch us some prey there."

He turned and padded off into the undergrowth; Ujurak followed, and Lusa had to go after them, casting a longing glance over her shoulders. *It's Toklo who's bee-brained. I* know *I can find food there!*

Once the flat-face dens were out of sight again, Toklo motioned Lusa and Ujurak to a hollow underneath a huge pine tree. "Wait here. I'll bring back some prey."

Lusa settled down, glad to be off her paws for a while. She could still hear the distant roar of firebeasts and pick up their harsh scent. She couldn't give up the idea of finding food in the silver cans that flat-faces kept outside their dens. *We'd have to wait until dark anyway,* she figured, glancing thoughtfully at Ujurak, who was snoozing with one paw over his nose.

Her head filled with thoughts of slipping off by herself while the others slept, and coming back with enough food to satisfy them all. *Toklo couldn't call me weak then!* But a pang of fear shook her like wind in a tree: Suppose they woke up while she was away, and went on without her?

The long day was drawing to an end before Lusa heard rustling in the undergrowth. She sat up, prodding the sleeping Ujurak, ready to flee in a heartbeat; then she relaxed as Toklo pushed his way out of the bushes with a single ground squirrel dangling from his jaws.

"Is that all you could catch?" she asked, dismayed.

"There's no prey anywhere," Toklo growled as he dropped the squirrel on the edge of the hollow. "The flat-faces must have scared it all away."

Ujurak got up and pressed his snout against Toklo's shoulder. "This'll be fine," he said. "We'll manage."

But the squirrel was old and scrawny; shared between the three of them, it was only a couple of dry mouthfuls each. Lusa's belly was still complaining when she had finished.

"*Now* will you try my plan?" she asked.

Toklo muttered something she didn't catch.

"We can't go on without food." Ujurak still sounded doubtful. "Maybe Lusa's right, and we should try the flat-face dens."

The big grizzly cub hesitated for a heartbeat, then shrugged.

"All right. But if it goes wrong, don't blame me."

Lusa took the lead as they padded back toward the dens in the gathering twilight. Her paws tingled with a mixture of excitement and fear. *I have to make this work!*

At last the cubs reached the edge of the stone path that separated them from the flat-face dens. Lusa stepped out confidently onto the hard surface; at the same moment a harsh beam of yellow light swept over her and a squealing firebeast rounded the corner. She leaped back just in time, feeling its hot sticky wind ruffle her fur as it passed. Her heart thudded hard enough to hurt; she almost wanted to turn back, but she knew Toklo and Ujurak were watching her. *I'll never hear the end of it if I give up now.*

Scared and embarrassed, she muttered, "Sorry," and looked both ways cautiously before venturing across, with Toklo and Ujurak close behind her.

On the other side of the stone path she followed the flat-face wall until she came to a gap blocked by wooden bars. Peering through, she saw an open, grassy enclosure at the back of a flat-face den; two of the big silver cans stood invitingly near the door.

Lusa sniffed, and her mouth started to water as she took in the tempting scents. "There's food in there," she said, dipping her head toward the cans. "Can you smell it?"

Ujurak nodded, but Toklo beckoned Lusa toward him with a jerk of his head. She padded over, blinking to get a piece of grit out of her eye. The firebeast had spat it at her as it roared past.

"We can't go in there," Toklo growled. "There's nowhere to hide."

Lusa let out an exasperated sigh. Did Toklo think the flat-faces were going to come out and give the food to him? They could only get the food if the enclosure around the den was empty. Didn't he know anything about flat-faces? Maybe he didn't. Maybe proper bears, bears who had always lived in the wild, didn't have to know about getting food from flat-faces. She felt her shoulders sag.

"Okay," she said. "We'll find somewhere better."

Silently they crept farther along the wall. The next gap opened to reveal an enclosure edged with thick bushes; the grassy space between them had another thicket in the very middle. Two more silver cans stood by the door, giving out more tasty smells.

"This is better," Lusa whispered. At least there were places to hide. Was that what a proper bear would look for?

Without waiting for Toklo to disagree, she clambered over the wooden bars and pushed her way underneath the nearest bush. Peeking out, she saw that one window of the den was lit, casting slices of yellow light on the grass, but thin, sharp-edged pelts were pulled across most of the gap; the flat-faces inside wouldn't be able to see her.

She shifted over to give Toklo and Ujurak more space as they wriggled under the branches to join her.

"Now what?" Toklo grumbled, squirming to unhook a twig from his ear.

"I'll go open the cans," Lusa replied. "You two watch what

I do, then you can try next time."

She slid out of the bushes and crept across the grass, keeping the central thicket between her and the den. She was more confident now; it felt good to be taking the lead and showing the others what she could do. When she reached the main clump of shrubs, she paused to check out the den. Flat-face voices came faintly from it, but the door and windows were all closed. Lusa emerged from her hiding place and padded across the grass to the silver cans.

Prying up the lid of the first can with her claws, she managed to lower it to the ground with no more than a few scraping noises. She cushioned the can with her paws, so it wouldn't give her away by clanging when she tipped it over. Two bulging shiny black skins tumbled out. Her mouth watering from the delicious smells that wreathed around her, Lusa ripped into one of the skins.

Among the flat-face trash she spotted a few of the potato sticks she had found before. Shoving her snout inside the skin, she crunched them up, reveling in the strong, fatty taste. Guilt swept over her as she remembered Toklo and Ujurak; glancing over her shoulder, she could make out their eyes gleaming from the edge of the bushes. *But there weren't many sticks,* she excused herself. *Not enough to share.*

Lusa investigated the other skin, but there was nothing in there good for bears to eat. She turned to the second can, but this time the lid was stuck; when she tugged at it with her claws it shot off unexpectedly, clattering down on the path beside the door.

Lusa froze, her ears flattened. Before the noise had died away, a dog started barking inside the den. All Lusa's instincts told her to flee. But she couldn't leave without finding something for her friends to eat. She tipped the silver can over, not caring this time whether it made a noise or not.

The door of the flat-face den flew open. A long-legged flat-face stood there shouting; a small white dog shot out from behind him, yapping.

Over the noise, Lusa heard Toklo barking, "Get out of there! Now!"

Panicking, she clawed at the skin inside the second can. A chicken carcass rolled out; she grabbed it up and raced across the grass toward the gap in the wall. With the dog snarling at her paws, she flung herself over the wooden bars and found Toklo and Ujurak pressed against the wall outside, their eyes huge with alarm.

"Come on!" Toklo huffed. His claws scraped on the stone path as he turned and led them back the way they had come. Lusa glanced behind her; to her relief, the dog was standing in the gap as if an invisible wall stopped it from stepping onto the stone path. Its ears were flattened and it was still yapping furiously. There was no sign of the flat-face, though Lusa heard a clattering sound as if the silver can was being picked up.

"Keep up!" barked Ujurak, and Lusa realized she had fallen behind the others. She put on an extra burst of speed and caught up to them at the edge of the stone path. There was no time to check for firebeasts; they raced across, and Lusa winced as her paws sank into sticky mud where the sun had melted the black stone. She hopped on three paws, trying to pull the mud off with her teeth, but the stench made her eyes water and her muzzle ended up as sticky as her paw.

"Come on!" Toklo called. He had pushed his back half into a bush with shiny dark leaves; Lusa could only see his shoulders and his face. She dived in beside him, almost squashing Ujurak, who crouched among the branches close to the trunk.

"Here." Lusa dropped the chicken carcass and tried not to gasp for breath too obviously. "I told you I'd find some food."

"You told us it was easy to get food from flat-faces," Toklo pointed out. His fur was sticking up in all directions, and one of his claws was bleeding. "You nearly got us killed!"

"No, I didn't!" Lusa protested. "It was just bad luck that the flat-face came out. That dog was too small to hurt us. And anyway, I *did* get us something to eat."

Toklo nosed the chicken suspiciously. "I'm not eating that," he grunted. "It stinks of flat-faces."

"What?" Lusa's pelt grew hot with anger. "So it's okay to eat food you catch, but not to eat what I find?"

"See? I *catch* food, you just *find* it. Or steal it from flat-faces. That shows how squirrel-brained you are," the big grizzly cub growled. "That's no way for a bear to hunt."

"Well, it's the way *I* hunt," Lusa retorted. "At least I got something. Do you want us all to starve to death?"

"You don't understand. You're not a proper bear." Toklo turned and pushed his way out of the bush, padding farther off into the woods.

Lusa met Ujurak's doubtful gaze. "You'll have some, won't you?" she pleaded. Her belly was still grumbling; the potato sticks hadn't been enough to satisfy her, but what she really wanted was to see her friends eating food she had provided.

To her dismay, Ujurak shook his head. "It's not natural to eat flat-face stuff," he said. "Besides, it smells yucky!"

"Fine!" Lusa huffed. "I'll eat it myself."

She gulped down the mouthfuls of chicken, crunching the bones, but it felt like chewing on wood. Toklo was right; she wasn't a proper bear. Her paws were meant for climbing trees, not for opening flat-face cans and stealing their food.

The chicken felt heavy in her belly as she and Ujurak followed Toklo into the trees and left the flat-face dens behind.

When Toklo and Ujurak found a hollow sheltered by bushes, Lusa climbed a tree and huddled miserably on a branch. She couldn't sleep. *They would be better off without me.*

The next morning Ujurak took the lead again, skirting the flat-face dens in a wide circle. The trees thinned out and gave way to tough moorland grass patched with clumps of thorn bushes. Lusa shivered as the chilly wind buffeted her fur. She felt vulnerable without branches overhead, without the comforting murmurs of the bear spirits. Ujurak led them straight across the moorland, their shadows padding dark alongside them as the sun reddened.

Rounding an outcrop of rock, Lusa halted in surprise to see three or four grayish white animals slowly wandering the hillside, their heads down as they nibbled the rough grass. "What are those?" she asked.

"Sheep," Ujurak replied, at the same time as Toklo growled, "Your next meal." Adding, "Stay back, both of you," he flattened himself to the ground and began to stalk the sheep, keeping downwind of them.

Making use of a dip in the ground where a tiny stream trickled along, Toklo crept almost close enough to touch the nearest sheep before he rose up on his hindpaws, roaring with his forepaws splayed. The group of sheep split up, letting out a terrified bleating as they ran in different directions. Toklo tried to drop down on one of them, but it leaped away; his forepaws grazed its rump as it fled.

Toklo let out a snarl of fury and gave chase. The sheep dodged rocks and scattered between bushes, but Toklo stayed hard behind one of them, whipping around to cut it off before it could escape. At last he put on a burst of speed and barged into its side, knocking it over. Lusa saw the sheep's legs kick frantically, and then it was still.

Toklo grabbed the sheep's neck in his jaws and dragged it back to where Lusa and Ujurak were waiting.

"Great kill!" Ujurak said, his eyes shining.

Toklo nodded to acknowledge the praise. He dropped the carcass at their paws. "Eat," he invited, settling down beside the sheep to tear off a huge mouthful for himself.

"Thanks, Toklo!" Ujurak dived in right away.

Lusa hesitated. She felt awkward and frustrated. Toklo had provided them with good food, and all she could do was eat it.

She still felt hot with shame when she remembered her own efforts at hunting.

"Thank you," she mumbled after a few heartbeats, and crouched beside Ujurak to eat. The meat of the sheep tasted rich and warm, but Lusa felt as if every mouthful would choke her. She didn't deserve it. She hated being so dependent on Toklo, when he clearly didn't like her and didn't want to talk to her.

He had judged her from the start, just because she had grown up in the Bear Bowl rather than the wild. If only he knew how much she had learned since leaving the Bowl, how much closer she was to being what he would call a proper bear now. She didn't always get things right, but she always tried.

Why does he have to be so angry? Hasn't he ever made a mistake in his life?

CHAPTER NINE

Lusa

That night the cubs sheltered among thornbushes, and the next day continued their trek across the moorland. Toklo pushed them on at a fast pace, and Lusa was panting when they finally reached the crest of the hills. In front of her paws the land fell away in long slopes to a valley. A river wound its way along the bottom; Lusa's claws dug into the grass when she saw how wide it was: She could hardly make out the opposite bank.

"Is that where we're going?" she asked.

Ujurak nodded. "The Pathway Star leads us across the river."

"And how do you suppose we're going to get to the other side?" Toklo growled. "I'm not going to swim."

"We'll find a bridge," Ujurak said.

Lusa nodded, secretly pleased that she wouldn't have to swim so far. She didn't doubt that she could, but she would feel very exposed, with no overhanging trees to hide her from passing firebeasts or flat-faces.

Twilight was gathering by the time the bears reached the

edge of the river. On the flat riverbank Lusa found her paws sinking into the grass and water welling up around her paws, soaking her fur. Padding alongside the river, she had to steer a winding course among clumps of longer grasses and reeds with feathery tops. The air was full of the scent of water and the thin, piping calls of strange birds.

"I hope we can find somewhere dry to sleep," she murmured to Ujurak.

Toklo beckoned them over to a hollow near a tumble of rocks, but the grass at the bottom was wet and spongy.

"This is no good," Lusa protested. "We'll get soaking wet."

"Then find somewhere better," Toklo snapped.

Lusa bit back a sharp retort. They were all tired and anxious; she knew it was important to find somewhere soon, because there was so little time to sleep now that the nights were so short. "But I'm not sleeping in a swamp," she muttered to herself.

"What about among the reeds?" Ujurak suggested. "We'd be hidden there."

"The reeds are *growing* in water, bee-brain," Toklo replied.

In the end they had to settle for a hump of tussocky grass with only a straggling bush for shelter. Toklo settled down with his back to the others and his paws clamped firmly over his snout. Damp and miserable, Lusa listened to his snoring, and to the quieter breathing of Ujurak. She peered upward for a glimpse of the Bear Watcher, wanting the reassurance she always felt under that quiet gaze, but clouds covered the sky.

At last she fell into a fitful doze, and was woken in the morning by the splashing of rain on the marshy ground. She crept out from the scant shelter of the bush, trying to shake water from her pelt. In front of her the river stretched out in a silver-gray expanse, reflecting the cloudy sky. Raindrops pitted its flat surface. The far bank was barely visible through the rain.

Behind her she could hear grunts and rustling as Toklo and Ujurak woke. The big grizzly padded past her without a word, heading toward the river. Ujurak followed him.

"If we have to swim we won't get much wetter," Lusa grumbled to herself.

Toklo's ears twitched. "I'm not going to swim. How many more times do I have to tell you?"

Ujurak found a track leading through the reeds to the edge of the river, where they could drink. The current rolled on, deep and silent, the surface bouncing with raindrops, and rain hid the far bank. Lusa stifled a pang of fear at the mist-shrouded emptiness.

A loud honking from overhead interrupted her thoughts. Lusa looked up to see a flock of geese swooping down out of the sky. They skimmed the surface of the river with tremendous squawking and clattering, to land on the grass a few bearlengths downstream.

"Could we catch one, do you think?" Lusa asked hopefully.

Before any bear could reply, a ripple of movement passed among the geese. *Maybe they heard me,* Lusa thought. The whole flock took to the air again; she watched as they whirled across the sky, then lined up in a ragged snout shape and flew off downriver to vanish into the mist.

"They've gone," Lusa said, disappointed. She turned to see if Ujurak was watching the geese, too.

But the small brown cub had vanished. Wildly she looked up and down the river, but all she could see was Toklo raising his snout from the water and shaking off the drops.

Lusa ran to his side. "Ujurak has gone! He was standing right beside me."

Toklo didn't reply. He just gazed downriver in the direction the geese had taken.

Lusa's belly lurched. "He changed, didn't he? He's flying away with the geese."

Toklo nodded, then settled down on his haunches and started grooming the knots out of his fur. Lusa watched him for a moment; she felt awkward because Toklo didn't seem to be bothered by the fact that their companion had vanished. "What if Ujurak doesn't come back?"

The big grizzly cub glanced up. "Don't worry, he will."

"But what if he doesn't? What will we do? We can't read the signs without him."

Toklo didn't reply, just kept on tugging at a particularly stubborn knot.

Lusa didn't dare go on asking. Ujurak *had* to come back! He was the only one who knew which way to go; he wouldn't just leave them like this. But she couldn't stop thinking how much easier it would be to reach the place where the spirits danced if you could wing your way through the sky in the shape of a bird, instead of trudging along on the ground as a bear.

Finally Toklo seemed satisfied that his pelt was as smooth as he could make it. He looked up and faced Lusa. "Ujurak *will* come back." His voice was full of confidence. "I know he will. We don't have to worry."

Lusa was startled by his faith. Toklo hadn't known Ujurak for much longer than he had known her, and yet he clearly trusted the younger cub. Even if he didn't trust her, it might be a sign that Toklo wasn't as scornful of other bears as he pretended to be.

She nodded. "Then we'll wait."

"You don't have to," Toklo said, a rare gentleness in his tone. Lusa could hear the words he hadn't spoken. *But I do.*

He needs *Ujurak!* The realization broke on Lusa like the sun rising, chasing away the darkness of the night. Compassion for Toklo filled her; he had just proven that no bear could truly exist alone. Not even Oka: Her choice to abandon her cub had driven her mad.

At least she wasn't alone when the flat-faces came for her. Lusa knew Oka had been glad of her company that long, echoing night.

Long grasses grew at the water's edge, trailing into the river. Lusa tore off a mouthful and chewed it, refreshed by the moist stems. After a few moments, Toklo padded down the bank for another drink, a few bearlengths farther downstream. Then he began to eat the succulent grasses, too.

Lusa crept along the bank until she was close enough to reach out and touch Toklo's shoulder with her muzzle.

Toklo jumped, almost choking on his mouthful of grass.

"Don't sneak up on me like that!" he spluttered. "What do you want?"

"Why won't you swim? I know you can. All bears can."

Suspicion flared in Toklo's brown eyes. "What do you want to know for? It's none of your business."

Lusa's instincts told her to turn away, not to bother him anymore. Instead she gathered her courage. "I thought you might tell me, that's all."

For a long moment, Toklo stared at her. Then he looked down at his paws. "I'm scared," he confessed.

"Why?"

"I—I can feel the spirits trying to drag me under." He didn't look up at Lusa. "I think maybe Tobi is trying to drown me, because he's lonely in the river, or maybe it's Oka, punishing me because I lived when her favorite cub died."

"But Oka wouldn't do that," Lusa said, trying to keep her voice steady. "She loved you very much."

The two cubs stared at each other for a long moment. Then Toklo turned away, his shoulders hunched. He tore up another mouthful of grass. "I don't care what my mother felt," he mumbled.

Please, Arcturus, Lusa prayed, *tell me what to say.*

"Flat-faces brought Oka into the Bear Bowl," she began. Toklo stiffened, but he didn't turn to look at her; he just kept champing on the grasses. "She was really thin, as if she'd been starving. She was so unhappy and so angry, and at first I didn't understand why. She had food and shelter, and the flat-faces were kind, they really were. But Oka didn't seem to care about getting her strength back. She just wanted to get *out*, back to the wild. She kept throwing herself at the fences, trying to break her way through."

There was no response from Toklo. Lusa just had to believe that he was still listening.

"I've always *known* bears don't have to live in a Bear Bowl," she went on, with an edge to her tone. *I'm not as dumb as he thinks!* "My father, King, was born in the wild, you know. I always loved hearing his stories of what life was like there. And I thought Oka might have some good stories, too. But she didn't want to talk to me. She just lay beside the fence with her eyes closed."

She wondered whether to tell Toklo about the time when Oka attacked a flat-face. She suspected that Toklo wouldn't share her feeling that the attack had been a dreadful thing to do; after all, he would have attacked a flat-face cub if Ujurak hadn't stopped him. But she couldn't leave it out, because it was why Oka had died without having a chance to find Toklo.

"Oka had been in the Bear Bowl for about a moon when she clawed a flat-face," she continued in a rush. "He'd come to feed her, and she charged at him and knocked him over." She suppressed a shudder as memories of the flat-face screaming and his blood splashing onto the grass flickered in her mind. "She held him down and clawed him, and he howled in pain. It was terrible."

Toklo's ears twitched; he was certainly listening now. "What does attacking a flat-face have to do with me?"

"Nothing. . . ." Lusa searched for the right words. "Oka was just so angry that she couldn't find you again. She had lost both her cubs—how do you think she felt?"

Toklo gazed out across the river. The rain had eased off and the clouds were breaking up, letting a gleam of sunlight through.

"Oka told me about you and Tobi." Lusa pressed on gently. "Because Tobi died, she thought you would die, too, and she couldn't bear it. That's why she sent you away to take care of yourself. She was so sorry. She didn't mean to hurt the flat-face, she was just grieving so much for you and Tobi."

A low, throaty sound came from deep in Toklo's chest, and he turned his head from side to side as if he were trying to shake off a stinging insect. For the first time he looked Lusa full in the face. His brown eyes were clouded.

Lusa wanted to press herself against his shoulder to comfort him with the warmth of her pelt, but she didn't quite dare.

"After the attack, the flat-faces took her away," she said. "She never came back. They . . . they wouldn't have returned her to the wild. Oka knew that. She was thinking about you, all the time. She was sorry for what she did to you. She—"

"She wasn't sorry!" Toklo growled. "If she had really cared, she wouldn't have sent me away."

Lusa's heart sank and she turned her head to look at the river sliding past.

Then she heard the beating of wings above her head. A goose was swooping down out of the sky, stretching out its legs for a landing. As soon as its feet touched the ground they began to thicken; its body expanded and brown fur flowed over it, swallowing up its feathers. Its wings became forepaws and its beak changed to a snout. Within a heartbeat Ujurak stood in front of them, a few bearlengths from the water's edge.

Lusa was too frozen by relief and astonishment to move. Ujurak trotted up to them. "Hi," he said. "Are you okay?"

"You came back!" Lusa exclaimed.

"Of course I came back. Did you think I wouldn't?" Ujurak gave her a friendly shove. "I'll always come back."

"Where have you been?" Toklo asked. His voice rasped with anger; Lusa wasn't sure if he was angry with her for telling him about Oka, or with Ujurak for taking off like that without warning.

"Flying with the geese," Ujurak replied, his eyes stretching wide. "They are so scared, and hungry. Their nesting grounds are shrinking, and they can find hardly anything to eat as they fly toward them."

"But did you see anything useful, like a place to cross the river?" Toklo prompted.

"Yes," Ujurak answered, the faraway look in his eyes clearing. "Farther downriver there's a flat-face bridge made of gray stone. It's huge, and there are firebeasts using it to cross."

"All right, let's go. Show us where it is." Ignoring Lusa, Toklo strode off downriver with Ujurak trotting behind him.

Lusa followed. She wished she could have done more to help Toklo understand his mother's sorrow. *It's my fault,* she told herself. *I didn't say it right.*

CHAPTER TEN

Toklo

"Where's this bridge?" Toklo called, glancing over his shoulder to where Ujurak and Lusa were padding along side by side.

"I'm not sure," Ujurak admitted. "Everything looks so different from up in the air." He paused, then nodded toward a clump of pine trees several bearlengths downriver, on the opposite bank. "I think we'll see it once we've passed those."

The rain had changed to a fine drizzle that misted like cobwebs on Toklo's pelt and trickled through to his skin, chilling him to his bones. "I wish I had wings," he grunted.

His belly still churned from the pain of what Lusa had told him, but he wasn't going to let her see.

Why should I care what Oka said before she died? She sent me away when I needed her. Nothing will ever change that.

The river seemed to wind on forever; the bank was covered with wiry grass that felt harsh underpaw, with never a sniff of proper prey. *What am I doing here?* Toklo grumbled to himself. *This isn't a good place for bears.*

They passed the trees that Ujurak had pointed out, but

there was still no sign of the bridge. "Are we ever going to get across?" Toklo muttered. "If we keep on like this for much longer, I'll have webbed paws."

"Sorry." Ujurak hunched his shoulders. "I guess it doesn't look so far when you're flying."

The pine trees were out of sight behind them when Toklo's ears picked up a rumbling noise ahead. It grew louder and louder, until he spotted firebeasts roaring along a BlackPath in an unending stream. They belched out a foul-smelling smoke that caught in Toklo's throat and made him cough.

"There." Ujurak nodded toward the firebeasts.

Lusa halted. "Wow! I didn't think there were so many fire-beasts, ever!"

Toklo stopped beside her, limbs stiffening and every hair on his pelt prickling with alarm. Ujurak had said the BlackPath was huge where it crossed the river, but he had never imagined it could be this big. *It's not meant for bears. . . .* Toklo pushed the thought away. They had to keep going; this was the only way they had of crossing.

When it reached the river, the BlackPath continued, stretching above their heads right across the water to the other side, supported by giant legs of the same shiny stuff the firebeasts were made from.

"We'll never get across there now." Lusa's fur stood on end and her eyes were scrunched up against the fumes and dust. "We should wait here until night comes. Maybe most of the firebeasts will have gone back to their dens by then."

"*I'm* not waiting here," Toklo protested, his muscles

tightening at the thought of staying out in the open where flat-faces could spot them easily.

"Let's go farther down the bank," Ujurak suggested. "We can hide there."

With a grunt of agreement, Toklo went first, scrambling down the riverbank until they reached a clump of bushes not far from the first of the bridge supports. He hadn't realized how massive they were until he saw it close-up; he had to tilt his head all the way back to see the top. He trotted up and gave it a sniff, but it didn't have much scent of its own, only the harsh tang of firebeasts.

Every heartbeat that passed made Toklo more convinced that something was wrong. He wondered if the others felt the same; perhaps they were angry with him for refusing to swim. Gazing out across the greasy brown water, he thought of what Lusa had told him: that Oka loved him, and wished she hadn't sent him away. That didn't make him feel any better about swimming. How could his mother *not* want to drag him under and drown him if she was so desperate to see him again?

Under the bridge the noise of the firebeasts clanged in his ears until his head hurt and he couldn't even hear his own thoughts. Toklo retraced his pawprints to where Ujurak and Lusa were nosing among the bushes.

"It's not too bad here," Ujurak said. "We can rest while we wait for nightfall."

"Hey, come over here!" Lusa called. "There are masses of berries."

Toklo turned to spot a flash of red among the tangling

branches. Padding closer, he saw Lusa standing beside a bush heavy with bright scarlet berries. She was reaching up to a branch, her jaws parted to bite down on the succulent fruit.

"No!" Toklo roared. "Stop!" Belly clenched with terror, he bounded over to her and roughly shouldered her away.

"Okay," Lusa said, scrabbling to get her balance and shooting him an aggrieved glare. "You can eat first if you want."

Toklo glared back at her. "No one gets to eat them. Those berries are deadly to bears," he growled. "Don't you know that? If you eat them you'll get horrible pains in your belly, and then you'll die."

Lusa began to back away, her annoyance changing to fear that made her eyes as big as moons. "I'm sorry," she said. "I didn't know."

"Of course you didn't," Toklo huffed, turning his back. *She'll never be a proper bear!* He shoved his way through the branches of the nearest bush and settled down close to the trunk with his nose resting on his paws.

In spite of the firebeast thunder, he dozed and dreamed of walking through his own territory in the forest, leaving his clawmarks on trees to mark his borders. Everywhere he walked belonged to him alone; there were no other bears relying on him to protect them and to find food. Full-fed, he lazed in a clearing with the sun warming his pelt. He could hear the gurgling of a river where he knew he could catch a plump salmon, and see the spot on the ground where a grouse had made her twiggy nest and filled it with eggs. Under a nearby tree was his den, where he could sleep, held safely by the earth.

He tried to enjoy the feeling of warmth and safety, but something was nagging at him. It niggled him with more and more urgency until he sprang to his paws. "Where are you?" he called to his dream-forest. "What do you want?"

He took off, charging through the trees, barking as he searched more and more desperately. He didn't even know what he was looking for.

"Toklo? Is it time to go on?"

Lusa's voice startled him; he realized he must have been barking out loud. He opened his eyes, and the sunlit forest slipped out of his mind. As Lusa scrambled out of their make-shift den, the branches shifted blackly against deep shadows, and Toklo saw that the long daylight had faded. The rumble of firebeasts crossing the bridge had eased, like the far-off rumble of a fading storm. Cautiously he stuck his head out of the bushes. The rain had stopped, though water still welled up around his paws when he trod on the sodden grass.

Lusa and Ujurak were waiting for him by the edge of the river; the water was thick and black now, and Toklo pushed down a bolt of terror that tried to choke him. *I'm not going near it,* he reminded himself. *Oka won't be able to grab me.*

Ujurak was letting out huffs of anxiety. "Toklo, we have to go!"

"Okay." Toklo scrambled back up the bank and to the edge of the BlackPath. The dazzling eyes of the firebeasts sliced through the dusk; a line of the huge creatures was still roaring across the bridge.

"I thought you said the firebeasts would have gone back to

their dens?" Ujurak said, blinking in the glare.

Lusa twitched her ears. "It's quieter than it was."

"We'll be okay if we keep to the edge," Toklo told them. "Come on. Follow me."

Keeping a cautious eye on the firebeasts as they approached, then roared away in both directions, he padded onto the bridge. Lusa pushed Ujurak into place behind Toklo and brought up the rear. Beside the BlackPath was a shiny wall, like thin silver saplings joined together. Through the gaps between the uprights Toklo could see the river below, foaming white as it churned around the supports of the bridge. It was a long way to fall; even though the uprights were too close together for a bear to slip through, Toklo felt dizzy when he looked down. After that first glance he kept his gaze firmly fixed on the BlackPath.

The ground at the edge of the BlackPath was filthy with greasy puddles and flat-face trash. The cubs splashed along; Toklo was blinded by the glaring eyes of the firebeasts that bore down on him, and flinched at the showers of filthy water their round black paws sprayed over him as they passed. Their wind buffeted his fur and made the air taste of grit and their choking fumes.

They had almost reached the halfway point when Toklo heard a deeper roar than before. A vast firebeast was heading right for him, its bulk blocking out the night sky. His gaze locked with its glaring eye-beams; he couldn't look away. He crouched down, trembling, convinced that the massive creature would charge straight over him, leaving his broken body behind. Lusa and Ujurak huddled beside him.

Then it was gone; Toklo glanced up to see two pairs of eyes gleaming as Lusa and Ujurak gazed at him, horrified. The red eyes in the vast firebeast's hindquarters were receding rapidly.

Toklo took a deep breath, trying to stop his heart pounding its way out of his chest. "Come on," he urged. "It didn't hurt us."

Lusa had overtaken Ujurak, who stood still, gazing down at the surging river through the gaps in the shiny wall. "Ujurak!" she urged. "We can't stay here. It's too dangerous."

When he was sure the smaller cub was following, Toklo set off again, hearing the pawsteps of his companions splashing behind. The firebeasts ruffled his fur and filled his nostrils with their stink. Toklo could see the flat-faces inside staring out at him and his companions. *Haven't you ever seen a bear before?*

One of the firebeasts slowed to a crawl, and a bright flash came from inside its belly. Toklo saw one of the flat-faces inside holding up a small black creature with a single huge eye. He bared his teeth and snarled; the bright flash came again, but the creature didn't dare leap out to attack him, and at once the firebeast roared away.

Scared, huh?

He felt as if he had been wading through trash and dirty puddles forever, but at last the far bank was only a few bear-lengths away. The shiny wall came to an end; the bank beyond, covered with bushes, sloped steeply down to the water's edge.

Toklo scrambled off the bridge, digging his claws into earth and roots to keep his balance as he climbed a bearlength down. Lusa followed him and turned back to wait for Ujurak.

As the small cub drew closer to the end of the bridge, another huge firebeast came roaring up behind him, its glaring eye-beams spilling over him.

"Look out!" Toklo barked.

Ujurak broke into a run, but his legs couldn't carry him faster than the firebeast's huge black paws, hissing nearer and nearer. The corner of the firebeast clipped his flank, tossing him up into the air. Ujurak let out a squeal. He hurtled onto the bank, his paws flailing, and slid downward until the branches of a bush brought him crashing to a halt.

"Ujurak!" Lusa cried, flinging herself down the slope to Ujurak's side.

For a few heartbeats Toklo stood frozen, gazing at the unmoving brown shape. He was thinking of another small cub who would never move again. Would they have to listen to Ujurak's breath growing slower and slower until it stopped? Would they have to cover him with leaves and moss, like Tobi? He remembered Oka's howls when she discovered that the cub she loved best was dead.

Panic slammed into Toklo's chest. *I can't remember the marks Oka made in the earth! I can't remember the words she said!* He wanted to howl like his mother, blaming the spirits for taking Ujurak away. He didn't dare follow Lusa down. While he waited here, he could try to tell himself that Ujurak would be okay. Guilt and anger churned inside him. He was the strong one; he should have protected Ujurak.

They should have swum across the river.

"Toklo!" Lusa called, looking up from where she crouched over Ujurak. "Come here!"

Toklo forced his paws to move, and scrambled clumsily down the slope to where Ujurak lay scrunched up. "Is he dead?"

"Don't be such a squirrel-brain." Lusa rested her paw on Ujurak's flank, drawing Toklo's attention to the faint rise and fall of his chest. "See? He's still breathing."

For a moment Toklo couldn't speak. He raised his head to stare out over the churning black water. He thought it looked hungry, swollen with the spirits of dead bears. *But you won't have another spirit tonight.*

Lusa bent over Ujurak again, swiping her tongue over his nose and around his muzzle. "Wake up, Ujurak. Please wake up," she begged.

Ujurak's eyes stayed closed. Toklo couldn't see any sign of injury on his body, except for a few scrapes on his fur, which probably came from roots and branches as he fell. He dug his claws hard into the ground. Ujurak had to wake soon, or he'd slip into death just as Tobi had. Leaning forward, Toklo sniffed Ujurak's fur. He didn't have the same sharp scent that had signaled Tobi's approaching death. Perhaps he would be all right after all. Dizzy with thankfulness, he closed his eyes, only opening them again when Lusa exclaimed, "He's waking up!"

Ujurak's chest heaved and his eyes flickered open.

"Oh, Ujurak!" Lusa's voice was husky with relief. "Can you stand up?"

The young cub blinked in bewilderment. "What happened? Where—" He tried to scramble up and collapsed again, his words ending in a gasp of pain.

"A firebeast hit you," Toklo said.

He wasn't sure that Ujurak understood. The small cub's eyes had closed again, and he kept whimpering as Lusa sniffed all over his body.

"I don't think you've broken any bones," she murmured reassuringly, smoothing Ujurak's fur with one paw. "Try to get up. We'll find a place to shelter."

"I can't," Ujurak moaned.

"Of course you can." Lusa bent down and gave the little cub's snout a comforting lick. "Remember when you were a goose, flying away on big, strong wings? You can do anything."

". . . not a goose now," Ujurak murmured, but he made a big effort and hauled himself to his paws.

"Lean on me," Lusa encouraged him, shoving her shoulder under Ujurak's for support. "There's a hollow not far away."

Staggering, paws weaving uncertainly, Ujurak let Lusa guide him down to a hollow just above the river, sheltered by a straggling berry bush.

Toklo plodded after them. "Ujurak, tell me about the healing plants," he urged. "I'll find some for you."

"Can't remember . . ." Ujurak breathed out the words, his eyes closing again.

Lusa curled protectively beside him, her eyes soft with sympathy. "Let him be. We'll ask him again in the morning."

Toklo nodded, and settled himself on the rim of the hollow. Ujurak had survived this time, but what about the next? This wasn't a place where bears should be. It was too dangerous.

It's all my fault, because I wouldn't swim the river. He made himself remember what Lusa had told him about his mother. *Was she right? Did Oka really love me?*

Toklo sighed. However he tried to excuse himself, he had been a coward. And his cowardice had nearly cost Ujurak his life. The young cub might forgive him, but Toklo knew he would never be able to forgive himself.

CHAPTER ELEVEN

Kallik

Kallik had lost track of time. She felt as if she'd been trekking across the empty landscape forever. The nights were so short; no sooner had the sun set than its glittering edge rose again from the flat horizon.

When the sun was at its fiercest and the flies were most troublesome, Kallik tried to find shade to sleep. Then she began trudging again.

Every so often she came across bear prints and droppings, and some of them were almost fresh. Once she saw a large male far ahead of her. She followed at a distance until he drew ahead and she lost sight of him.

As she trekked, she often thought about the family of bears she had seen set down by the metal bird. Kallik imagined playing with the she-cub and her brother, chasing them and scampering through the snow.

But most often, she thought about her mother and brother. All kinds of things could spark her memories. She could be curled behind a rock, sheltering from the sun, and suddenly she'd remember being safe and warm, curled up with Nisa and Taqqiq in the birth den, listening to Nisa's stories of Silaluk and how she was chased by Robin, Chickadee, and Moose Bird. Or she'd be clawing the hole of a mouse in the hard ground and she'd remember crouching next to Taqqiq beside an ice hole, while Nisa taught them how to catch a seal. Even in this sunburnt wilderness, Kallik's paws tingled with excitement as she remembered how Nisa had dragged her prey up onto the ice; she could almost taste the rich fat as she sank her teeth into the meal her mother had provided.

Then, one morning, the sun grew hazy and soon it vanished altogether in a misty white cloud. The cloud sank lower and lower, unrolling across the plain until Kallik could barely see her own paws, and the sound they made was muted, as if she were padding across a covering of feathers. It was cold, too: not the hard, bright cold of the ice, but a raw chill that sank into her pelt and invaded her body with every breath. It was spooky to set her paws down when she had no idea of what lay ahead. She was walking blind, more alonc than she had ever been before.

Kallik's eyes began to ache from the bright sheen of the mist around her, dazzling in the light of a sun she couldn't see. Gradually, the glare softened as the sun dropped in the sky, and then she felt like she was walking on the bottom of the sea. She must have slept, and she woke to see the same white mist, brightening then softening as the sun climbed and dropped in the sky for several days.

Once, to break the deathly silence, she let out a bark, but

her voice sounded feeble in the surrounding nothingness. Then she shivered as she wondered if something might have heard her, and be stalking her, creeping up on her unseen. From then on she padded as softly as she could, even trying to suppress the sound of her own breathing.

All she could feel was the hard ground under her paws and the chill of the mist that crept into the depths of her pelt. The marshes around her, with the pools and reeds and buzzing insects, might have vanished altogether.

Kallik wondered if she would spend the rest of her life padding through this unbroken whiteness.

And then came the bad memories. They seemed so real that it was like they were happening all over again. She saw her mother, Nisa, being pulled under the water by the orca. She called to her brother, Taqqiq, through the white mist.

"Taqqiq!" she cried.

Kallik started running through the wall of mist, bounding over sharp stones and spiky bushes.

"I'm coming, Taqqiq! I'll save you!"

Suddenly, she skidded to a halt. Ahead she could pick out two hazy shapes. White shapes, scarcely visible against the background, one much bigger than the other. A full-grown white bear was walking ahead of her, with a small cub at its side.

The cub spoke. "I'm tired! Let me ride on your back, please."

Taqqiq!

Kallik watched the mother bear crouch down to let the cub scramble up into her fur. Then they set off again, with the cub riding on his mother's shoulders. Their scent trail drifted behind them, tickling Kallik's nose. Scents she had thought she would never smell again.

"Mother! Taqqiq! It's me, Kallik! Wait for me!"

She hurled herself forward, but however fast she ran, the mother and cub stayed the same distance ahead of her, even though they didn't seem to be hurrying.

How could Nisa be here, when Kallik had seen her slip beneath the waves, dragged down by the orca? How could Taqqiq be with her, unless he were dead, too?

Kallik only knew that she had heard her brother speak, and she could pick up the familiar scents of Nisa and Taqqiq on the damp air. Her heart pounded as she raced along. But even when she put on an extra burst of speed, she knew she was dropping behind. Thicker mist surged between them, blotting her mother and brother from Kallik's sight. She let out a wail of desperation.

"Wait!" she begged. "I'm coming!"

The mist swirled; the indistinct figures of the two bears appeared again, Taqqiq still crouched on Nisa's back. They were even farther ahead now; they didn't turn their heads to look at Kallik as she panted along behind them, as if they didn't know that Kallik was there, or didn't care. Her muscles ached and her heart thudded hard enough to burst out of her chest. But it was no use; the faint shapes of Nisa and Taqqiq melted back into the fog.

"Don't leave me!" Kallik shrieked.

She ran on and on, calling for her mother, though now

the fog was as blank and empty as before. Suddenly a mound of white rose up in front of her; unable to stop in time, she crashed into it and felt the softness of fur.

"Mother?" she gasped.

The next thing she felt was a stinging cuff around her ear. Yelping with pain and shock, Kallik looked up. A female bear stood glaring down at her, but it wasn't Nisa.

Disappointment surged over Kallik. "You're not Nisa."

"No, I'm not, whoever she might be," the she-bear growled. "Now go away and leave me alone."

"But there was a cub with you," Kallik persisted. She might have been mistaken that she had seen her mother, but she had definitely heard Taqqiq's voice. "Where is he?"

"There's no cub. Go away."

Kallik gazed around desperately, but Taqqiq's shape had vanished into the mist. "He was here," she insisted. "Did you see where he went?"

"How many more times?" the she-bear snarled. "No."

Kallik stared down at her paws. She felt exhausted and confused.

"Are you still here?" the bear asked bad-temperedly.

Kallik crouched low to the ground. "I'm sorry I ran into you," she said. As the bear turned and began to pad off, she added, "Are you going the same way as the other bears?"

The she-bear paused and gave her a curt nod.

"Do you know where the tracks lead?" Kallik burst out.

The other bear let out a grunt of surprise. "You don't know? Well, you're only a cub, I suppose. This is the Claw Path. It leads to a lake where bears meet in peace on the Longest Day. No bear will raise claw against another while they stay beside that lake."

"Why not?" Kallik asked, trying to imagine somewhere she would be allowed to eat her kill without worrying that a bigger bear would steal it from her.

"It's the place where the white bears meet to call back the ice. We order the sun down from the sky so the cold can return and we can go out to feed once more."

Kallik stared at her in astonishment. "Can we really do that? Make the ice come back?"

The she-bear nodded solemnly. "Once the lake was connected to the everlasting ice," she continued. "But the ice shrank and melted, cutting the lake off and trapping the bear spirits that live under the surface. Many bears gather there now, and pay respects to the deep, still water. We never forget that once, long ago, it was ice."

"The spirits are there?" Kallik's belly lurched. Did that mean she would be able to see her mother again, as well as find her brother? Perhaps that was why she had seen Nisa and Taqqiq in the fog; they must be traveling toward that sacred place, too.

The she-bear didn't seem to have heard Kallik's question. She was gazing into the mist, as if she could see something there that Kallik could not. "They say the lake is on the route that leads to the Place of Everlasting Ice."

"Oh!" Kallik exclaimed. "The Place of Everlasting Ice is real!"

"Some bears say the place is nothing more than a legend. I *know* it is real, but it's very far away—farther than your paws could take you."

"I have to get there," Kallik insisted. "I'm looking for my brother." Hopefully, she added, "May I travel with you? I'd help you find food."

The female grunted. "Eat all mine, more like. No, it's best to travel alone. One mouth to feed, one pelt to protect."

Kallik's heart sank. "But what about all the other bears?" she protested. "The ones who left tracks here?"

"Just because many bears have passed this way doesn't mean they were traveling together," the other bear replied, beginning to pad away. Glancing over her shoulder, she added, "Didn't your mother tell you that white bears live alone?"

Only when they're old enough, Kallik thought, digging her claws into the ground. She knew it would be no good to follow the she-bear; she wasn't like Nanuk or the she-bear who had been dropped safely from the metal bird, willing to help a strange cub. So she sat and waited until the huge white shape melted into the mist.

Loneliness flooded through Kallik, as cold and heavy as the fog. She was going the right way, but it seemed so unfair that she still had to be on her own. If she had really seen Nisa and Taqqiq traveling toward the lake, why hadn't they waited for her? And if Taqqiq was with their mother now, that must mean he was dead. So what was the point of going to the Place of Everlasting Ice to look for him?

Then Kallik's pelt prickled as she asked herself why Nisa's

spirit had appeared to her. *She must have been showing me the way to go! She said she would take care of me.* Kallik knew that she had to keep going; besides, she wanted to see the lake the she-bear had told her about. Even if she didn't find Taqqiq, she might hear news of what had happened to him. She heaved herself to her paws and kept on walking.

A faint breeze sprang up, pulling the fog into thin shreds. Soon Kallik could see where she was going again, following the bear trail through the same bleak, unfriendly expanse of mud and reeds and stunted bushes. Far ahead, she could make out a white dot that she thought was the she-bear; peering past her, Kallik picked out two or three more white dots, moving in the same direction. She headed after them, but didn't try to catch up. None of them was Nisa or Taqqiq, and she guessed she wouldn't be welcome to travel with them.

The breeze stiffened, blowing toward Kallik, until she was fighting for every step against a raw wind that flattened her fur to her sides and blew stinging debris into her eyes. Gray clouds rolled across the sky. Rain began to fall, harder and harder; the wind drove it into Kallik's face in cold flurries. Soon her pelt was soaked; she waded through a sea of mud that splashed up and streaked her white fur. Head down, she struggled on, almost as blind as she had been in the mist. Every pawstep was more of an effort than the last.

"I've got to find shelter," she muttered.

Glancing around, she couldn't see anything except the sweeping rain; she was almost ready to lie down in the mud and let it wash over her. But she was afraid that if she did that she would never get up again.

Then she saw something dark looming up, a couple of bear-lengths away from her path. She veered toward it. *Maybe it's a cave, like the one where I hid from the insects.* But when she reached it she saw it was only an outcrop of rock poking up out of the mud. Sick with disappointment, she turned away, then looked back.

You won't find anything better, seal-brain!

The outcrop wasn't a real shelter, but at least it blocked out the worst of the wind. Kallik crouched at its base, huddling against the rock wall beneath a shallow overhang. Exhaustion swept over her; she didn't think she could have gone any farther if she had tried. Letting out a faint moan, she closed her eyes and listened to the buffeting of the wind and the lashing of the rain. She longed to feel the comforting touch of her mother's fur, to burrow into Nisa's side, where she would be warm and safe.

"Nisa, can you hear me?" she whispered. "Please help me. I don't think I can go on anymore."

Kallik was drifting into sleep when she felt movement beside her; something was wriggling between her body and the rock. She started back and opened her eyes; blinking in astonishment, she saw the Arctic fox with the torn ear. Its pelt was drenched, showing every one of its ribs, and it was shivering wretchedly. Its terrified gaze locked with Kallik's; it was tense with fear and ready to flee if she showed the least sign of a threat.

A spark of warmth woke inside Kallik at the sight of the

pathetic bundle of fur and bones. She wasn't the only one to be alone and miserable.

"It's okay, fox," she murmured. "You can stay."

She didn't think the fox understood her, but her tone must have been reassuring. It relaxed, and burrowed even deeper into the gap between Kallik's body and the rock. Kallik shifted protectively to give it as much shelter as she could. It felt good to be helping her companion, who had been with her ever since she first turned her back on the smell of the sea.

Gradually the fox's shivering faded; faint grunts and snores told Kallik it was asleep. Its body was a tiny core of warmth in the midst of the storm. Letting out a long sigh, Kallik closed her eyes and let sleep wrap itself around her.

CHAPTER TWELVE

Lusa

Lusa woke with the sun on her face. Blinking, she parted her jaws in an enormous yawn. She was lying in a hollow among the roots of a small tree; it was too short and prickly for her to climb, but the feel of the trunk against her back was reassuring, as though the tree's bear spirit was guarding her.

Lusa wriggled and looked out at the new day.

The sun was glittering in the sky, drawing out the delicious scents all around her. Her belly rumbled and she silently thanked the Bear Watcher for these long days for hunting and traveling, and for the trees that provided rest and shade.

Leaves crackled underneath her; Ujurak, who was curled up beside her, raised his head, instantly awake. "Hi," he murmured, stifling a yawn. "Is it time to go on?"

"Soon," Lusa replied. "How do you feel?"

Ujurak got up and stretched each leg in turn. "Much better. The leaves I asked you to gather are really working."

"Do you want some more?" Lusa asked. "I know where to find them."

Ujurak shook his head. "I'll be fine now." Scrambling out of the hollow to look around, he added, "Where's Toklo?"

For the first time Lusa noticed that Toklo's nest in the hollow was empty, only squashed leaves and fading scent showing that he had ever been there. For a moment her heart raced: What if Toklo had abandoned them? *He wouldn't do that,* Lusa tried to tell herself, but the big grizzly cub had been silent and grumpy ever since they crossed the bridge, and she couldn't be sure.

Lusa caught a faint whiff of his scent. She climbed out of the hollow and looked around, sniffing the air. The sun was rising from behind a ridge of hills in the distance. It cast its bright yellow light on smooth green meadows patterned with the long shadows of bushes and trees.

Toklo appeared from farther down the bank with a hare dangling from his jaws. He padded over and dropped it beside her and Ujurak.

"Great! Thanks," Ujurak yelped, crouching down to eat.

Toklo settled opposite him, but Lusa hung back. She still felt guilty that she couldn't hunt; it didn't seem fair that Toklo had to do all the work. Her mouth watered at the sight of the hare, but she made herself turn aside and take a mouthful of leaves from a nearby bush.

"What's the matter?" Toklo called. "There's enough for all of us."

Lusa searched for a reply, but before she could speak, Toklo added, "You've earned it, if that's what's bothering you. You found the herbs to make Ujurak better, so that's your way of being useful."

Lusa huffed gratefully at him, surprised that Toklo seemed to know what she was thinking. But as she crouched to eat her share of the prey, she couldn't help wondering how she could go on being useful now that Ujurak was well again.

The hare was bigger than most of the prey they had found on the mountain, but it didn't take long for them to finish it.

"Which way now, Ujurak?" Lusa asked. "Is there a sign?"

Ujurak stood on his hind legs and looked around, screwing up his eyes as he thought. "Yes!" he exclaimed at last, pointing with his muzzle. "See that cloud, just above the ridge? What does it look like?"

Lusa studied the cloud. It was squarish, with a pointed bit at one end and four squat clouds hanging just below. The pointed bit looked like a muzzle if she half-closed her eyes, and the little clouds could be short, sturdy legs. . . . "It's just like a bear!"

"Then that's the way we have to go."

Toklo took the lead as they headed toward the ridge. Lusa followed, feeling light on her paws for the first time in days. The sun was hot on her pelt, the air full of warm scents and whispering breezes. A small stream chattered across their path; they dipped their snouts for a drink, then leaped over it and went on.

Ujurak was padding happily from side to side, stopping to sniff a flower or a bush, then bounding to catch up.

Toklo halted, looking over his shoulder as the younger cub

nibbled a patch of juicy grass. "Are you going to stand there all day?" he called.

"Coming!" Ujurak launched himself forward and hurled himself at Toklo. "*You're* the slowfoot around here!"

Toklo let out a growl, and the two cubs rolled over and over, snapping playfully with open jaws. Lusa hesitated, then jumped forward and threw herself on top of them. She felt Ujurak's paws pummeling her belly, while Toklo gripped her shoulder gently in his mouth. She knew they were curbing their strength so they wouldn't hurt her; she wrestled back, slapping them with her front paws and wriggling away when they tried to catch hold of her. Black bears might be small, but that made them slippery as fish!

Finally Toklo pulled away, slapping a paw at Ujurak as the younger cub tried to burrow into his side with a squeal of excitement. "Be quiet," he huffed, sniffing the air. "I can smell another bear."

Lusa rolled over and sat up. "Where?"

Toklo's eyes were wary. "I'm not sure. Stay there."

Lusa and Ujurak watched as Toklo padded across the hillside, his neck stretched out to sniff the plants that edged the trail. Finally he halted beside a bush that grew on the bank of another stream. "A brown bear has been here," he said.

Ujurak bounded across to see what he had found, and Lusa followed more slowly. Close to the bush, she could make out the distinctive brown-bear scent, and spotted a single pawmark on the damp earth. It looked as if a full-grown bear had made it.

Toklo was examining the bush. "There are no clawmarks," he reported, "so we aren't in his territory. But we still need to be careful."

They padded on quietly, alert for any more signs of the strange bear. Lusa spotted a few chewed-up berries, and Ujurak found a dent in the earth under a rocky overhang. The bear scent hung around it, and there were more pawprints.

"All the prints are pointing the same way," Toklo said. "That means the bear was just passing through. If we're lucky, we might not meet him."

"Are all the marks from the same bear?" Lusa asked.

Toklo replied, "Probably," but he looked uneasy.

Sunhigh came and went as the cubs plodded up to the top of the ridge. Lusa thought the brown-bear scent was growing stronger—so strong that she kept looking around, expecting to see the bear heading toward them. Then as she drew closer to the ridge she realized that it wasn't only one bear she could smell; there were a lot of them!

"Toklo . . ." she began.

Toklo signed her to be silent with one paw. His eyes were watchful, flicking from side to side as he took in the bent twigs at the side of the path that suggested bigger bears had gone this way. Ujurak's eyes were huge and round, as if he couldn't imagine that many bears following the same trail as they were. Lusa's paws began to tremble.

They kept on climbing, veering toward a rocky outcrop at the summit, where they could hide until they saw what lay on the other side. As they reached the top Lusa's ears pricked at the sound of voices growling or calling out, and the excited yelps of cubs. She peered out from behind the rocks.

On the other side of the ridge the ground fell away more steeply. At the bottom was a huge lake. It was so wide that Lusa could only just make out the far shore, a dark smudgy line. Many bearlengths toward where the sun rose, thick woodland grew right up to the water's edge, but the rest of the lakeshore was bare ground, dotted with rocks and occasional clumps of spiky dark green grass. The water reflected the blue sky and glittered in the rays of the sun.

Between Lusa and the lakeshore was a huge mass of brown bears. She could see bears so old that their muzzles had turned gray, and cubs even smaller than Ujurak, bouncing around excitedly until their mothers drew them back and made them stay close to their side.

"So many bears!" Ujurak whispered, peering over Lusa's shoulder.

"I thought brown bears lived alone," she gulped.

Toklo was staring down with an unreadable expression in his eyes. "They do."

"Then why are all these bears here?" Lusa asked. "What's happening?"

"I don't know," Toklo snapped. "I never heard of anything like this." He gazed down in silence for a few heartbeats, then added, "Which way now? Can we get around this lake without meeting all those bears?"

"If we can, I think we should," Lusa said, hoping her voice

wasn't shaking too much.

"No," Ujurak protested. "This is the place. This is where the signs have been leading us."

Toklo snorted. "Brown bears don't follow the sorts of signs you're talking about. There must be prey here. There must be salmon in the lake."

"I think we should go down there," Ujurak said.

Lusa wasn't so sure. She flinched as two young males reared up on their hind legs, batting at each other with their fore-paws, their jaws wide as they roared ferociously. "If they're friendly, I'm a squirrel," she muttered.

"They're only playing," Ujurak pointed out, watching the bears break apart and butt each other in the shoulder with their heads. Their slow, shambling movements weren't meant to hurt, just show off their size and strength. "Come on!"

"Okay. . . ." Toklo still sounded doubtful. "But we should—"

"Great!" Ujurak shot off without waiting for him to finish, bounding down the slope toward the gathering of brown bears.

"Bee-brain," Toklo muttered as he followed, and added to Lusa, "Keep close to me. Your black pelt will stand out here like a pine tree on a bare mountain."

Reluctantly Lusa padded beside him, following Ujurak down into the crowd of brown bears.

CHAPTER THIRTEEN

Lusa

Lusa stuck as close as she could to Toklo. There were so many bears, huge adult males pacing the ground, adult females watching over their cubs, older bears picking fleas out of their fur, and young bears play-fighting.

She caught scraps of their talk, or brief snatches of stories as they passed.

"The river has dried up completely where we live," one skinny she-bear fretted, looking down at her two cubs. "I can't remember the last time we ate salmon."

"Nor can I," an old male bear replied. "There's still a river in my territory, but all the fish have gone."

"I just hope there's food here," the mother bear sighed. She nudged her cubs with her muzzle until they began to trot toward the lake.

Just beyond them was another male bear with a wary look in his eyes. "Where do I come from?" he echoed to a younger she-bear who was questioning him. "Uh . . . over the mountains. There are slim pickings in my territory now. Too many flat-faces."

Is every bear short of food? Lusa wondered.

A little farther on her attention was caught by another female, frail and grizzled with age, who was pushing a stick toward two small cubs. "Now, imagine this is a salmon. What are you going to do?"

"This!" one of the cubs squealed, leaping for the stick.

But the old she-bear pushed the stick rapidly forward so that it slid underneath the cub as he jumped, and his paws came down on the bare ground.

"Hey, that wasn't fair!" he complained.

"Let me try," his sister begged. "I think I get it."

The old bear retrieved the stick and pushed it toward the she-cub. The cub leaped and Lusa shook her head, expecting her to land short of the mock prey. But the old bear kept the stick sliding forward at the same pace, and the cub landed exactly on top of it. She let out a squeal of triumph as her claws closed over it. "See, squirrel-brain!" she taunted her brother.

"Well done," said the old bear. "Remember that the salmon won't lie there and wait for you to catch it. You have to jump where it's going to be."

"Can we try it for real now?" the male cub asked. "Please?"

"Soon, but first—"

"Hey, you!" a rough voice exclaimed.

Startled, Lusa looked up to see a half-grown male grizzly standing right in front of her, his eyes glittering with hostility.

"Yes, you, black bear," he went on. "What are you doing here? This is our place."

"I—I'm sorry," Lusa stammered. "I'm with my friends." She looked around anxiously, but she couldn't spot Toklo and Ujurak among the mass of furry brown bodies. She tried not to panic.

"Your *friends* aren't here." Another voice joined in: it belonged to a young male, even bigger than the first, with a freshly healed scar stretching from his ear to his muzzle. He gave Lusa a shove that nearly knocked her off her paws. "They're over there." He jerked his head in the direction of the trees near the waterline. "So get out."

"Go now." The first grizzly raised a threatening paw. "You don't belong here."

Lusa looked at the trees. Toklo and Ujurak hadn't said anything about going into the woods. And anyway, how did this brown bear know who her friends were?

"Okay, I'll go and look for—" she began, breaking off in confusion as Toklo appeared from the crowd of bears.

"Come on, Lusa," he said quietly, and added to the two young males, "Leave her alone. She's with me."

The two grizzlies muttered to each other, still looking hostile, but didn't say any more to Lusa. She followed Toklo toward the lakeshore.

"I *told* you to stick close to me," Toklo grunted, though he sounded more anxious than angry.

"Sorry. I was watching some cubs."

Lusa stayed close to Toklo until they came to the water's

edge. There she spotted Ujurak talking to an old, toothless bear with white whiskers.

"The ceremony will take place at the next sunrise," the old bear was saying to Ujurak, "when the Longest Day begins."

"What's the longest day?" Ujurak asked.

"You don't know? You've not heard of the Longest Day?"

"No," Ujurak replied.

The old bear huffed. "In my day cubs were taught the old ways by their mothers," he grumbled. "Cubs these days—"

"Please tell me," Ujurak asked.

The old bear scratched the fuzzy fur on his shoulder with one hindpaw. "Have you noticed the days getting longer, little cub?" He lifted his snout and sniffed the breeze. Lusa noticed that his eyes were gray and watery. "The sun has always been the friend of the brown bears. After the dark, hungry time of earthsleep, the sun puts food in the water, under the soil, in the trees—food for brown bears. On the Longest Day, the sun defeats the darkness altogether, and we bears gather to thank the spirits."

He dropped his snout and squinted at Ujurak. "But now the sun has stopped providing food for brown bears. The spirits are displeased."

"He's got bees in his brain," Toklo whispered to Lusa.

"Hey, look at that *black* bear!"

Lusa turned around to see a grizzly she-cub bounding up to her; the cub looked younger than she was but was much bigger. "Get out of here!" she growled. "This is brown bear territory."

Lusa edged closer to Toklo as the mother bear loomed up behind her cub. *She'll tear me apart!* she thought.

But the mother cuffed her cub over the ear. "Come away," she huffed. "Does this little bear look as if she could do us any harm?"

The she-cub shot a hostile glance at Lusa, then bounded away with her mother.

Lusa felt a large snout nudge her side. The old bear pushed his face close to Lusa's, his watery eyes squinting to see her. "A black bear, hey? You shouldn't be here, you should be with your own kind."

Lusa stared at him in astonishment. "There are black bears here?" she squeaked. "Where?"

The old bear turned his head and pointed with his muzzle along the shore to where the trees came down to the edge of the lake. "Where would you expect to find black bears, young one?" He shook his head, then slowly plodded away along the lakeshore. "Cubs these days don't know anything," he grumbled.

Lusa stared at the dark line of trees. "There are black bears here!" she said.

"You should go find them," Ujurak said. "There'll be trouble sooner or later if you stay here."

"But what about our journey?" Toklo asked.

"My paws led us here for a reason. I want to stay for the Longest Day and I want to find out what it is."

Lusa looked at her two grizzly friends. "Will I see you again?"

"If we stay in one another's thoughts, we'll find each other," Ujurak replied.

Toklo gave Lusa a poke in the shoulder with his snout. "Don't worry. He's not so easy to shake off," he said, amusement flickering in his eyes.

Lusa exchanged an excited glance with Toklo and Ujurak. She felt a wave of affection for both of them. She didn't want to leave them, but the longing to see other black bears was too strong.

"Good-bye," she said, touching her muzzle quickly to theirs.

"The spirits go with you," Ujurak responded.

"Good-bye," Toklo grunted. "Look after yourself."

Lusa's paws felt as heavy as rocks as she turned to pad away. She realized how much she had come to depend on Ujurak, and even prickly Toklo, and how much she would miss them. *But we'll see one another again,* she promised herself.

CHAPTER FOURTEEN

Lusa

Lusa scurried as fast as she could away from the edge of the lake, splashing through marshy ground toward the trees. She dipped her head, trying to avoid making eye contact with the brown bears, but she could hear their growls around her and sense their dark eyes glaring at her.

As she reached the forest her belly tightened with excitement. She slowed, savoring the strong scent of black bears. She hadn't smelled that scent since the Bear Bowl! There were lots of them here, judging by all the scents; more black bears than she'd met in her whole life. She ventured underneath the outlying pines, treading cautiously over the uneven ground, thick with fallen needles. The soft murmuring of bear spirits was all around her in the whispering branches.

Soon, Lusa began to hear the voices of bears up ahead. Their scents grew stronger, pulling her on. Above her head, the branches of a tree waved wildly as if a bear were climbing there, though she saw nothing. The voices grew louder; Lusa scrambled up a steep bank and found herself on the edge of a clearing. Warily she peered out from behind the nearest tree.

The clearing was full of black bears. Lusa could hardly see the ground between them as they jostled for space. One bear close to the tree where she was hiding gave the bear next to him a hearty shove.

"Watch where you're putting your claws! That was my hind leg."

"Sorry." The other bear sounded grumpy. "There's no space to breathe here."

A little farther away, a couple of she-bears were touching noses. "It's good to see you again, Issa," said one. "Is this your cub? She looks a fine, strong one."

The little cub pressed herself into her mother's pelt, and peeped out shyly at the speaker.

"Yes, the spirits have blessed us this suncircle," Issa replied. "And how about you, Taloa?"

"I've had a terrible journey to get here," Taloa replied, shaking her head. "So many flat-faces! I thought a firebeast would get me for sure. But it's good to be here," she added.

A couple of half-grown males bounded past. "You stole a fish from me last time!" the one in the rear shouted.

The other bear glanced back. "I'll steal another one this time, you dumb chunk of fur!"

His pursuer leaped at him and knocked him over; the two of them rolled over and slammed into an older bear, who huffed at them in annoyance. The two young males broke apart, scrambled to their paws, and dashed off together, seemingly friends again.

Lusa began to realize that the bears in the center of the clearing were older, with shrunken bodies and grizzled snouts, while the younger adults were gathered around them, with most of the cubs on the outside under the trees. She looked longingly at two cubs about her own age, who were chasing each other up and down a tree.

"I'm faster than you!" one of them called out.

"No, you're not! You're slower than a fat rabbit."

Lusa's paws itched to join in their game, but she suddenly felt very shy. She couldn't walk into the middle of all these bears and introduce herself. Step by step, she crept back from the edge of the clearing, until she was brought up short by a tree. She looked up; the trunk stretched high above her head until it divided into a thick tangle of branches.

Lusa started as rustling sounded behind her. She bounded up the tree, never stopping until the branches concealed her. Peering down, she saw a young black bear padding past to join the other bears in the clearing.

"Hi, Pokkoli!" a bear called. "Over here!"

Lusa climbed the rest of the way up the tree. It was good to feel the rough bark under her claws and the trunk swaying with her weight as she neared the top. She hadn't climbed a tree for a long time. Wind ruffled her fur; the rustling of the branches blended with the lapping of waves on the shore of the lake.

Looking out, Lusa saw that her tree was one of the highest in the forest. From her vantage point she could see farther, and she realized that the lake she had thought so big was only one branch; the main body of water, the tree trunk, stretched into the far distance until it was lost in a shimmering haze. Did it stretch all the way to the end of the world?

Lusa stared over the murmuring canopy of the forest. Beyond the trees, she could see the gathering of brown bears swarming across the open shore. She tried to pick out Toklo and Ujurak among the shifting mass of bodies, but she was too far away to see any of them clearly, and besides, her traveling companions were small enough to be completely hidden by the full-grown bears.

Hugging the trunk with her front paws, Lusa wriggled around until she was facing the other way. Not far off, the trees came to an abrupt end, leaving an endless stretch of bare earth. Marshy pools dotted the ground, reflecting pale light from the sky. Reeds grew around them; rocks jutted from the earth and there were a few scrawny bushes, twisted into weird shapes by the sweeping wind. After that, just empty, empty space; flat, windswept land with no trees, no friendly bear spirits, nothing at all as far as she could see.

Lusa was clinging to one of the last trees in the world.

CHAPTER FIFTEEN

Kallik

Kallik woke up blinking in bright sunlight. She lay huddled at the base of the rock; her pelt and the muddy ground all around her steamed gently as the hot rays dried them out. For a few moments she kept still, letting the warmth soak through her fur, then she tried to stand. Wincing as she stretched stiff muscles, Kallik looked for the Arctic fox, but it had gone. She tried to stifle a pang of loss. *It's only a fox.*

An enticing scent tickled Kallik's nostrils. Food! Her belly rumbled and saliva flooded her jaws as her gaze fell on the body of a hare, stretched out on the ground beside her. The scent told her it was freshly killed.

Puzzled and a little afraid, Kallik looked around. She longed to sink her teeth into the prey, but she knew what a risk it could be to eat another bear's kill. She pictured a huge white bear roaring as it bore down on her, its claws outstretched. Then she spotted the fox, its eyes gleaming from underneath the low branches of a thornbush.

Warmth flooded over Kallik. "*You* caught it, didn't you?" she said.

The fox twitched its ears.

She had sheltered the fox during the storm, and now it had brought her a gift. That was what friends did for each other. She had a friend!

"Thank you," she said, dipping her head.

She tore at the delicious hare meat, savoring every mouthful as she felt it slide warm into her belly. It tasted even better because the Arctic fox had brought it for her.

Kallik was so hungry that she could have eaten the hare twice over. But she stopped when a haunch was left, and backed well away. She wondered if the fox trusted her enough to come close now that the desperate need for shelter from the storm was past. It crept up, more confidently now, and settled down to eat with a bright-eyed glance at Kallik.

With her belly full, Kallik set out again. *I am on the Claw Path!* she thought, excitement fluttering inside her. As she trekked, she began to notice large pawprints and droppings, and the occasional bunch of white hairs snagged on a bush. She knew that other bears had passed this way. Here and there, she found a few berries, but she guessed that most of the bushes along the Claw Path had been stripped by the bears who had gone before her. The fox had watched her leave the rock where they had spent the night, and she didn't know if it was still following her, out of sight. She hoped it was, but she knew that she had to concentrate on her journey, not the fox's, and at last she was sure she was going the right way.

"Thank you, spirits, for guiding me here," she whispered.

The sun was sliding down the sky when Kallik spotted movement on the ground a few bearlengths ahead of her. Padding forward curiously, she spotted a snow goose fluttering in a muddy hollow. It kept trying to take off, then falling back again, as if one of its wings was damaged.

Kallik crept toward it, remembering to keep downwind, and killed it with a quick blow to the neck. She ate her share, recalling what Nisa had told her about not bolting her food. Then she raised her head and looked around.

"Are you there?" she called to the fox. "This is for you."

A russet snout poked out from behind a rock; the fox's eyes gleamed as it crept forward. Kallik backed away. She left it gulping down its share of the prey, but now she knew she would see it again.

I wonder if we'll go all the way to the Endless Ice together.

Thirsty, she veered from the track toward a pool fringed with reeds. She dipped her head to drink. Above her the sky was still light; there was no moon or friendly star-spirits reflected in the water. Even the water tasted thin and empty, compared with the sea. She looked up as the Arctic fox stepped to the opposite edge of the pool and started lapping.

"I'm glad you're here, with me," she said softly.

The day stretched on. Kallik had to rely on the traces of other bears to be sure she was still going the right way. She began to fear that she would never reach the bears' meeting place, or it would take her so long that the Longest Day would be over before she arrived there. Maybe the Longest Day had been and gone without her noticing; she didn't know exactly how long the nights were compared with the days because she was asleep. And how would she know the way from the lake to the Endless Ice? What if there were no other bears going there? She remembered the she-bear she had met in the mist telling her that it was too far for her paws.

"It's *not* too far," she muttered determinedly. "I *will* get there."

The fox was traveling in sight of her now, trotting a little way ahead with its bushy tail sweeping the ground. The tip of the tail left a tiny line in the dust, like a burntpath for ants.

Halfway up a grassy slope, the Arctic fox halted, sniffing the air. It crouched low with its tail flat on the ground.

"What is it?" Kallik barked.

A gentle breeze was blowing down the slope into her face, and she sniffed, drawing in a familiar scent. It was the scent of bears. Her heart flipped with excitement. "We made it!" she yelped. "We found the gathering."

The fox turned and scurried a short way back down the slope. It stopped and looked back as if wondering whether Kallik was coming, too.

"It's this way," Kallik said.

The fox crouched in the grass, its nose twitching.

"I understand," Kallik said. "This is not the place you're going. What would you want with a gathering of bears?"

Kallik knew that the fox didn't belong by the lake. To other white bears, an Arctic fox would be prey, and her friendship would be over in a few greedy mouthfuls.

"I hope we meet again, little one," Kallik murmured.

The fox flicked its ears, then began stalking through the grass, its nose to the ground. Suddenly it pounced into a clump of bushes and a hare sprang out, dashing away down the slope. The Arctic fox darted after it.

At the foot of the slope the fox stopped. It looked back at Kallik, then it dashed away on the trail of the hare.

Kallik watched it scamper out of sight. "Good-bye," she murmured. The fox had been her only friend since Nanuk died, and she would miss it. But white bears would make better friends because she could talk to them—and she was about to meet lots of them, including the white bear she had been looking for all along. She turned around and started running up the slope.

"I'm coming, Taqqiq!" she called, bounding as fast as she could.

The smell of the bears grew stronger and she could hear their faint sounds. She skidded to a stop at the top of the ridge and stared, feeling her eyes stretch wide with astonishment. Whatever she had expected, it hadn't been this.

Ahead of her, the ground fell away in a long slope, all the way to the shores of a lake. Kallik hadn't seen so much water since she left the melting ice. And along the shore were more white bears than she had ever imagined could be in one place, even more than at the gathering place beside the sea where she had been born. More bears than she'd dreamed existed.

She had reached the bear lake. She'd reached the gathering for the Longest Day.

CHAPTER SIXTEEN

Toklo

Toklo's belly rumbled. "I'm hungry," he told Ujurak. "I'm going to catch a fish."

"Fine. I want to talk to more bears," Ujurak said.

Toklo lowered his head and touched Ujurak's snout with his own. "Suit yourself," he muttered. "Just be careful, okay?"

Ujurak bounded off along the water's edge. "I will! See you later!"

Toklo watched him go, splashing water over the other bears with his thundering pawsteps. Toklo snorted with amusement as older bears jumped out of the way and glared after Ujurak. Then the bear cub vanished in a sea of brown bodies, and Toklo was truly on his own.

"So we're all here for the Longest Day," he murmured, glancing around at the brown bears. "I hope they haven't caught all the fish in the lake yet."

He padded down to the water's edge, weaving his way among strange bears. They all seemed to know one another either as friends or longtime enemies. Toklo felt uncomfortable, squashed, his ears full of grumbles and huffs as the bears squabbled for a patch of ground to call their own.

"Watch out!" he snarled as a small cub bundled into him. Then he spotted a she-bear lumbering toward them; she gave the cub a gentle cuff around the head.

"Come away!" she scolded. "What have I told you about going too near bears you don't know?" She locked her gaze with Toklo's, as if daring him to challenge her; Toklo gave her an awkward nod and padded on.

A few bearlengths from the lake, he spotted a large male grizzly gnawing on a fish. Hunger clawed in his belly. He couldn't remember how many sunrises had passed since he last tasted salmon. Now that he didn't have to worry about Ujurak and Lusa, he could keep all his prey for himself, but the thought didn't feel as good as he had expected. He glanced across at the forest and hoped Lusa had made it safely to the trees. He wondered if he'd ever see her again.

Stop being so salmon-brained! he huffed to himself. *Since when do brown bears and black bears live together?*

Toklo turned back to the lake and walked straight into a massive grizzly who was lumbering out of the water.

The adult bear loomed over him. "Watch where you're going," he growled.

Toklo ducked his head. "Sorry," he muttered.

There was a long silence. Eventually Toklo dared to look up. The big grizzly's muzzle was gray with age; scars raked across it and there were more on his shoulder and along his side.

He's been in more battles than I've seen sunrises. To his surprise the bear didn't look angry anymore.

"Where are you going in such a hurry?" he grunted.

"Down to the lake," Toklo replied. "I want to catch a fish."

The grizzly huffed out his breath. "You'll wait a long time. Oh, there are fish in there, but they're few and far between. Not even enough to keep a scrawny cub like you alive."

Toklo looked around wildly. "Then what are all these bears going to eat?"

The old bear stared at Toklo for a few moments. Toklo shifted his front paws on the pebbles, feeling his fur itch.

"What's your name, young one?" the big grizzly asked.

"Toklo."

"And I am Shesh. Now look out across the water, Toklo. What do you see?"

Toklo gazed at the gray, ridged water, wondering what the old bear was getting at. "Um . . . waves."

"And what else?" Shesh persisted.

"An island," Toklo replied. "With bushes . . . and some trees."

"This lake has been here since the time before bears," Shesh told him. "It was a cold and barren place. The wind swept over it, snow and rain and sunlight fell onto the ground, but it never changed. No creatures dared to live here. Then the great bear Arcturus came this way. He was searching for a great wilderness where he could live all alone. He strode across the lake and where he set his paw, an island sprang up. Fish thronged around it and he ate his fill before he journeyed on. And ever since then we bears have taken this lake for our own, and every suncircle, on the Longest Day, we return here to remember that bear's journey and to give thanks to his spirit."

That must have been a massive bear, Toklo thought. *I wonder where he is now.*

"Come with me to the parley stone," Shesh said, turning away from the water. "There you will hear more tales."

"But I'm hungry!" Toklo protested.

"We are all hungry, little one," the old bear replied.

Shesh led the way along the lakeshore until he reached a flat-topped stone that jutted out over the water. Many grizzlies crowded around it: mostly older bears, Toklo noticed, though there were some mothers with cubs. Toklo spotted Ujurak on the opposite side, looking around him with bright-eyed interest. The crowd parted for Shesh with nods of respect, so that he and Toklo could make their way to the foot of the rock.

The old bear Ujurak had spoken to earlier stood on top of the rock. A breeze flattened his pelt against his thin frame, but he held himself more proudly than before.

"That is Oogrook," Shesh murmured into Toklo's ear. "The oldest and wisest of us all."

Oogrook lifted his muzzle and let out a long low moan that echoed around the lakeshore. The bears near him sank into silence; then he stopped and began to speak."This will be my last Longest Day Gathering," he began, his voice as thin as a reed and faint as the wind on the water. "At sunrise tomorrow I will give thanks to the sun, and to the spirits for—"

"What do you want to *thank* them for?" A she-bear spoke

up, her hackles raised. "They're supposed to bring us food, but we're all hungry. I thought there'd be plenty of fish in the lake, but it's as bad here as everywhere else."

A few of the bears growled at her for interrupting, but Oogrook silenced them with a raised paw. "What our sister says is true. In some places rivers have dried up, while in others they burst their banks and drown the land around for many bearlengths. There are fewer fish to eat, fewer roots and berries to be found."

"True, true," a mother bear grunted, giving her cub a comforting lick on its shoulder.

"So what should we do, Oogrook?" another voice cried from the opposite side of the stone. "If we can't find food, we'll all die!"

A chorus of voices joined in. "Yes, tell us what to do!"

"Where can I find food for my cubs?"

"The fish must have gone *somewhere*!"

Once more Oogrook held up his paw for silence. "We are here to thank the spirits for what should be the time of best prey. And why should we only blame them for the lack of food? Could it be our fault, for not living the way of true brown bears? In such bad times, a demonstration of courage and strength is needed to show that brown bears are still strong, still worthy of being fed by the river spirits."

"How do we do that?" a bear burst out.

The ancient bear nodded. "A good question. I believe that we can bring the salmon back by following in the pawsteps of Arcturus, the great bear who once walked across the lake. He was brave enough to make the journey alone, and he found a place where he could live and eat and find shelter."

"What has this got to do with bringing the fish back?" demanded the she-bear who had spoken first.

"I believe that a bear should make the journey to Pawprint Island," Oogrook replied. "Alone, because that is how brown bears live—alone, proud, hunting for themselves. Then perhaps Arcturus will look kindly on us, and send back the fish."

Silence followed his words as the bears looked at one another, with doubt or dawning hope in their expressions.

"It might work," Shesh said thoughtfully.

"I'll go! I'll go!" squeaked a tiny cub, bouncing up and down with excitement.

"Don't be squirrel-brained," his mother said, calming him with a paw on one shoulder. "You're far too young."

"Why don't you go, Hattack?" one of the young males suggested, nudging his companion. "You're always saying what a good swimmer you are."

Hattack looked at his paws. "Well, I would," he mumbled, "but I've got a cramp in one hind leg."

"Then I'll go," his companion announced. "*I'm* not scared."

Toklo looked at the lake. Waves hissed on the shore; the island looked a long way away. He imagined the great bear Arcturus striding across the water, pulling the island up by his claws and scooping out huge mouthfuls of fish.

He glanced back at the bears gathered around the parley stone. Ujurak was squeezing forward through the crowd. For a moment Toklo was afraid that he was going to volunteer; the younger cub was certainly bee-brained enough. But Ujurak just listened intently to what the other bears were saying.

A voice spoke behind Toklo. "Here's the bear who should go!" At the same moment a heavy paw landed on his back.

Toklo sprang to his paws and spun around. "What—"

The speaker was a huge bear with a ragged pelt and a hump. Toklo thought he looked familiar, but he couldn't remember where they might have met before.

"Why do you say that, Shoteka?" Oogrook asked, raising his voice above the murmurs of surprise from the other bears.

Memory struck Toklo like a blow in the belly. He remembered a wide salmon river below a mountain, many sunrises ago. And he remembered the grizzly who had tried to drown him there. Toklo's jaws gaped in horror. "Shoteka!"

"I didn't expect to see you again," the humpbacked bear snarled. "I thought you would have died long ago, with no mother to protect you."

A pang of grief and anger shook Toklo as he recalled how Oka had defended him from this bear who tried to kill him.

"Shoteka?" Oogrook's voice had an edge of impatience as he waited for an answer. "Why do you choose this cub?"

Shoteka shrugged. "One bear has to go: Why not this one?" More quietly, he added to Toklo, "But you're too weak. No wonder your mother abandoned you."

"Don't talk about my mother!" Toklo snarled.

The grizzly's eyes glittered with hostility. "Try stopping me."

"Oogrook." Shesh drew closer to Toklo's side. "This journey

is too dangerous for a cub."

"Yes, he's too young," a bear shouted from the other side of the parley stone. "Why don't you go yourself, Shoteka?"

"I chose him *because* he's young," Shoteka replied. "He will go a cub but return a full-grown bear, like Arcturus."

"I think Shoteka's right," one of the she-bears added. "A cub should go. They are the future of all the bears."

"Spirits save us!" Shesh growled. "We cannot risk the life of a cub, not even for this."

All around the stone, the bears erupted into growls and snarls, huffs and snorts, gesturing at Toklo as they argued. Toklo looked across the choppy waves to the island. He imagined how quiet it would be there, away from all these noisy bears.

Shoteka put his muzzle by Toklo's ear. "You're just like your mother, weak and scared," he whispered. "Sooner or later the flat-faces will come and take you away, and you'll scream for help. Just like Oka did. Scared as a squirrel, she was, begging and pleading as they dragged her into the firebeast."

Fury surged through Toklo like flame. "I'll go!" he roared at the top of his voice.

The bears stopped arguing and turned to look at him.

"If you survive the challenge, Arcturus will know that brown bears are worthy of being fed for the next suncircle," Oogrook said.

"*If* you survive," Shoteka hissed in his ear.

"You don't have to do this," Shesh said quietly beside him. "You're only a cub. No bear will think worse of you."

"I'll do it, I'll go," Toklo insisted.

"That is bravely spoken, young one," Oogrook said. "May the spirits go with you."

"Thank you, Oogrook," Toklo replied, surprised that his voice sounded clear and steady. Glancing at Shoteka, he added, "I hope I meet you again, when I'm bigger!"

"I won't hold my breath," the grizzly retorted. He turned and padded away from the parley stone.

The other bears began to move away, too; Toklo felt very small when the older bears nodded to him in respect as they went by, while the young ones glanced nervously at him and whispered to one another as if he weren't a regular brown bear anymore, but some kind of spirit-bear.

Ujurak wriggled his way to Toklo's side. "Hey, Toklo, are you really going to swim all the way out there?"

Toklo looked out at Pawprint Island, trying not to let Ujurak see the fear swirling inside his belly. "I'd do anything for a bit of peace and quiet," he said gruffly.

Shesh padded up to Toklo and stood beside him, gazing out at the island. It seemed to move farther away with every wave that lapped at his paws.

"What should I do when I get there?" Toklo asked the old bear.

"Feel the strength and pride of Arcturus, young bear," Shesh told him. "Rake your claws down a tree. Catch some prey. Defend your territory. For the Longest Day, Pawprint Island belongs to you. Then return to us after the sun has touched the horizon."

Toklo gulped. The old bear's obvious concern for him made

him suspect that this was going to be even harder than he had thought.

"You should rest for a while and build up your strength, so you're ready," Shesh said.

A she-bear padded up with a small fish in her jaws, and laid it on the pebbles beside him. "May the spirits go with you," she murmured.

"Er, thank you," Toklo said, feeling very embarrassed. "Uh . . . do you want some?" he offered to Shesh and Ujurak.

Ujurak shook his head.

"That is yours," Shesh explained. "You deserve it for the task you have undertaken. If you succeed, then every bear will have all the fish they can eat."

That didn't stop Toklo from feeling guilty as he lay down and ate it up. It didn't fill his belly but it was good to eat something that wasn't leaves or berries. His eyes felt heavy with sleep. But when he closed them, the words of the she-bear echoed in his ears: *May the spirits go with you.* Didn't she know it was the spirits he was afraid of? Waiting just below the surface, waiting to pull him down, his fur as heavy as stones, until water rushed into his nose and mouth and his breath was sucked away . . .

Opening his eyes again, he let his nose rest on his paws and stared out at the lake, watching the water turn pale gray, then pink as the sun slowly dipped behind the forest.

Shesh appeared beside him, his paws crunching on the stones. "It is time," he said gently.

Toklo rose to his paws. With Ujurak at his side, he padded

the few paces that took him to the very edge of the lake. The island looked impossibly far away, almost hidden by white-tipped waves with birds bobbing on them.

I can't do this.

He glanced back and nearly yelped with surprise. The whole gathering of brown bears had come down to the shore and was watching him. There were more bears than he could count: huge adults, groups of young cubs, scrawny bears, old bears, bears sitting and bears standing on their back legs. Toklo's own legs felt wobbly, but Shesh was calm and approving as if he trusted Toklo to do this, while the ancient Oogrook's eyes were filled with hope. Only Shoteka, standing off to one side, looked scornful.

Ujurak pushed his muzzle into the fur on Toklo's shoulder. "Look at the lake," he whispered. "It's a good sign."

Toklo turned toward the lake again. In the evening sun it had turned bright pink, the color of salmon.

"You'll be okay, I promise," Ujurak said. "You *can* swim, just remember that."

"Thanks," Toklo replied.

Ujurak bounded up the beach to stand beside Shesh. Toklo knew there was no going back now; he had taken the challenge and what happened next was in the paws of the spirits. The spirits waiting to drag him under . . .

Oka? Tobi? Do you really want to see me again?

Slowly, he padded forward, the lake water lapping cold and soft over his feet. Behind him, he could hear the other bears murmuring excitedly.

"The salmon will return to us."

"The cub is brave."

"Arcturus! Honor this cub by bringing us prey."

They wouldn't honor him when he didn't come back, and they stayed hungry. But at least he wouldn't be here to see their disappointment. Maybe this had been meant to happen all along; he had brought Ujurak and Lusa safely to the lake, and other bears would journey with them now.

The water crept cold up his legs as he waded farther from the shore. He could feel bear spirits tugging at his paws already, pulling him into the water, and thought he could hear the voices of his mother and Tobi. *Come to us,* they whispered. *Come into the water. . . .*

For a heartbeat he froze, fighting the impulse to gallop back to shore.

Why did I agree to this? It's all Shoteka's fault. I hope a tree falls on his head. I hope he's attacked by a firebeast.

He took another step and felt the water lifting him off his paws. Water filled his nose and splashed over his eyes. He stretched his muzzle up to breathe and kicked off from the pebbly bottom.

Slowly, Toklo began dragging himself through the water, closer to Pawprint Island.

CHAPTER SEVENTEEN

Kallik

The sun was setting as Kallik ran down the slope to join the other bears. Her body felt light as goose feathers and she couldn't feel the cuts on her paws.

She had reached the Longest Day Gathering! *Maybe Taqqiq will be here!*

She passed bears sitting in groups, their heads together as if they were talking. Others padded up and down the edge of the lake, or stood with their forepaws in the water, dipping their muzzles to drink.

" . . . shot by a flat-face," she heard as she passed the first group. "And her cubs left with no mother to care for them."

A pang of pity clawed Kallik's heart as she pictured that unknown bear and her cubs. She knew how the cubs must have felt, left alone to look after themselves.

"The ice is melting sooner every suncircle," another bear put in. "We're here to call it back, but will the ice spirits hear us? That's what I'd like to know."

The bears were crowded more closely together as Kallik

approached the lake. She began looking around, hoping to spot Taqqiq, but every bear she saw was a stranger. Some of them raised their muzzles to sniff her, or swung their heads to follow her with a suspicious gaze as she padded past.

She drew near to a larger group of females and their cubs; memory stabbed her heart like a splinter of ice when she spotted two cubs wrestling together. She and Taqqiq had played just like that.

"I'm an orca, and I'm going to eat you," one of the cubs squealed, pouncing on her brother.

"Oh yeah? Well, I'm a walrus, and I'm going to eat *you*!"

The two cubs rolled over and over until they bumped into one of the she-bears, who swiveled around to glare at them. "That's enough!"

"Sorry, Mother." Both cubs sat looking at their paws until the she-bear gave them each a gentle cuff on their shoulders. Then they scampered off again, chasing each other in a circle.

"Has any bear seen Nanuk?" the she-bear asked another bear standing close by. "I expected her to be here by now."

Kallik's ears pricked. *Does she mean* my *Nanuk?*

"No, Qanniq," the bear replied. Her fur was thin and patchy and her body shrunken with age, but there was wisdom in her pale eyes. "You know that Nanuk prefers to travel alone, ever since she lost her cubs last burn-sky."

Yes! Kallik padded up to the she-bear who'd spoken first. "Do you know Nanuk? A bear with a flattish muzzle and tiny ears?"

The bears turned and stared at her.

"Yes, I know her," Qanniq replied. "Why? Have you seen her?"

Kallik shook her head. "I'm so sorry," she said. "Nanuk is dead."

"No!" exclaimed a younger she-bear who had padded up to listen.

The oldest bear's eyes were filled with sorrow. "I grieve to hear that. May her spirit travel safely to the sky."

Qanniq asked, "How do you know? Were you with her?"

Kallik nodded.

"What happened?" the younger bear asked.

"I was captured by flat-faces," Kallik explained, feeling a little awkward to be the center of so much attention. She wasn't used to talking this much, and her throat hurt as if she'd been eating prickers. "They . . . they put me in a cage, and that's when I met Nanuk. The flat-faces made us go to sleep with pointy sticks. But that wasn't what killed her," she added quickly, as the mother bear began to growl deep in her throat. "When we woke up, we were both in a net, carried way up in the sky by a huge metal bird."

"Carried in the sky?" the younger she-bear scoffed. "I think you ate a bit of bad fish and had a nightmare."

"I did not!" Kallik retorted indignantly. "It was real. Later on I saw another metal bird putting a she-bear and her cubs down."

"It's true, Imiq." The oldest bear gave Kallik an approving nod. "The same thing happened to me, many suncircles ago.

The flat-faces carried me in a flying firebeast and took me back to the ice. Go on, young one."

"That's what Nanuk said! That the flat-faces were taking us to the place where the ice comes first. But then a storm came, and the metal bird fell out of the sky. We landed in deep snow . . . and when I woke up, Nanuk was dead." Kallik's voice shook.

"Flat-faces!" The younger female, Imiq, spat out the words. "Even when they try to help, they bring trouble."

"They do their best," the oldest bear said gently. "Bears make mistakes, too."

"I can't believe we'll never see Nanuk again," the mother bear murmured. "She wasn't always easy to get along with, but she had a kind heart."

"And she was a good mother to her cubs," the oldest bear added. "She went without food to feed them, but they still died of hunger."

"*I* heard that when they were dead she ate them," Imiq said, an edge of spite in her voice.

Kallik whirled to face her. "Nanuk would *never* have done that. She loved her cubs. She was still sad about them when I knew her."

Imiq looked taken aback. "I'm only saying what I heard," she muttered.

"You shouldn't spread wicked rumors like that," Kallik told her.

The oldest she-bear put a comforting paw on Kallik's shoulder. "Steady, young one," she murmured. "Imiq never thinks before she speaks. Few bears will believe that tale. Most of us will grieve for Nanuk and honor her memory."

"I miss her so much," Kallik said, looking down at her paws. "She told me about the place of endless ice, where the spirits dance in the sky. She said it was a real place, not just a story. I wish we could have gone there together."

A respectful silence fell, in which Kallik could hear the soft lapping of waves on the lakeshore and the distant voices of other bears.

"I know of that place, too," the mother bear said at last.

Kallik pricked her ears. "Have you ever been there?" she asked hopefully.

Qanniq shook her head.

"I have," the older bear said. "Once, many burn-skies ago, when I was young. It is true that the spirits dance there. I have seen them."

Kallik stared at her. "What are they like?" she breathed.

"Tell us, Siqiniq," the mother bear urged.

"They're very beautiful," Siqiniq replied. "Their faces and legs and arched backs fill the sky with light. They're the only color in that place of snow and ice. I've heard they dance here, too," she added to Kallik's surprise. "But we can't see them because the sky is too bright, and there is no true night."

Kallik tipped her head back to look at the sky. It was still light, streaked with glowing pink. She wondered if there were spirits hovering above her now, hidden from her. *Mother, if you're there,* she begged silently, *show me where I can find Taqqiq.*

"Spirits!" A loud voice from behind interrupted Kallik's

thoughts. Startled, she saw a group of young male bears charge past, jostling one another and sending the two young cubs scampering back to their mother's side. "There's no such thing as spirits in the sky," one of them jeered.

Siqiniq faced him calmly. "Maybe you think that now. But when you are older, you will be wiser."

The young male looked unsettled for a moment; then his eyes hardened. "Old fool," he snarled, and dashed on after his companions.

"They have no respect for any bear," Imiq huffed. "How dare he tell us he doesn't believe in the spirits of the ice?"

"Half-grown males," Qanniq growled. "What do you expect?"

"They're getting worse," Imiq pointed out. "Chasing and fighting and making noise when other bears are trying to get a bit of sleep. And I saw with my own eyes one of them stealing a fish from old Anarteq."

"They do that all the time," Qanniq put in, gathering her cubs closer to her. "They'll steal from any bear who's too weak to fight back."

Siqiniq sighed. "I remember a time when there was enough food for every bear, and there was no need to steal. It was a time when every bear knew that their ancestors were looking down on them."

"Well, talking catches no fish," Qanniq said, rising to her paws and prodding her cubs, who were huddled together at her side. "Come on, you two. There's not much fish in the lake, but we'll see what we can find."

She led the way down to the edge of the water. That was the signal for the group to break up, some following the mother bear, others padding off along the shore. Siqiniq settled down for a nap on the stones, folding her scrawny haunches underneath her.

"Thank you for telling me about the ice," Kallik said, dipping her head politely.

"Thank you for telling us about Nanuk," the older bear responded. "It is hard to lose a friend and not know why."

Kallik felt encouraged by the warmth in her voice. "Please, can you tell me more about this Gathering?" she prompted. "I know we're here to call back the ice, but I've no idea how we do that. My . . . my mother never told me."

Siqiniq shifted around to find a more comfortable position. "The Longest Day begins at sunrise," she began. "Every bear will gather on the lakeshore to tell the sun its reign is ending. And we call to the bear spirits to bring back the dark so that we can see them shining in the sky."

"And the ice will come back?"

Siqiniq nodded. "Every suncircle, the ice comes back. The other bears are here, too," she added, twitching her ears. "But they welcome the sun at the peak of its journey, while we send it away."

"What other bears?" Kallik asked, puzzled.

"The brown bears and the black bears." Siqiniq pointed with her muzzle. "They meet on the other side of the lake."

Kallik stared at her, digging her claws into the rough shingle. *How can bears be brown and black?* She would have told any other bear that their brain was full of feathers if they told her there were different-colored bears, but her respect for Siqiniq was too great to argue. She gazed across the lake to the other side, a skylength away. The sky reflected in the water, turning it pink. Straining her eyes, Kallik thought she could make out movement over there, but it was too far to see if there really were bears with black and brown pelts. *I wonder if I'll get to see them?*

"I've got so much to learn," she murmured, half to herself.

"Where's your mother, young one?" Siqiniq prompted. "Hasn't she taught you these things?"

"My mother is dead."

Siqiniq bowed her head. "I'm sorry. Did she die when the firebeast fell from the sky?"

"No," Kallik replied, her belly churning as she remembered the terrible day she lost her mother. "Orca took her."

"Orca," Siqiniq echoed with a sigh. "They have taken many good bears. One of my cubs died like that." She closed her eyes and let her muzzle rest on her paws. "Many suncircles ago, but I will never forget. . . ." Her voice died away.

Kallik realized the old bear had drifted into sleep. *I never asked her if she'd seen Taqqiq,* she thought, annoyed with herself. *Maybe later.*

She wandered along the shore, watching tiny waves rippling over the pebbles. Several bears were standing in the shallows, their eyes fixed intently on the water. As Kallik watched, one of them plunged his snout into the water and pulled it out again with a fish wriggling in his jaws.

Hunger griped in her belly; perhaps she could catch a fish, too. She waded a few pawsteps into the water, enjoying the cool sensation on her sore pads. She stared down; the water was clear, giving her a good view of the pebbly bottom, but at first she couldn't see any movement. Wind ruffled her fur, ridging the surface of the water. *Spirits, please send me a fish,* she begged.

Just at the edge of her sight, she glimpsed a flicker of silver. Thrusting off with her hindpaws, she pounced, but when her forepaws landed her claws gripped nothing but pebbles. Water splashed up around her, soaking her legs and belly fur.

"Watch out," an older male bear growled from a few bear-lengths away. "You'll scare away what fish there are, bouncing about like that."

"Sorry," Kallik muttered.

She bent her head and concentrated once more on the lake bottom. It seemed a very long time before she saw the next faint movement in the water. She forced her paws to stay still as the fish swam along the bottom with little flicks of its tail. It was coming closer; Kallik held her breath, then lashed out with one paw, pinning her prey down. Then she plunged her muzzle into the lake and sank her teeth into the fish just behind the gills.

Triumph flooded over her as she straightened up, the fish in her jaws. *I caught one!*

But before she could turn to go back to shore, a bear crashed into her side, pushing her over. Water frothed around her, blinding her as paws pummeled her flank. The fish was wrenched out of her jaws.

"No!" she spluttered, getting a mouthful of lake water. "Stop it!"

The pummeling stopped and she heard pawsteps splashing away. Scrambling to her feet, water streaming from her pelt, she spotted a young male bear heading back to land with her fish in his jaws.

"Hey!" she yelled. "I caught that! Give it back!"

The bear ignored her. Furious, Kallik splashed after him. He had joined three other young bears at the water's edge; they tore her fish into pieces and gulped it down before Kallik could reach them.

Kallik's belly was bawling with hunger and every hair on her pelt was hot with rage as she stood stiff-legged at the edge of the lake. "Thieves!" she snarled. "Why can't you catch your own fish?"

The young bear who had attacked her glanced around. "Shut up, seal-brain."

Kallik got a good look at him for the first time. Something about him was oddly familiar . . . the shape of his ears . . . the way he ran with his paws splayed out. . . . No, he was too big.

But I'm bigger now, too.

"Hey, Taqqiq, that was a good catch!" one of the other bears said, nudging him with his shoulder. "Can you get us another one?"

Kallik caught her breath. *It* is *him!* "Taqqiq!" she cried. "Taqqiq!"

Her brother narrowed his eyes. "Who are you? How do you know my name?"

"I'm . . . I'm Kallik," she stammered. "Your sister."

"My sister's dead," Taqqiq growled. "She and my mother were killed by orca."

His companions were gaping at Kallik; one of them nudged Taqqiq. "Ignore her, she's crazy."

"I'm not crazy. I'm *alive*. Nisa pushed me onto the ice before the orca dragged her down. But you were on the other side of the water, and I couldn't get back to you."

Taqqiq padded over to her, his huge feet crunching on the pebbles, then stretched out his neck and sniffed her. "You *are* Kallik," he whispered, his eyes widening.

"Of course I am!" said Kallik. "And I found you!"

Taqqiq glanced at his friends, then back at Kallik. "What are you doing here?" he hissed. "I didn't ask you to come looking for me!"

Kallik felt her heart turn to ice and her legs went very wobbly, as if they weren't going to hold her up for much longer. This wasn't how she had imagined her reunion with her brother.

"Are you staying there all day?" one of the other bears growled. "We're going to look for some more food. If you want any, you'd better come." He padded away, closely flanked by the other two.

Taqqiq turned and followed them up the shore. "Leave me alone," he snarled to Kallik over his shoulder. "I have my own friends now."

"Wait!" Kallik called after him. "What are you doing? It's

wrong to steal food. Why can't you catch your own, like our mother taught us?"

Taqqiq stopped and curled his lip, revealing strong yellow teeth. "Things are different now. If Nisa wanted to show us how to survive her way, she shouldn't have died and left us alone."

"Our mother didn't choose to die." Kallik's heart twisted at the bitterness in her brother's voice. "Her spirit is still here, watching over us."

But Taqqiq kept walking up the beach and didn't look back.

Kallik gazed after him, the cold lake water washing around her paws. In all the times she had imagined finding her brother at the end of her long, long journey, she had never once dreamed that he would not be pleased to see her.

CHAPTER EIGHTEEN

Lusa

"I can't stay in this tree forever," Lusa decided.

She felt too exposed at the top of the tree; the sight of so much open space made her dizzy—and frightened. She had never imagined that the trees would just *end*, that there would be endless empty land with no bear spirits at all. She scrambled down into the thicker branches to crouch in a fork where she could keep watch on the ground below. No bear padded past, though she could still hear the murmur of voices from the big clearing. In spite of her anxiety about the end of the trees, her pelt prickled with excitement at the thought of meeting real wild black bears. *I wonder if any of them knew King?*

Lusa had just begun to climb farther down when something big crashed into the tree above her. The branches waved wildly and Lusa lost her balance, swinging upside down from the branch with the ground rocking sickeningly above her head. Letting out a squeal of shock, she clung on with her hind claws, remembering how her father had told her that black bears never fall out of trees. *Not unless some bee-brain shakes it around.*

As the branches grew still again, she looked up. Another black bear cub had appeared in the tree above her. He was gazing down at her with bright curiosity in his eyes.

"Sorry," he yelped. "Are you okay? I didn't see you there."

You didn't try looking. Lusa bit back the sharp retort. "I'm fine," she puffed, clambering up onto the branch again. "You startled me, that's all."

The other cub peered at her more closely. "I haven't seen you before, have I? My name's Miki."

"I'm Lusa."

Miki scrambled down the tree until he could crouch on the branch next to her, so close that their pelts brushed. He reminded Lusa a bit of Yogi. He was younger and smaller, but he had the same splash of white fur on his chest.

"So you just got here?" he said. "Have you come far?"

"A long way," Lusa replied. "All the way from the Bear Bowl."

Miki put his head on one side. His ears were round and very fluffy, like the rest of him. "What's a Bear Bowl?"

Lusa wondered if she should have admitted right away that she wasn't a wild bear. But Miki would be bound to find out sooner or later. She wouldn't be able to hide that she didn't know all the things the other bears knew.

"A Bear Bowl is a place where flat-faces keep bears," she explained. "They feed us and look after us."

Miki looked confused; he raised one paw to scratch his ear. "I always knew flat-faces were weird. What do they do that for?"

"So other flat-faces can come and look at us, I think," said Lusa. "They were quite friendly."

Miki let out a disbelieving huff. "I don't like flat-faces. My mother and father went into some flat-face dens to look for food. And they never came back." His eyes glazed with grief as he added, "It was on the way here. They told me to wait under a bush at the edge of the dens. I waited and waited, but they didn't come."

"Oh, that's terrible!" Lusa knew how hard it had been for her to leave Aisha and King behind. It must be much, much worse to lose your parents and not know what had happened to them, or whether they were still alive. "What did you do?" she asked.

"I went into the dens to look for them." Miki was rigid with sadness. "But I couldn't find them. The trail of their scent stopped in a place that smelled sharp and smoky. Then I met some other bears. They said I should go with them, that they'd look after me now. I didn't want to at first, but . . . I knew I'd never see my mother and father again. As well as the smoky smell, I could smell blood. I . . . I just hope they didn't hurt for long."

Lusa leaned over to push her muzzle into the fur on Miki's shoulder. "I'm glad you didn't have to travel alone," she murmured.

"But you came here alone, didn't you?" Miki asked, shaking

himself as if his bad memories could be flicked off his pelt like water.

"No, I traveled with other bears." Lusa wasn't ready to admit that they were brown bears.

To her relief, Miki didn't ask her where those bears were now. He sat up, balancing on the branch as it swayed. "I'm starving!" he announced. "Let's go find something to eat."

"Okay." Lusa followed him as he bounded down the tree, her stomach growling.

"You're a great climber!" Miki exclaimed as she landed neatly beside him.

Lusa stretched up proudly. "My father, King, taught me, back in the Bear Bowl."

Miki lifted his muzzle into the air and drew in a huge breath. Lusa copied him; there was a tang on the air that reminded her of the scent of the fruit in the Bear Bowl.

"Over there?" she suggested, pointing with her nose.

"Hey, well scented. Let's go!"

Miki bounded off, with Lusa hard on his paws, weaving among the trees until they came to a more open space. The ground sloped upward, covered with low-growing bushes; they had glossy green leaves and bright red berries. The sharp tang surrounded Lusa now and her mouth watered.

Other black bears were already feeding in the thicket, stripping the berries from the branches with sharp pointed teeth. Not far from Lusa two adult bears were bending the branches down so that their young cubs could reach the fruit.

"Don't gulp them too fast," the mother bear said. "If you

do, they'll give you a bellyache."

Miki plunged into the nearest bushes under the trees and began to munch the berries. Lusa checked at the edge of the bushes. "Won't they mind?" she asked, jerking her head in the direction of the other bears.

"No, 'course not," Miki reassured her. "We have to take what we can get. Come on," he urged as Lusa still hesitated. "They'll all be gone if you don't hurry."

Lusa padded up to the nearest bush and tore off a mouthful of the berries. *Yuck!* She curled back her top lip. The berries looked juicy, but they were hard and dusty, and close up she could see that the sun had shriveled some of them. But if the other bears were eating them, so must she, because it meant there wasn't a better supply of berries somewhere else.

"There should be more than this," Miki muttered.

"It's so long since I saw any berries worth eating, these don't taste too bad," Lusa admitted, stretching up to reach the fruit growing on the topmost branch.

Miki grunted. "The bears you came with can't have been much good at finding them," he mumbled through a mouthful.

A few other bears had arrived, standing at the edge of the thicket and huffing anxiously as they looked for a clear space where they could feed.

"About time," one of them complained as Lusa and Miki finished stripping their share of berries from the bush and padded back under the trees.

They settled down in the shadows. The light was fading

out of the sky, and the forest was growing darker. The bear spirits whispered softly above Lusa's head as she licked berry pips from her paws. She wondered if they were saying sorry for the meager food supply.

Miki blew out a long breath. "I'm still hungry!" he complained. He hauled himself to his paws and padded a couple of bearlengths to a moss-covered stone at the foot of a nearby tree. "Hang on, I think there might be something under here. . . ."

Lusa joined him, puzzled. It looked like a perfectly ordinary stone. "You can't eat that," she said. "Unless you mean the moss is good to eat?"

"Well, it would be okay if you were really hungry," Miki said. "But I can show you something better. Watch."

He hooked a paw under the stone and flipped it over. Lusa peered down; the soil he had exposed was covered with fat white wriggling things. They smelled damp and earthy.

"What are those?" she asked.

Miki's brown eyes shone. "Grubs. They're pretty good. You want to try?"

"Mmm . . ." Lusa's mouth watered again. "They smell really juicy!"

She and Miki crouched down at the edge of the soil and began to eat. Lusa crunched up the grubs, enjoying the way they burst in her mouth and the taste of the fat white bodies. "They're really good!" she exclaimed.

Behind her she heard the pad of pawsteps, and a voice whining, "My tummy's empty!" Turning her head, Lusa saw a thin she-bear with a cub even smaller than Lusa and Miki.

The cub was butting its mother in the side. "I'm *hungry*! I want something to eat *now*!"

"I'm looking for food." The mother bear sounded harassed. "You'll have to wait till I find something."

Reluctantly Lusa got up from the soil patch, where there were still plenty of grubs left. "Come on," she said to the she-bear. "You can have some of these."

The she-bear gazed at her in disbelief, while her cub instantly darted forward and plunged its muzzle into the wriggling grubs. "It's okay," Lusa said softly. The mother bear gave her a quick, awkward nod and crouched to eat beside her cub.

Miki got up and joined Lusa. "You must have bees in your brain!" he muttered into her ear. "Giving away food? No bear would care if you starved to death."

Lusa looked at him. "But I would care if another bear starved to death because of me."

Miki sighed, swiping his tongue around his muzzle. "I guess we've had enough for now." Giving Lusa a nudge, he added, "Let's climb."

Lusa yawned; she really wanted to curl up and sleep. But she followed Miki to the nearest tree, watching how expertly he raced up the trunk to a high branch. Lusa bounded up after him, pleased that she was nearly as good as he was.

From up here, she could see above the other pines to the shore of the lake. Black bears were emerging from the trees, each with a spray of leaves and berries in their jaws. They laid them at the water's edge, beginning to form a twiggy barrier just out of reach of the waves.

"What are they doing?" she called to Miki, who was clinging to a swaying branch on the other side of the trunk.

"I think they're getting ready for the ceremony," he replied. "I've never seen it before, but the bears I came here with told me about it. At dawn, we'll all gather by the lakeshore, and the oldest bear will welcome the sun on the Longest Day."

"What are the berries for?" Lusa's stomach growled at the thought of all that food, even dry and dusty berries, just lying there.

"To honor the spirits." He didn't tell her how, exactly, and Lusa suspected he didn't know. "I'm going to sleep," he added with a huge yawn. "It's safe up here. The brown bears won't bother us." His voice sank to a whisper. "One of the bears I traveled with said she'd seen a grizzly bear kill a black cub and eat it!" He shivered. "Best to stay away from them."

"Grizzlies don't eat black bears!" Lusa protested.

"How do you know?" Miki twitched his ears in surprise. "Were there brown bears in your Bear Bowl?"

"Y-yes."

"And you all lived together?" Miki sounded disbelieving.

"Not exactly." Lusa squirmed; Miki's questions felt like ants crawling in her pelt. "The brown bears were in a different part of the Bowl. We could talk to them through the fence, though."

"So they *might* have eaten you, if they could have gotten at you." Miki sounded triumphant, as if he had proved his point.

"The flat-faces knew, or why would they keep the brown bears away from you? That proves they're bad."

"No, they're not!" Lusa blurted out, irritation getting the better of her. "I traveled here with two brown bears, actually." *At least, I suppose Ujurak is a brown bear. Most of the time.* "So I *do* know what they're like. They looked after me and fed me. We were friends."

"Friends?" Miki's eyes stretched wide. "I've never heard of that before. Whatever made you want to travel with grizzlies?"

"It's a long story," Lusa began. Quickly she told Miki how Oka had come to the Bear Bowl, and sent Lusa to find her son Toklo with a message. "When I found him, he was with another grizzly cub, called Ujurak. He's the most amazing bear!" She leaned closer to Miki, eager to make him understand just how remarkable Ujurak was. "He knows stuff other bears don't know, and he's on a journey to find the place where the spirits dance in the sky. I didn't have anywhere else to go, so I decided to go with him and Toklo." She was about to tell him how Ujurak could change into other animals and even birds, but Miki interrupted her.

"Well, you've found black bears now," he said, as if that was all that mattered. "So this is where you belong." He shifted on the branch until he had wedged himself into a comfortable position, and closed his eyes. Almost at once his slow, regular breathing told Lusa he was asleep. He wasn't interested in hearing about brown bears. He was a black bear: He obviously thought Lusa was only traveling with brown bears until she found bears just like her.

Lusa settled down with her pelt pressed close to his, but she stayed awake, listening to the murmured conversations of the black bears nearby in the forest.

Miki's right, she thought. *This is like coming home, among other black bears. I'll be a proper bear with them. I'll be able to hunt for the same food and stay under the trees, close to the bear spirits. I've even made a friend,* she added, as Miki let out a little grunt.

As she drifted to sleep, Lusa gazed out through the branches at the lake. The sun was touching the horizon on the far side, staining the water pinkish red like the color of berries. A dark shape was bobbing among the waves, halfway between the shore and a distant island. Lusa blinked, peering at it more closely. *Is that a* bear *out there?* Drowsily, she wondered what it was doing. *I'm glad it's not me.*

She yawned and closed her eyes. The bear in the lake had nothing to do with her. She was safe with her own kind, and that was where she would stay.

I'm going to miss Ujurak and Toklo.

CHAPTER NINETEEN

Toklo

I am with you, Toklo, the waves hissed.

"Go away!" Toklo growled. "I don't want to be dead like you. Leave me alone!"

By now he was so far out that the choppy water was buffeting him from both sides, making it hard to swim in a straight line toward the island. He spluttered as a wave broke over his nose, and his head went under. Flailing his paws, he struggled up again; he was so low in the water that he could barely see the island, and the weight of his sodden fur was dragging him down.

I'll never make it, he thought despairingly.

His limbs felt heavy like lumps of wood. He had never been so tired. It was a massive effort to keep on paddling and kicking out with his hindpaws, and he couldn't tell if he was making any progress.

Maybe Shoteka was right. I am *weak. Mother? Tobi? Can you see me now?*

The voice echoed inside his head. *You are strong, Toklo.*

Toklo felt bulky fur, slick with water, brush against his flank. His head whipped around, but he couldn't see anything except the choppy lake water. The sensation came again, more strongly this time, and with it a once-familiar scent.

Oka was swimming with him.

On his other side he became aware of a smaller shape, stick-frail among the waves, but pressing strongly against his side. *Tobi!* They had come to drown him, just as he knew they would.

Panic gripped Toklo in icy claws. He didn't want to drown! He lashed out with both forepaws, trying to thrust the shapes away from him. Thrashing frantically, he gulped in another mouthful of water and went under again. As the water closed over his head he found that he was trapped in an eerie, gray-brown world of strange shadows and flickering shapes. Faint outlines of two brown bears, one large and one pitifully small, spiraled around him.

You're drowning me! he raged. *Let me go!*

His paws flailed and his limbs grew heavier, and he began to sink down to the bottom of the lake. Pain clawed through his chest as he fought the urge to breathe. It would be a relief to give in.

Okay, you win. Oka, Tobi, here I am.

Toklo shut his eyes and let the black cloud fill him up, first his paws, then his legs, then his body sinking lower and lower, and finally his head, until his ears buzzed with nothingness and he saw nothing but darkness behind his eyelids. *Is this how it felt when you died, Tobi?*

There was a jolt, and Toklo's eyes flew open. Water dragged at his muzzle, which was moving steadily up toward a shimmering light. He felt himself being shoved again, harder this time, on both flanks. One push was stronger than the other, so he swerved through the water toward the lighter push. He fought to look back. The two bear spirits were behind him, nudging him with their shoulders.

Up, Toklo! Swim toward the light!

Toklo flailed his front legs, trying to drag himself through the water. The light rushed nearer and nearer, and suddenly his head broke the surface and he was gulping air, the best air he had ever tasted, which filled him up and sent the heavy black cloud spinning out of his head.

That's right, Toklo! Breathe! The high-pitched voice of his brother rang in his ears.

Swim, Toklo! his mother urged him, her bulk still supporting him in the waves.

Swim! Tobi added. He sounded much stronger and happier than he had been when he was alive. *Swim with us, Toklo. I'll help you.*

Their bodies surged underneath Toklo, bearing him up. Some of his exhaustion ebbed away, and suddenly swimming wasn't as hard as it had been before. He stretched out his front paws and scooped the water behind him, sending his body slick as a fish through the waves.

"I'm swimming!" he shouted.

Yes, you are, said his mother. She sounded proud and sad at the same time.

Toklo tried to look around, but waves splashed in his eyes and he couldn't see the bear spirits anymore. "You saved me!" he barked. "You didn't let me drown!"

"You are my son, and I love you. I want you to live for a long, long time. Tobi and I will be waiting for you, always. But not before it is your time to join us. Go carefully, precious Toklo."

"I will," Toklo replied, with a strange choking feeling in his throat that made it hard to speak. "Good-bye, Mother. Good-bye, Tobi."

Good-bye!

Good-bye!

Toklo faced ahead again, and felt his mother and brother fade away from his sides. He didn't need them to help him swim now. He was pulling himself through the water, keeping his muzzle above the waves and breathing steadily. Oka and Tobi hadn't wanted to drag him down with them, and now he missed them even more.

He was leaving the open water behind at last; the waves stopped splashing over his muzzle, and the surface flattened enough for him to catch a glimpse of the pine-clad island ahead. It loomed above him, a dusty mound of earth and brittle grass, dotted with tall skinny trees.

"Pawprint Island!" he whispered.

Toklo felt his forepaws scrape on shingle. He dug in with his claws and stood up, bracing himself against the waves rolling in behind him. The water reached up to his shoulders. He began to wade to the shore. As the water grew shallower, he turned once more and looked back at the rippling black lake.

The silence pressed around him, deafening him. Suddenly, he didn't want to be alone.

"Mother! Tobi! Don't leave me!"

With water washing around his paws, he wondered whether he should go back into the lake to look for them.

No, Toklo, whispered the waves. *It is not your time.*

Toklo swung around and trudged up the shelving lake bottom until he could clamber onto a boulder. He shook the water out of his pelt and looked around.

"I've done it," he said aloud.

The sun had dropped below the horizon but there was still a pale light in the sky, and the night wasn't entirely dark. Only the lake was black and the hills around it, silhouetted against the gray sky. On the distant lakeshore he could just make out the shapes of brown bears, and farther around the lake where the forest reached down to the water, he spotted the shadows of black bears under the trees. He wondered if Lusa was among them, but the bears were too far away for him to make out one particular cub.

Toklo turned away from the lake. *I have to spend the Longest Day here, so I might as well explore.*

The ground sloped gently up from the water. The shingle beach gave way to grass, and then to shrubs and a few stunted trees. Toklo pushed his way into the undergrowth. It felt dry and crackly, as if it hadn't rained for a long, long time. There were no bear scents here, no pawmarks or droppings to suggest that he was not alone. *This is* my *territory,* he reminded himself, pushing down the empty feeling inside him. He reared up on his hindpaws and scored his claws on the trunk of the nearest tree. They left deep, satisfying scratches behind. Even if there were no other bears to see them, Toklo knew they were there, and knew they meant that this place belonged to him.

Padding farther into the undergrowth, he spotted a weasel slinking under the bushes, its body low as it searched for prey. Instinctively Toklo began to stalk it; saliva filled his mouth as he crept forward, setting his paws down one at a time on the brittle pine needles. The weasel was scratching the ground underneath the bush. Toklo paused; the breeze was blowing in his face, carrying the creature's scent into his jaws and over his tongue. Toklo lunged under the bush and slammed his paws down on the weasel, snapping its neck. He scooped it up with his claw then crouched low, sinking his teeth into its warm flesh, savoring the juices as they filled his belly.

Oogrook had told him that the fate of all the bears rested on his shoulders. Toklo didn't know how swimming to the island would help, but he had done it. Perhaps the sight of the weasel was an omen of more prey for all the bears, not just him. He stood up and began to climb the low, scrubby hill in the center of the island. He felt the tingle of renewed strength in his limbs, and as he padded along he wondered if this was what Shesh had meant by the spirit of Arcturus coming to him on the ancient Paw Print.

From the summit of the hill, he could see the entire island. On the side where he had swum ashore, the ground climbed steadily upward, covered by trees and bushes. On the other side, the hill fell away more steeply, covered by thin, tough grass. It ended in a cliff, with the lake water washing around sharp rocks far below. Toklo shuddered, glad he hadn't come ashore on that side.

The wind buffeted his fur and stung his eyes as he stood facing into it. It carried the scents of salt, ice, and fish, and the strange scent of bears that seemed to be a mixture of all three. Toklo peered into the gloom; these were bears he had never encountered before, and his pelt tingled with a mixture of curiosity and alarm. On the distant shoreline he could just make out their shapes, huge figures that looked carved out of ice against the gray rocks. The wind carried the sound of roaring to him across the water; they sounded fierce. Toklo was suddenly very glad to be alone on the island, and hoped that the strange bears didn't like swimming.

He trudged back across the stretch of grass and into the trees. He decided to make himself a den, and sleep until the sun rose on the Longest Day. He remembered seeing a comfortable-looking hollow near the beach, with a twisted pine tree hanging over it, shedding its needles on the ground to make a soft nest. He retraced his pawsteps and found the hollow, which was a bit too shallow to shelter him if it rained, but judging by the dust on the ground, that was unlikely. He snapped off some thin twigs that might scratch his eyes when he crawled into the hollow. Then he wriggled in and lay down, shifting around among the pine needles until he was comfortable.

Toklo closed his eyes. The soft lap of the waves on the shore seemed full of spirit-voices as he drifted into sleep.

* * *

The barking of bears woke Toklo; from his den under the pine tree he could see across the lake to the shore where the brown bears were gathering. They were crowded together at the water's edge, around the parley stone, but they were too far away for Toklo to see exactly what they were doing, or hear their voices clearly. Above his head the sky was flushed with dawn; the glittering disc of the sun was floating into the sky once more, already too bright to look at. Toklo's paws tingled. *This is the Longest Day!*

A bird in the branches above his head let out an alarm call. Clambering out of his den, Toklo spotted movement on the beach. Something was bobbing in the waves at the edge of the lake, something far too big to be a bird or a weasel. Toklo ducked behind the pine tree above his sleeping hollow and peered out. Scrambling out of the water, shaking himself dry, was a ragged-pelted grizzly with a distinctive hump between his shoulders. Toklo's heart sank.

Shoteka!

CHAPTER TWENTY

Toklo

Toklo waited in the cover of the pine tree as Shoteka scanned the shore in front of him. After a moment's ominous silence, the grizzly opened his jaws in a roar. "Come out!"

Toklo's first instinct was to hide. *But he'll find me. It's a small island. And he can track me by my scent.*

"Come out, coward!" the humpbacked grizzly roared again.

"You shouldn't be here," Toklo hissed through gritted teeth. "I'm supposed to be *alone.*"

Glancing at the waves, he wondered if Oka and Tobi were watching him, telling him to be brave. *I'll make you proud of me,* he promised as he stepped out onto the shore and faced the humpbacked bear. Just for a heartbeat he caught a glimmer of shock in Shoteka's tiny, hostile eyes.

"What do you want?" Toklo demanded.

The humpbacked bear let out a huff of contempt. "You think *you* can bring the fish back? A useless, weak bear like you?"

"I am *not* weak!" Toklo snarled.

"Weak bears should be killed," Shoteka said, ignoring him, "before they weaken all of us. I don't know why your mother bothered protecting you. After all, she was weak, too. She couldn't even look after you!"

Toklo's anger erupted in a red flash of rage. "Oka did the best she could," he growled.

"It was a poor best," Shoteka sneered.

Letting out a roar, Toklo charged down the pebbly shore. Surprise gave him the advantage. He managed to rake his claws down Shoteka's side as he dashed past, before the other bear could do anything to defend himself.

Toklo whirled to attack again, in time to see Shoteka rear up on his hindpaws with his forepaws splayed out, his claws tearing at the air. Shoteka bellowed so loudly that a pair of large white birds flapped out of a tree behind Toklo. For a heartbeat he hesitated: This bear was nearly twice his size! His legs were like tree trunks, and his body was almost as big as a firebeast's.

You're smaller, but you're faster, Oka's voice whispered in Toklo's mind.

Shoteka loomed over Toklo, ready to fall on him and crush him like a beetle. Darting forward, Toklo dodged the outstretched claws and slashed Shoteka's exposed belly. Blood sprang along the line of his claws, and Toklo smelled its hot scent. He leaped out of the way as the grizzly dropped to four paws again.

Toklo felt teeth meet his neck fur. He squealed as Shoteka

lifted all four of his paws off the ground, shook him as if he were a hare, then flung him onto the stones. Toklo lay still, half-stunned, trying to remember how to breathe; pain pierced him as claws raked over his shoulder and down his side.

Through blurred vision he saw the big grizzly standing over him, his teeth bared, ready to bite down on his neck. The reek of his hot breath swept over Toklo. "Are you ready to swim with the spirits, weakling?"

Desperately Toklo wriggled onto his back and battered at the humpback's belly with his hindpaws. He heard a grunt and his opponent moved away, enough for Toklo to scramble to his paws again.

"I'm not swimming with any spirits yet," he growled.

He rushed in to give one of Shoteka's paws a sharp nip, before springing back out of range. He could feel blood trickling from his wounds, and felt as if his strength was trickling away with it. *I can't keep this up much longer.*

The humpbacked bear was wary now, circling him with hatred in his eyes. Toklo's courage surged up again. "Now who's weak?" he taunted.

Shoteka lunged at him; Toklo dodged at the last moment and managed to get another blow in on the bear's rump. The humpback let out a shriek of frustration.

Before Shoteka could turn to face him again, Toklo scrambled up onto the other bear's back. He raked his claws across the humpback's head, tearing out huge clumps of fur. Shoteka's blood spattered on the pebbles. He started to rear up again; Toklo half-jumped, half-fell off the bear's back and braced himself for the next blow.

But the grizzly didn't attack. Instead, he dropped his forepaws to the ground and stood shaking his head. Toklo watched him, terrified that Shoteka was gathering his strength for a quick revenge. Panting, he crouched on the stones, feeling them dig into the scratches on his flanks.

But Shoteka turned away and shambled a few paces farther down the beach. Toklo stared after him in startled silence as the humpbacked bear paused for a couple of heartbeats, then began to wade out into the lake.

With water halfway up his legs, Shoteka turned to look over his shoulder. "You are not worthy to honor Arcturus," he snapped. "I may have spared you today, but there will come a time when you'll wish that I'd killed you. Your mother shamed me, and I will have my revenge. For now, I will let you live. But there are worse times to come, little bear, believe me. This is only the beginning."

He waded out farther until the water reached his shoulders and he began to swim. Toklo watched his bobbing dark head vanish among the white-tipped waves.

So that's why he came looking for me, he thought. *Because my mother saved me before. Oka, you were right to save me then. I'll never regret that, never!* He pushed away the memory of Shoteka's last words, about worse times lying ahead. Those were just the words of a defeated bear; they meant nothing. Toklo would never wish he had died!

He waded into the lake until he could lie on one side and let the waves lap against his wounds. He took a few mouthfuls of cool water. *My first battle,* he thought. *I defended my territory.*

Heaving himself out of the water, Toklo limped back across the foreshore and curled up in the hollow underneath the pine tree. The sun was well above the horizon now, its warm rays soothing his battered body.

This was what it meant to be a brown bear. To live alone, powerful and fierce, so that every other bear would respect and fear him.

I want it to be like this always, he thought. *I don't want to be responsible for any other bears. Just myself, guarding my territory alone like the star that is chased around the sky.*

CHAPTER TWENTY-ONE

Kallik

Kallik dozed uneasily through the short night on an uncomfortable bed of stones. The older bears had taken all of the best sleeping places, though she noticed that Taqqiq and his friends had found a soft patch of grass to rest on, after they chased off a she-bear and her cub.

But it was not just the stones digging into her that kept Kallik awake. Her quest to find her brother was over. But it had all gone wrong. She didn't recognize Taqqiq in this rough bully who thought nothing of stealing another bear's prey and scorned the other bears when they talked about the spirits. He cared more about his cruel friends than he did about her. And she had no idea what she ought to do now.

Kallik raised her head as other bears brushed past her, heading down to the lakeshore in eerie silence. The old she-bear, Siqiniq, whom Kallik had spoken to the day before, was standing on a rock at the water's edge. As the other bears crowded around her, Kallik got up and followed them, full of curiosity.

The sky was stained red from the approaching sunrise. A hush fell over the assembled bears as the glow grew brighter. In the silence, Kallik heard a yelp from behind, and turned her head to see Taqqiq and his friends wrestling together at the edge of the crowd. An older bear snapped at them, but they didn't stop.

As the glittering rim of the sun edged above the horizon, Siqiniq stood taller on the rock and raised one paw. "Sun, we welcome you on this Longest Day," she began, her voice ringing out clearly. "Now hear my words: Your reign is ending. From now on, the dark will return at the end of each day, bringing with it snow and ice, and striking stillness into the melted water. White bears will be able to return to their feeding grounds once more."

A sigh swept through the bears. The ice could not return too soon to ease their hunger. Still sleepy, Kallik stifled a yawn, and hoped no bear would think she was being disrespectful.

"Bear spirits," Siqiniq went on, "bring back the dark, so that you may shine again in your tiny fragments of ice. Drive the sun lower in the sky, so that we can honor you from our ancient home on the ice."

She fell silent, and all the bears waited until the whole disc of the sun had cleared the horizon. Kallik could still hear scuffling and muffled yelps from the direction of Taqqiq and his friends. *Shut up!* she thought fiercely. *I don't care if you don't believe in what Siqiniq is saying. Other bears have the right to listen to her.*

Once the sun was up, all the bears bowed their heads

toward it. Kallik bowed, too, feeling awestruck that she was here to witness the beginning of the return of the ice, and the power of Siqiniq, who could even command the sun.

Then the gathering began to break up, the bears going back to their sleeping places, or farther up the beach to forage in the undergrowth. A few of them waded into the lake, peering in hopefully for fish. Kallik realized how hungry she was; she headed for the lake, too, wondering if she could hide anything she caught from Taqqiq and the others.

Her brother and his friends were tussling with one another at the water's edge, splashing around noisily and not even trying to fish.

"Hey!" one of them barked, breaking away from the scrimmage. "There's Namak with a fish. Let's go grab it!" He pointed to a much older bear, slowly heading away from the water with a fish in his mouth.

The rest of the bears sat up, then sprang to their paws. They ran after the older bear and encircled him, pushing and shoving him from all sides and batting at him with their claws. Confused, Namak tried to shoulder his way past them, but they wouldn't let him go. He let out a growl of frustration and dropped the fish.

Immediately all four of the bears pounced on the prey and tore it apart, gulping the scraps down until it was gone. Namak stood watching them, his lips peeled back in a snarl, but there was nothing he could do. His shoulders drooped and he trudged to the edge of the lake and waded out into the water.

"That's right, old seal-brain!" one of the young bears yelled. "Catch us another one!"

Angry and discouraged, Kallik turned away from the lake. She wasn't going to catch a fish to feed Taqqiq and his horrible friends. Instead, she headed for the undergrowth at the top of the beach, where a few bears were feeding on leaves and berries. Kallik found a bush in a quiet spot where she could munch on the foliage, wishing it were succulent fish instead. She was still struggling to swallow her first mouthful when she heard approaching pawsteps and stiffened at the loud voice of one of Taqqiq's friends.

"This will do. No bear will hear us."

Kallik peered out from behind her bush. A couple of bearlengths away, the four young bears were settling themselves down, breaking branches to make enough space and tearing off mouthfuls of leaves, only to spit them out with disgusted noises.

"This is worse than rotfood," one of them whined.

"Yeah, you're right, Manik," said another. "It's not fit for bears."

"Complaining's no good, Iqaluk. We'll starve if we don't *do* something," a third bear growled. He was bigger than the others, with heavy shoulders and a narrow face. "There has to be food somewhere. If we can't catch it ourselves, we'll have to take it."

"But Salik, where can we take it from?" Taqqiq objected. "These scrawny bears can't catch any prey worth eating. They're only strong enough to beg the sun to go away."

"There'll be food in the forest over the other side," Salik snarled. "Animals to prey on, roots and berries to eat. The bears over there are far better off than we are."

"Yeah," Manik agreed. "It's not fair that we're stuck here while they're in the forest stuffing themselves."

"That's what I was going to tell you." Salik, who seemed to be the leader of the group, leaned forward, his eyes slitted. "It's not fair, so we should do something about it. Let's raid their dens and drive them out! Then we can take their food!"

Kallik listened in horror. Attacking a whole group of other bears? Stealing all their food? Surely Taqqiq wouldn't go along with this!

Before she could call out to him, she heard the sound of another bear pushing his way through the undergrowth. She looked up to see a full-grown bear who strode up to Taqqiq and the others.

"What did I hear you say?" he demanded. "Raiding the forest? Have you got feathers in your brain?"

"Shove off, old goose," Salik retorted, rudely turning his back on the older bear. "This has nothing to do with you."

"It has everything to do with me, and every other bear here," the bear replied. "Stealing food from other bears? *Fighting* with other bears? On the Longest Day?"

His voice had reached the ears of more white bears, who padded down the foreshore or waded up from the lake to see what was going on. They crowded around Taqqiq and his friends, their voices raised in shock and anxiety.

"What's going on? What did they say?"

"You can't do that! Show a bit of respect!"

Kallik wriggled out of the bushes and squeezed herself through the crowd of tightly packed bodies.

Salik and the older male were glaring at each other as if they were a heartbeat away from a fight. Taqqiq and the other two had bunched together, their lips drawn back in a snarl as they stared defiantly around.

"Have you no respect for tradition?" quavered a high-pitched voice.

The bears parted to let Siqiniq pad into the center. Her body was frail and old, but her eyes blazed. "Don't you know that this is a day of truce, to honor the spirits of the ice? That's why we're here, not to fight and steal and make enemies of other bears."

Salik huffed out a breath of contemptuous laughter. "Every bear knows there are no spirits. That's just a tale to frighten cubs."

"Right. We don't believe in that garbage anymore," Taqqiq added.

Kallik gasped. Was this really Taqqiq talking, who had curled up with her in their BirthDen and listened to Nisa's stories about Silaluk and the hunters? "Taqqiq, no . . ." she pleaded, but other voices drowned her out.

"If I were your mother, I'd give you a good clawing," a she-bear spat out.

"My mother's dead," Taqqiq retorted. "And you can't tell me what to do."

"Are we going or not?" Salik demanded. "The rest of you

can sit here and starve, for all I care," he snarled at the crowd. "Wait and see how much your precious spirits will do for you."

"Yes," Iqaluk put in. "We need food, and we'll do whatever it takes to get it. It's not our problem if you're too scared."

With Salik in the lead, all four bears shoved their way through the crowd and disappeared into the bushes.

"Kunik, we have to stop this," Siqiniq said, her eyes wide with distress.

The older male who had spoken first looked grim. "We can't fight them, or we break the truce, too. Do you want to make the ice spirits angry with all white bears?"

Siqiniq's claws scraped the ground in front of her. "Then what will happen?"

"That is in the paws of the ice spirits," Kunik replied.

Kallik pushed her way through the edge of the crowd and out into the open. She could see Taqqiq and the others running along the lakeshore.

"Taqqiq! Wait!" she cried.

If her brother heard her, he gave no sign of it. He raced along in Salik's pawsteps; Kallik flung herself after him.

"Wait for me!" she panted.

She forced her paws to move faster, dodging other bears, ignoring the sharp stones that stabbed her pads. Pelting all out, she couldn't avoid a thorny bush growing in the gap between two boulders, and the sharp spines tore at her fur. Stubbornly, she didn't slow down, just wrenched herself through the narrow space and kept running. But the other bears were drawing steadily away, toward a line of dark trees.

She wondered what the ice spirits would do to bears who broke the truce. Maybe Taqqiq would never become a star, never be with their mother, Nisa, again, shining in the sky.

Though she was falling farther and farther behind, Kallik ran on, trying to ignore her aching leg muscles and sore paws.

Oh, spirits, help me, she begged. *Somehow I have to stop him.*

CHAPTER TWENTY-TWO

Kallik

Kallik paused, panting, her heart thumping as if it were about to burst out of her chest. She had lost sight of Taqqiq and the others; she didn't think they could have reached the forest yet, so where had they gone?

The hard ground where the white bears were gathered had given way to marshland. Small streams meandered through muddy grass and reeds, with a few twisted bushes where the ground began to slope upward to a ridge. The wind dropped for a moment, and Kallik heard the raucous voices of young bears coming from inland, behind the ridge. She paused, sniffing, and from the mingled scents of white bears she picked out the familiar one that was her brother's.

"Taqqiq?" she called.

There was no reply but the whispering of the wind as it carried the bear scent toward her, along with the scent of mud and reeds and empty places. Following the sound of the voices, Kallik climbed up to the top of the rise. On the other side, she saw muddy banks leading down to a small, reed-fringed pool.

The bears were rolling around in the mud, plastering it on their fur and splashing one another, then flinging themselves down the muddy slopes until they landed in the water at the edge of the pool.

Kallik took a few paces down the slope, mud squelching between her toes. "Taqqiq, what are you doing?" she demanded. She felt small and shrill beside the bigger male bears.

There was a sucking sound as Taqqiq pulled himself up out of the mud. "Oh, it's you again. What do you want?"

Kallik wanted to wail out loud. What had happened to her brother since they shared their games on the ice? "I want to talk to you."

"Tell her to go away." Salik flicked a glob of mud at Taqqiq; it hit his neck and slid stickily down into his fur. "We don't want her hanging around."

Taqqiq glanced back at him. "I'd better see what she wants. She'll never leave us alone if I don't." Wading out of the mud, he came to a halt in front of Kallik. "Well?"

"What are you all *doing*? Why do you want to play in that disgusting stuff?"

"We're not playing," Taqqiq said loftily. "This was Salik's idea. He's very clever."

Kallik gave a disbelieving sniff.

"It's to disguise us when we get to the other bears' territory," Taqqiq went on. "With mud plastered all over our pelts, they'll never notice us sneaking up."

"You think it hides your scent?" Kallik couldn't believe that any bear could be so stupid. "Well, it doesn't. It just makes you smell like filthy bears."

Taqqiq turned away with an offended grunt, and took a couple of paces back toward the muddy pool.

"No, Taqqiq, wait! That's not what I wanted to say."

"What, then?" Taqqiq still looked unfriendly.

"I want to know why you've started stealing food from other bears. That's not what our mother taught us."

"But she isn't here now, is she?" Taqqiq growled. "We're doing it because we don't want to starve."

A tiny spark of anger woke in Kallik. "But it's okay if other bears starve?"

Taqqiq's eyes hardened. "Rather them than us."

"I can't believe you're saying that!" Kallik exclaimed, the spark of anger fanned to flame. "Don't you remember how it felt when bigger bears stole our food?"

Taqqiq shrugged. "*We're* bigger now. Bigger and stronger."

"But it's wrong, Taqqiq." Kallik shook her head hopelessly. "There has to be a better way."

"Then you go and figure out what it is," Taqqiq snarled, facing her with sullen fury in his eyes. "The spirits of the ice have abandoned us. They've turned their backs on us, so it's time for us to turn our backs on them."

"Back there"—Kallik jerked her head toward the place where the other bears had gathered to greet the Longest Day—"you said you didn't believe in the ice spirits. Or was that just when Salik was listening?"

Taqqiq shrugged again, uneasily this time. "I dunno. But if they do exist, they don't care about us, so what difference does it make?"

Kallik felt despair, like the orca dragging her down into darkness. "I've looked for you for so long," she murmured. "Sometimes I thought you were dead, but I never stopped looking."

"I saw our mother die." Taqqiq's voice shook a little. "I thought you were dead, too. I've done what I had to survive."

"And so did I!" Kallik burst out. "It was so hard. We were too young to be left alone." Anxious to keep him talking, she added, "What happened to you, after we were separated?"

"I was scared," Taqqiq admitted quietly, as if he didn't want the others to hear. "I watched the orca drag our mother down, and then I couldn't see you anymore, either. I thought they must have taken you as well. I knew I had to get to land, but I didn't know which way to go. I just ran along the ice until I couldn't run anymore."

As he was talking, Taqqiq settled down beside his sister, nestling his haunches into the prickly grass. A glint of hope kindled in Kallik, bright as the Pathway Star.

"The next day was clear again. I looked for you and couldn't see you, so I swam across to the next piece of ice."

"But I came back to look for you!" Kallik exclaimed. "I never saw you."

Taqqiq looked at his mud-stained paws. "There was so much ice and sea. . . . I could scent the land, so I just kept on going until I got there. I was so hungry. I saw a mother bear giving some fish to her cubs, and I stole some when she wasn't looking."

"Did you try eating grass?" Kallik asked. "I did, but it's not very nice."

"Grass!" Taqqiq huffed. "That's not food for bears. I found some berries, though. They were okay. I tried following other bears, to see what they did; if you're careful, they'll lead you to food."

Kallik shuddered. "I was too scared to get close. Our mother said that adult bears sometimes eat cubs, remember?"

"Well, they didn't eat me!" Taqqiq boasted. "I used to creep up and hide, and made sure the wind didn't carry my scent to them. And sometimes if they quarreled over some prey, I could take it while they were fighting."

"I met a bear called Purnaq who showed me the place where all the bears were waiting by the sea."

"I was there!" Taqqiq exclaimed. "I looked for you, but I didn't see you."

"I looked for you, too." Kallik shivered. She had been so close to her brother and had never realized it. Did the spirits have some purpose in keeping them apart until the Gathering here beside the lake? "But there were so many bears there. . . . Did you see the old bear with the torn claws?"

"Yes—stupid creature," Taqqiq scoffed. "Calling out to the spirits—like they're going to listen!"

A pang of pain clawed at Kallik's heart. She had felt sorry for the old bear.

"I saw him attack the white firebeast," she said. "That was brave."

Taqqiq scratched his ear. "Brave but stupid. I'd bet you a whole seal that the no-claws wouldn't come anywhere near the bears if they knew we could hurt them."

"I suppose . . ." Kallik agreed reluctantly. "It was weird: all those no-claws inside the firebeast, staring at us."

"Yeah. The firebeast is stupid, too. We tracked it the whole way into the no-claws' dens."

"We?" Kallik echoed, with a flicker of apprehension.

"Salik and the others." Taqqiq glanced down at the pool where the other three were still throwing mud at one another. "Salik is a good bear to be with. He's strong and clever. He makes sure his friends get enough to eat."

Even if he steals from other bears?

"I went into the no-claws' place, too," she said, changing the subject. "That was where—"

She wanted to tell Taqqiq about the no-claws with the firesticks, and how they had tried to take her and Nanuk back to the ice. Would Taqqiq ever believe that she had flown underneath a metal bird? She had so much to tell him! She wanted to pour out everything about her travels, to let her brother share how scared she'd been and how she had managed to struggle through. *Except for the fox,* she told herself. *If Taqqiq thinks it's okay to steal from other bears, he'd never understand about the fox.*

But a shout came from Salik, interrupting her. "Taqqiq, are you going to sit there all day?"

Taqqiq hauled himself to his paws. "Coming!"

"No," Kallik begged. "Taqqiq, please stay with me. It was much better on the ice, when we helped each other. Remember how you said you'd protect me in the sea, when Nisa first said we had to swim?"

For a long moment Taqqiq gazed at her. Then he shook his head. "That was then," he growled. "Everything is different now. There's no ice here, and bears have to do what they can to survive."

The other three bears had dragged themselves out of the mud and padded up the slope to join Taqqiq. Salik was in the lead. He stalked up to Kallik and glared down at her; Kallik's nose wrinkled at the rank smell of the mud clinging to his pelt.

"*Don't* follow us again," he snarled, and added to Taqqiq, "I don't care if she's your denmate. If she doesn't leave us alone I'll claw her pelt off."

"He means it," Taqqiq warned her.

And you would let him? Kallik shrieked inside.

"Go back to the other bears," Taqqiq went on. "Just stop following me around, okay?"

Kallik nodded. With a last snarl at her, Salik turned away, leading the others around the lake toward the line of dark trees where the other bears were. Kallik watched them racing along the shore until they crashed into the trees and disappeared. Then she rose to her paws and followed cautiously, taking advantage of every dip in the land and scrawny bush for cover.

You can't tell me what to do, Taqqiq. I want to know what you're up to.

At last she reached the outermost trees and paused briefly, sniffing their warm scent and listening to the rustle of wind in the branches. Padding forward, she felt the odd, spiky sensation of needles under her pads. She looked around warily, but she couldn't see or hear Taqqiq and the others, though she caught a trace of their fading scent. There were no other white bears, either.

Then she heard pawsteps on the other side of a patch of bushes. Kallik pushed her way through, glad that they didn't have thorns this time, and halted in amazement. A small group of bears was foraging across an open patch of ground, pausing beside the bushes to strip berries and leaves with sharp, clever white teeth. But these bears were tiny.

And their fur was *black*!

CHAPTER TWENTY-THREE

Lusa

"Wake up!" The excited voice roused Lusa from sleep and a paw prodded her sharply in the side. "Come on, Lusa, hurry!"

Lusa grunted and opened eyes bleared with sleep to see Miki's excited face peering into hers. "What's the matter?"

"It's the start of the Longest Day! We've got to be there for the sunrise ceremony."

Lusa yawned and rubbed her eyes. "Okay, I'm coming."

She scrambled down the trunk after Miki and headed through the trees toward the lakeshore. More black bears were emerging from the forest, crowding together along the water's edge, just inside the barrier of leaves and berries she had seen them building. They waited in silence; near Lusa, a tiny cub squeaked with excitement and was hastily hushed by his mother. Lusa recognized the she-bear Issa, whom she had seen in the clearing the day before.

The sky was streaked with red, and an intense golden glow on the horizon showed where the sun would rise. A breeze flattened Lusa's fur as she stepped into the open, making the trees whisper, rattle, and hum. The lake water was rough with ridges of gray water; Lusa wondered if the bear she had seen the day before had made it to the island.

"There's Hashi," Miki whispered. "He's the oldest bear."

Lusa watched as a plump male bear clambered onto a rock at the edge of the lake. Leaves and berries were heaped at its base. He turned to face the glow in the sky, where a dazzling point of light blazed out as the sun struck the surface of the world. At the same moment the wind dropped; although there were still waves out on the lake, the trees where the bears were gathered became still.

"Spirits of the trees," Hashi called, lifting his snout to the open sky, "we thank you for the long days of sun that have brought us berries and other food."

"Too much sun if you ask me," some bear muttered behind Lusa; she turned her head and spotted one of the half-grown cubs who had been playing in the clearing the day before. "It makes the berries all dry and yucky."

"*And* it's too hot," his friend agreed.

"That's enough." An older she-bear—Taloa, Lusa thought—cuffed the first speaker over his ear. "Show a bit of respect."

The young bear rolled his eyes, but stayed silent.

"We beg you for more berries to feed us as the days grow shorter," Hashi went on, "enough to sustain us through the dark times until the sun comes again."

"Fat lot of good asking for more berries." The bears behind Lusa were muttering again. "As soon as the bushes grow, the flat-faces dig them up and leave them to die."

Issa let out a long sigh. "That's true," she whispered. "And they cut the trees down. So many bear spirits are being lost—when we die, will there be any trees left for our spirits?"

Lusa shivered. If flat-faces were cutting the trees down, there might soon be a world without any trees at all! Everything would look like the empty land she had seen when she climbed the tree at the edge of the forest. Where would the black bears live *before* they died?

Hashi saluted the rising sun with both forepaws raised. Lusa and the other bears copied him. Rocking back onto her haunches until she was sitting upright, she felt warmth and strength flow into her as the first pale rays struck her belly fur. Then the bears all remained still until the whole of the sun's disc had appeared above the horizon. Lusa thought they were waiting for something.

Then some bear cried, "There's no wind! The spirits aren't speaking to us!"

"Have we made them angry?" another bear fretted.

"Maybe the spirits know the flat-faces have defeated them!"

More anxious cries and murmurs rose from the assembled bears. Hashi raised a paw for silence, but the clamor didn't die down until an old she-bear scrambled onto the rock beside him.

"The spirits will never give up fighting," she announced. "Don't be afraid. Trust them to take care of us as they always have."

"But how do you *know*?" Issa persisted.

Miki poked Lusa in the side. "This is boring. Let's go play."

Lusa would have liked to stay and listen. She was a proper black bear now, and she needed to understand their worries. But she didn't want to lose her new friend, so she turned and followed Miki back into the forest.

Pressing herself close to the ground, Lusa crept around the thornbush. Her paws scarcely rustled on the dead leaves that covered the ground. Pausing, she sniffed the air and cast a cautious glance behind her before creeping on again.

As she rounded the bush, she spotted Miki; he had his back to her, intently scanning the undergrowth in front of him.

But you're looking the wrong way!

Lusa bunched her muscles and pounced; Miki let out a squeal as she landed on top of him. The two cubs wrestled together among the bushes, rolling over and over and batting each other lightly with their forepaws; Lusa felt a delighted huff welling up inside her. This was like playing with Yogi in the Bear Bowl.

The branches of a nearby tree waved up and down; Miki sat up with bits of leaf stuck all over his pelt as a bear's face poked out from between the leaves.

"Hi, Ossi!" Miki called. "Come down and meet Lusa."

A young male bear, bigger than Miki but not full-grown yet, swarmed down the tree, followed by a she-bear of about the same age. Both their pelts were a warm russet-brown color, and Lusa liked the lively sparkle in their eyes.

"This is Ossi and his sister Chula," Miki introduced them.

"I met them on the way here. This is Lusa," he added. "She came all the way here from a . . . a Bear Bowl."

Chula gave Lusa a friendly sniff, while Ossi asked, "What's a Bear Bowl?"

Lusa explained again, while the two cubs' eyes stretched wide with astonishment.

"And you came all this way by yourself?" Chula asked when she had finished.

"No, I was with some other bears . . . brown bears."

Ossi looked shocked. "Rather you than me."

"No, they were—" Lusa hesitated. *Weird? Difficult? My friends?* "They were okay," she said at last.

Ossi shrugged. "I wouldn't want to travel with grizzlies. They're dangerous."

"We ran into a grizzly on the way here," Chula put in. "He was huge!"

"What happened?" Miki prompted.

"We were traveling through a forest," Ossi said, "and we must have missed his markings on the trees, because he suddenly leaped out at us, roaring that we were on his territory."

Lusa remembered the brown bear who had almost killed her not long after she left the Bear Bowl. "What did you do?"

"Climbed trees," Ossi replied. "Fast."

"And then we crossed his territory, jumping from tree to tree so we never had to touch the ground," Chula went on, her eyes dancing. "That stupid old grizzly followed us all the way, growling about what he would do to us when he caught us."

"But he didn't catch us," her brother finished. "Because we were always out of reach!"

"I would have been *terrified*!" Lusa said admiringly.

"Well . . . I was a bit scared when the branch I leaped onto bent over, and there I was dangling with the brown bear's jaws snapping just below me," Ossi admitted.

His sister gave him a friendly shove. "I've never seen you climb so fast!"

"I'm hungry!" Miki announced, springing to his paws. "Let's see if we can find some food."

Ossi leaned forward, glancing around to make sure no other bears could hear him. "I know where there's an ants' nest."

Lusa remembered eating ants in the Bear Bowl. She liked the taste, but they were hard to catch, and tickly if they got into your pelt.

"Ant grubs." Chula swiped her tongue around her jaws. "Yum!"

"Let's climb." Ossi headed for the nearest tree. "We don't want every bear asking where we're going."

Lusa followed, clambering from tree to tree while the branches waved around them. She'd never traveled like this before, and she found it hard to keep her balance as the branches dipped under her weight, lurching her close to the ground—which looked awfully hard from this high up.

"Don't aim for the ends of the branches when you jump," Chula advised her. "They bend over; that's how the grizzly nearly caught Ossi. It's much safer to keep nearer to the trunk."

Lusa found Chula was right; once she knew what to do, it was easy. Her paws tingled with excitement. Toklo and Ujurak had never climbed through trees like this, and never thought of looking inside an ants' nest for food.

They skirted the clearing where she had seen the bears assembling when she first arrived in the forest. Hashi and a few of the other adult bears were sitting there now; their voices rose up into the trees. Lusa paused to listen.

"I can remember when a bear could travel through the forest for day after day and never see a sign of a flat-face," Hashi said. "Now they're everywhere with their stone paths and their firebeasts and their dens. Where are we supposed to live?"

"That's right," a she-bear agreed, casting an anxious look across the clearing to where two small cubs were chasing each other around a tree. "And if it isn't flat-faces, it's grizzlies. One of them drove me and my cubs out of territory where black bears had lived forever."

"There's never enough food," Taloa complained. "You can search all day and never find—"

"Hey, Lusa!" Startled by the sound of Miki's voice close to her ear, Lusa nearly lost her balance and had to make a grab for the trunk. "What are you doing?"

Lusa jerked her snout to point out the bears in the clearing. "Hashi said—"

"Oh, you don't want to listen to him." Miki let out a huff.

"He's always going on about how everything was better when he was a cub. Some of the others think he's wise, but . . ." He shrugged, flicking his ears as if Hashi were an annoying fly. "Come on, or that greedy pair will have eaten all the ants!"

Scrambling in pursuit, Lusa tried to forget what she had just heard. But it reminded her too much of what Ujurak had said, when he had taken the shape of the goose and the deer and the eagle. All the animals were suffering, not just bears.

Soon she arrived at the edge of another clearing, where Ossi and Chula were already sniffing around a huge mound of earth.

"Is that the ants' nest?" she asked Miki as they scrambled down.

"That's right," Miki told her. "And it's a big one. I'm surprised no bear has found it yet."

As Lusa approached the nest she became aware of a pungent scent coming from the ant colony. She blinked stinging eyes. "There was an ants' nest in the Bear Bowl, but it didn't smell like that. It was only a little one, though."

Her belly rumbled impatiently. Back in the Bear Bowl she'd never been hungry enough to do more than taste the ants, just for a change. Now she eyed the big, juicy nest hopefully; there should be a good meal in there.

Chula had already found a hole in the mound and stuck her long tongue down it. Ossi shoved a forepaw inside, gave it a swift lick, then stuck his whole muzzle into the gap. Trying to ignore the awful smell, Lusa tentatively poked a hole into the mound and stuck her tongue inside. She pulled it out covered with ant grubs: tiny specks that hardly looked as if they would make a meal. *But there are lots of them,* she thought, and drew her tongue back into her mouth.

Chula had been right. The grubs *were* delicious!

Enthusiastically Lusa probed the mound for more. This was even better than the salty potato sticks that she had found among the flat-face garbage.

At last they had eaten enough; holes gaped in the ant mound and the earth was scattered. Ants were scurrying around distractedly among the wreckage.

Ossi stretched his jaws in a vast yawn. "Time for a nap," he declared.

He climbed a tree and settled himself in a fork in the branches. His sister pulled herself up after him and found a place for herself a bearlength higher. Their russet-brown pelts were almost lost among the dappled sunlight as sunhigh approached.

"I'm not sleepy," Lusa said. She padded to the edge of the trees and looked out across the marshy landscape. "What is it like out there?" she asked as Miki joined her.

Miki shrugged. "I don't know. Cold, I guess. And a bit windy." His fur fluttered around his face, and he shivered.

"Let's explore!" When Miki hesitated, Lusa added, "Come on—it'll be fun!"

"Okay. Keep your eyes open, though. If any bear sees us, they won't be pleased. Black bears are meant to stay under the trees."

Venturing out from the shelter of the trees, Lusa sniffed the land ahead: a watery, boggy scent, full of reeds and mud. The ground was covered in tussocky grass, interspersed with sharp stones and clumps of reeds dotted here and there. Wisps of white mist clung to the ground; the air felt damp and clammy, and Lusa shivered. Somewhere a bird was piping a thin call, but she couldn't see it.

"Careful!" Miki whispered.

Intent on the new smells, Lusa hadn't noticed the scent of bears, or the sound of pawsteps behind them. She glanced back to see a couple of full-grown black bears ambling along at the edge of the trees. They might be angry to see her and Miki straying outside the black bears' gathering place.

"Quick, Miki, this way!" she gasped.

Just ahead was a shallow, muddy stream, fringed with reeds. Lusa slid into the water and pressed herself down until only her snout was showing.

"Yuck!" Miki grunted as he joined her. "I can't believe I'm doing this."

Within a few heartbeats the adult bears disappeared back into the forest. Lusa clambered out of the stream and shook muddy water from her pelt.

"They didn't see us," she breathed in relief.

Miki hauled himself out with a disgusted huff and Lusa set off again, farther out into the empty land. She didn't like this place: There were a few windswept bushes, but none of them had leaves soft enough to eat, or any sign of berries. It was windy, cold in spite of the sun, and the ground was sticky with drying mud. There was no shelter for black bears, not even anywhere to play. She led the way out into the open, feeling her pelt prickle as the comforting shelter of the trees and the murmur of bear spirits fell farther behind.

"Do you think anything lives here?" Miki whispered.

"I wouldn't think so." Lusa was whispering back; somehow it didn't seem right to speak in ordinary voices. *And something might be listening,* she thought, hiding a shudder.

She glanced at her surroundings, but nothing moved; the bog stretched all around her, blocked only by the dark line of the forest they had just left. Somehow the trees looked a long way away, much farther than they'd walked.

Suddenly a screech sounded from a clump of reeds just ahead. A big white bird shot upward with a loud beating of wings, rattling the tops of the reeds. Lusa jumped, gasping in panic, then tried to pretend she hadn't been scared.

Miki had leaped almost a bearlength backward as the bird screeched. "Well, there's nothing to see here," he said, trying to sound nonchalant; Lusa caught the fear in his voice. "It's boring. I'm going back."

He turned and began to trot toward the forest, then picked up speed until he was racing full tilt back to the trees. Lusa bounded after him, feeling the cold, wet grass brush her belly fur. Stones stabbed her paws; she was suddenly so frightened that she didn't have time to avoid them. Being away from the trees was *scary*. It felt as though some vast invisible bird, its wingspan even greater than an eagle's, was swooping down on her, ready to sink its talons into her exposed flanks.

Neither of the cubs stopped until they were safely under

the shadow of the forest, with the reassuring voices of the tree spirits above their heads. Miki hurled himself up the nearest tree, and Lusa followed, flopping down on the branch next to him.

"Well, that was interesting," said Miki, casually licking a paw.

"But I don't think we need to go back there," Lusa panted, trying to get her breath. "There's nothing out there for bears. The forest is the place for us."

And this is where I'll stay, she decided. *I don't ever want to leave the forest again.*

CHAPTER TWENTY-FOUR

Lusa

Lusa dozed in the tree beside Miki, and woke to the sound of bears pushing their way through the undergrowth. Raising her head, she quickly checked that she and her friend weren't visible from below, then gave the air a good sniff.

It was bear scent she could smell, but not the scent of black bears—or of brown bears, either.

Lusa reached out with one paw and prodded Miki's shoulder; as soon as his eyes opened she twitched her muzzle at him for silence.

"Sniff," she whispered.

Miki's eyes stretched wide in alarm. "Strange bears!"

Lusa peered down through the branches, trying to see the intruders. Every hair on her pelt was standing on end; somehow, she knew that the strangers shouldn't be here, and that something really bad was about to happen. Below her, the bushes rustled more loudly, and a massive shape pushed its way into the clear space underneath Lusa's tree.

White bears!

Lusa's heart leaped and she nearly lost her grip on the branch. It was so long since she had seen white bears in the Bear Bowl, and she had never expected to see any here. "What do they want?" she hissed.

"I don't know," Miki replied, "but it can't be good." He pressed close to Lusa and they both stared down in mounting horror.

The white bear below them was a male, much bigger than Lusa, but not as big as the white bears she remembered in the Bear Bowl; she guessed he was a half-grown cub. His white pelt was plastered all over with mud and he smelled of earth and fish mixed together.

Three more white bears followed, padding with long strides over the pine needles. They looked strong and fierce, their hackles bristling as they swung their pointed muzzles from side to side, searching for . . . *what*? Prey? *Black bears?*

As they crossed the open space and disappeared into the forest on the other side, Miki whispered, "This is terrible. They shouldn't be here. The white bears are supposed to stay on the other side of the lake."

"We'd better follow them and see what they do."

Miki nodded. "Okay."

They scrambled from tree to tree; Lusa kept as quiet as she could, trying not to make the branches shake, but it was hard when her legs were shaking with fear.

The white bears didn't look up, just kept peering into the trees with their beady black eyes, and Lusa and Miki tracked them until they came to the clearing with the berry bushes where they had fed the day before. Two full-grown black bears were searching the bushes for berries, accompanied by three cubs, smaller than Lusa.

"Hey! Climb a tree!" Miki barked.

"White bears are coming!" Lusa yelped.

Before the family of bears could react, the white bears burst out of the undergrowth at the edge of the clearing. "Get out of our way!" one of them snarled. "Get out, or we'll rip your fur off!"

The she-bear clacked her teeth with fright and shoved the nearest cub up a tree, then the next one. The male black bear bravely faced the white bears, hunching his shoulders so the fur stood up.

"You get out. This is our territory."

The third cub scrambled up into the tree and their mother followed. All four of them crouched among the branches, gazing down at the white bears with wide, terrified eyes.

The white bear in the lead cuffed the black bear hard over his head. "The forest is ours now. There's nothing you can do to stop us."

The black bear tumbled onto the ground from the force of the blow, scrambled to his paws, and hurled himself up the nearest tree. From his refuge on a branch he hissed furiously at the white bears. "The trees belong to black bears! The spirits will repay you for this."

The white bears ignored him. They blundered through the bushes, trampling the branches and stripping off leaves and berries to shove into their mouths.

Miki's eyes stretched wide with alarm. "They're stealing our food! We've got to go warn the others."

He took off through the trees, not caring about being seen or heard anymore, heading for the clearing where most of the black bears gathered. Lusa followed him, suddenly feeling clumsy and too heavy to be running through slender branches.

"Come on!" Miki urged her.

They were only a few bearlengths from the clearing when Miki leaped for the next tree, and Lusa heard the ominous crack of the branch as he put his weight on it. Miki let out a squeal of shock, scrabbling with his claws as he tried to scramble closer to the trunk. But the branch snapped; Miki crashed through the branches underneath and fell to the ground with a loud thud.

"Miki!" Lusa shrieked; she peered down, but there were too many branches in the way, and she couldn't see him.

"What was that?" huffed a voice from the clearing.

Another voice answered it. "Prey!"

Lusa slid down the tree until she could balance on a lower branch and see through the leaves. Miki was lying in a black huddle on the ground, his legs twitching.

"Miki!" Lusa cried. "Get up! The white bears are coming!"

Miki lifted his head; he looked half-stunned. Lusa bunched her muscles to jump down beside him, but it was too late. The white bears came charging through the trees.

Miki struggled to his feet, shaking his head. He stumbled toward Lusa's tree, but the leader of the white bears cut him off, thrusting his snout into Miki's face and letting out a fierce huff. The other three white bears closed in on him, surrounding him and pushing him with their massive front paws.

"He's nice and fat," one commented.

Miki struck out with his claws, but the white bears were too big and too many. One of them fastened his teeth in Miki's scruff and swung him off the ground, shaking him like a rat.

"Get off! Put me down!" Miki lashed out, but the white bear took no notice.

"Let him go!" Lusa barked from the tree.

One of the white bears raised his head and growled at her, but she was too high up for them to reach.

"Help! Help!" she called. "They've got Miki!"

No black bears appeared. *They can't have heard me,* Lusa thought despairingly.

The bear who was holding Miki dragged him through the bushes; Miki kept on kicking and clawing, but the white bear was too strong for him. Lusa heard his cries grow fainter.

"Help! White bears!" she shouted.

She flung herself into the next tree, heading for the big clearing. The sun was beginning to slide down the sky; its rays dazzled her, but she kept going, even when she could hardly see the branch she was leaping for.

When she reached the big clearing, she found Hashi resting under the trees, surrounded by more of the older bears. A couple of them were asleep. At the far side, Chula and Ossi were playing with some of the other cubs.

"Help!" Lusa gasped, scrambling down the tree and leaping

the last bearlength to stand in front Hashi. "White bears have taken Miki!"

"White bears?" Hashi sprang to his paws. "Where?"

"Where all the berry bushes are." Lusa jerked her head in that direction. "Hurry, please!"

Hashi bounded up the nearest tree, but to Lusa's horror he didn't head deeper into the forest. Instead he settled himself where a branch forked from the trunk and crouched there, digging his claws into the bark.

Spinning around, Lusa saw that the rest of the black bears were making for the trees, too. "Don't you understand?" she said. "They'll kill Miki if we don't help him. I think they're going to eat him!"

Ossi raced over from the edge of the clearing, with Chula close behind her. "We'll come with you," he panted.

"You will not!" One of the she-bears gave Ossi and his sister a sharp cuff around the ear. "Up the tree with you, right now! Black bears can't fight white bears."

Chula gave Lusa an apologetic glance, but she and Ossi trotted after the she-bear—their mother, Lusa guessed—and climbed the nearest tree.

"But Miki will die!" Lusa protested. "Aren't you going to do something?"

"Lusa, get off the ground at once," Hashi ordered. "You're in danger down there."

Lusa looked around. The clearing was empty. The black bears were all crouching in the trees like enormous furry berries. She hauled herself into Hashi's tree, not because she wanted to hide, but because she needed to make him listen. She was only just in time. As she swung herself onto the branch just below Hashi, three white bears burst into the clearing.

Where is Miki? They can't have eaten him already!

The white bears scattered the branches the black bears had been sharing, trampling the stems, then gulped the leaves and berries down and looked around for more. Spotting the black bears in the trees, they stretched up and growled at them, but the black bears were out of their reach, and the white bears were too big and heavy to climb.

Lusa looked down into the hostile eyes and gaping jaws of the biggest white bear. "Where is Miki?"

"You have to leave," a bear barked from a different tree. "This isn't your territory."

"It is now," the white bear snarled. "You're all cowards, stuck in the trees. It's not your territory if you can't defend it."

"What have you done with Miki?" Lusa called.

"The forest is ours now, along with everything in it. We can take what we like. You had better leave the forest, cub, or we will come back for you next!" He slashed his claws angrily across the bark and dropped to all fours again to join his companions, who were searching the clearing for more food. One of them, sniffing around at the edge, called out, "Hey! Berries!"

He pushed his way into the bushes and his companions followed him.

"White bears in our territory," Ossi's mother, in the next tree, whimpered. "What does this mean?"

"It means Miki is in trouble," Lusa retorted. "Isn't *any* bear going to help?"

"These are dark times," Hashi growled. "Nothing is the same as it used to be."

"The white bears *never* used to trespass on our territory." Taloa spoke from a nearby tree. "Why are they doing it now?"

"They're hungry," Ossi's mother replied. "We all know that food is harder to find."

"That doesn't mean they get to steal ours," Taloa retorted.

Lusa couldn't believe that these bears were talking about food, when they should have been planning to rescue Miki. *Don't they care at all?* she asked herself, choking back her fury. Maybe they were cowards, like the white bear had said.

The white bears had finished stripping the berry bushes and were prowling into the clearing. Lusa spotted a flicker of movement at the edge: A squirrel whipped around and scurried away as soon as it saw the white bears.

But the white bears had seen it, too. "Squirrel!" one of them growled. They charged across the open land and vanished; a heartbeat later a shrill squeal came from the forest, abruptly cut off. Lusa could hear snarling as the white bears squabbled over their prey.

"We've got to fight them!" Ossi barked. "Force them out of our territory before we have nothing left to eat!"

"You stay where you are," his mother snapped. "Do you want to end up like that squirrel?"

"Then what about Miki?" Lusa cried.

"The white bears are too fierce and strong," Hashi said. "We'd never win against them in a fight."

"Then why don't we go talk to them?" Lusa begged, gazing up at the old bear on the branch above her. "I *know* bears of different kinds can get along together. Maybe all we need to do is ask, and they'll let Miki go."

Hashi blinked solemnly at her. "We can do nothing for Miki. His fate is in the paws of the spirits."

Lusa clung to her branch as a chilly breeze sprang up, rustling through the trees. The voices of the bear spirits were all around her.

Hashi raised his head. "Spirits," he called. "The forest is our home. Do not let the white bears take it from us. We ask this of you, Bear Watcher. Before the sun touches the horizon, and the Longest Day is over, prove to us that our territory is safe. Bring us a sign!"

The voices of the bear spirits murmured on, but Lusa couldn't understand their reply. "What happens if the Bear Watcher doesn't bring a sign? What will you do then?"

"Then we fight the white bears!" Ossi growled. "We can—" He broke off with a squeal as his mother raked her claws over his ear.

"If we try to fight, we'll all be killed," she snapped.

"I don't know why we're even talking about this," a voice came from the branches of the next tree, from a bear Lusa couldn't see. "There's nothing we can do, and that's that."

Hashi rose to his paws and balanced on his branch. "If the spirits do not help us, then I will never come to Great Bear

Lake again for the Longest Day."

For a moment there was silence except for the growls of the white bears somewhere in the forest.

"Hashi, have you got honey between your ears?" Ossi's mother said. "Haven't you been listening? If the spirits don't help us, *there will be no* forest for black bears. Great Bear Lake will belong to the white bears!"

A chorus of growls and huffs broke out from the other bears.

"The spirits have abandoned us!" Taloa snarled.

"This is not going to help Miki!" Lusa exclaimed.

No bear answered her. *I have to do something!* As quietly as she could she scrambled through the branches until she could climb down the tree on the opposite side from the clearing.

I'm going to find Ujurak and Toklo. They'll know what to do to help Miki. If it isn't too late.

She crept through the trees, heading for the shore. From there it was only a short journey to the brown bears' territory. She could already see the rock where Hashi had stood to greet the sun when she heard a roar from behind her, and the sound of heavy bodies crashing through the undergrowth.

"I can see you!" one of the white bears roared. "You won't get away!"

Lusa's heart stopped for a moment. Then she started to run. She could hear the white bears pounding after her and imagined their teeth meeting in her scruff. They would pick her up and shake her just like Miki, and then probably eat her.

No! Lusa wasn't going to let that happen. Bears did *not* eat other bears, especially not on the Longest Day. She broke out into the open on the lakeshore. The wet rocks were sharp and slippery under her paws, and once she left the trees behind there was nowhere to hide. Glancing over her shoulder, she saw one white bear hard on her paws. She wanted to race along the shore, but her pursuer forced her to swerve toward the waterline, scattering the barrier of leaves and berries and breaking twigs under her paws.

Now the spirits will be angry with me!

As she tried to scramble over a slanting boulder, the white bear barged into her. Lusa's paws skidded on the wet rock; with an icy shock the lake water surged around her and her head went under.

Paws flailing, she forced herself back to the surface, to see the white bear sliding into the water nearby. Lusa began to paddle furiously, swimming out toward the middle of the lake. She knew she was a good swimmer, but when she looked back she could see that the white bear was gliding through the water much faster than she was, his nostrils flared and his black eyes half-closed against the waves.

Then she heard a faint cry from the receding shore. "Iqaluk! Leave her—she'll have to come back eventually!"

Glancing over her shoulder, she saw the other two white bears had appeared from the trees. The bear chasing Lusa gave up his pursuit and began to head back to the shore. "I'll be waiting, little bear!" he snarled as he paddled smoothly away.

Lusa stopped to catch her breath, treading water, and looked around. She had already swum a long way out, and her legs ached from her dash through the trees. The breeze was strengthening and the lake water grew choppy. She didn't dare swim straight back to shore, because the white bears would be waiting for her. She needed to head for the brown bears' territory, where she could find Toklo and Ujurak and get their help to chase out the white bears, but that was much farther away.

I'm not sure I can make it, Lusa thought wearily as she struck out.

Closer than the shore she was making for, she spotted an island covered by trees. Lusa began to swim toward it; she would rest there for a while, then swim directly back into brown bear territory to look for Toklo and Ujurak. Every stroke was an effort now; waves splashed into her face and it was hard to keep her muzzle clear of them. She choked and spluttered as a wave broke over her face, and for a moment she felt the dark water pulling her down. . . .

Suddenly her paws scraped against stones; with a huff of relief she managed to stand up and wade out of the lake. Exhausted, dripping water, she scrambled over the rocks and onto a pebbly stretch of ground that separated the lake from the trees in the center of the island.

There was a furious roar behind her. She spun around as a brown bear sprang toward her with his claws stretched out. As he knocked her over and landed hard on top of her, she gasped, "Toklo!"

CHAPTER TWENTY-FIVE

Toklo

Toklo stared at the black bear cowering under his paws. "Lusa!"

"Toklo, let me up!" Lusa barked urgently.

Startled, Toklo backed off. *If she followed me here to talk about Oka, I'll claw her fur off!*

Lusa scrambled to her paws and shook herself; Toklo sprang farther back to avoid the water and grit spattering from her pelt.

"What are you doing here?" he demanded. "How did you know where to find me?"

"I didn't know." Lusa's eyes stretched wide. "Toklo, I need your help!"

"What's the matter?" Toklo asked. "Is it Ujurak?"

"No, I haven't seen him—but we need to find him, too. I'm sure he'll know what to do."

Irritation pricked every hair on Toklo's pelt. "I still don't know what you're talking about."

Lusa flopped down on the pebbles, panting from her swim. "I told you, I need your help. I—"

"Come farther up," Toklo interrupted. He didn't want another bear on Pawprint Island with him, but there was no need for Lusa to shiver in the wind. "There's a place to rest under a pine tree."

"There's no time. The white bears have taken Miki! He's a black bear cub, a friend of mine," Lusa went on quickly.

"What do you mean, white bears have taken him?" Toklo managed to get a word in.

"They came around the lake and invaded the forest. They're not supposed to—they're supposed to stay in their own territory, on the other side of the lake. They're so big! And so white, like snow. They started scaring the black bears, and taking our food. Miki and I were up a tree. We tried to find the others to warn them, but a branch broke and Miki fell. One of the white bears picked him up and carried him off. We've got to rescue him!" Lusa finished breathlessly.

"I can't." Toklo shook his head. The white bears must have been the pale shapes he had seen across the water. How strange, a bear that wasn't black or brown. They'd find it hard to stalk prey because their pelts would stand out against trees or grass or even rocks. "The brown bears chose me to stay on this island for all of the Longest Day, to please the spirits. Then they'll give us back our salmon."

Lusa stared at him. "But Miki will die!"

"That's not my fault." Toklo bristled. "I don't have to look after black bears!"

"I don't believe this!" Lusa flared up, fury blazing in her eyes. "You're just scared."

"I'm not scared. But I've never met Miki. Why should I risk my neck to help him?"

"Because no other bear will, and I can't do this on my own," Lusa said quietly. "Come with me, Toklo, and we'll find Ujurak, too, and—"

"And then what? Do you think that the three of us can take on all the white bears? They'll kill us, as well as your friend, and what good will that do?"

"I'll think of a plan." Lusa spoke confidently. "You'll see."

Toklo huffed. "I won't see, because I'm not going with you."

"I wish Ujurak were here," Lusa said. "Ujurak, where are you?"

"I'm sorry, Lusa," Toklo said. "But Miki isn't my problem. I am a brown bear. Brown bears don't meddle in the affairs of other bears. We live alone."

Lusa gave Toklo a long look. *She's not going to talk me into it,* he told himself. *I've already fought one battle today. I have nothing to prove, especially not to black bears.*

"All right," Lusa said at last. She took a deep breath and rose to her paws. "I'll go alone."

For a few heartbeats Toklo wanted to stop her. She was going to throw her life away for nothing. But he was a brown bear. He was here to honor Arcturus, and help to bring the salmon back. He couldn't get involved in the troubles of black bears.

"Good luck, Lusa," he murmured.

Lusa didn't reply. Turning away, she padded back to the

lake and waded out into the water.

Toklo stood at the water's edge, watching her bobbing black head as she swam toward the opposite side of the lake, where the white bears gathered.

Suddenly, a feeling of dark emptiness opened inside him like the jaws of an angry bear. Instead of the lake before him, he saw Ujurak being hit by the firebeast at the end of the bridge; then the vision of Ujurak turned into his brother, Tobi, cold on the mountainside, covered in dirt and twigs. He rubbed his eyes and the lake returned, and far out in the water, the small black cub swimming away from him.

Was he sending Lusa to her death?

"Come back!" he called, but his voice was whipped away by the wind.

He curled up beside a stone, dark thoughts swarming like bees in his brain.

Did Oka feel like that when Tobi died? Did she abandon me because she couldn't face feeling that way again? But she should have protected me. I was her cub, too.

CHAPTER TWENTY-SIX

Kallik

Kallik spun around and fled from the forest. Black bears! She had seen black bears, eating bushes in a clearing. That couldn't be right. Siqiniq had told her there were black bears and brown bears on the other side of the lake, but Kallik hadn't really believed her until she had seen them for herself. And even though they were much smaller than white bears, she was afraid. They were so different!

At last she had to stop and catch her breath, glancing back to make sure the strange-colored bears hadn't followed her. To her relief, the dark line of the forest was still and silent. Crouching among the reeds, Kallik watched the waves washing in and out. The sun was sliding down the sky, turning the lake water to dazzling gold. Above the waves, birds swooped for insects, calling out in harsh voices. Kallik started as she spotted movement at the edge of the forest. She raised her head, her ears pricked. A single white bear, tiny at that distance, had just emerged from the trees. Kallik couldn't see any sign of the other three.

As the bear drew nearer she realized it was Taqqiq. He was carrying something black and awkward in his mouth, something that moved jerkily. At first Kallik couldn't make out what it was. She stared, her eyes watering in the sharp breeze, as he splashed his way toward her. She blinked. He was holding a small black bear cub, twisting and struggling to free himself from Taqqiq's grip on his scruff. The wind carried his frightened whimpering across the marshes to Kallik.

No! He's brought one of the black bears!

Springing to her paws, she rushed toward her brother, and met him as he leaped one of the small streams that wound its way into the lake. She stopped dead in front of him to block his path. "Taqqiq, what have you done?"

She stretched out her neck to sniff the tiny cub; his warm black fur smelled of leaves, trees, and earth rich with worms.

Taqqiq dropped the cub and slammed a paw down on his neck to stop him from running off. The cub let out a squeal of pain and terror. Abruptly Kallik's suspicion turned to pity. This black cub was a bear like her, as frightened as she would have been if a bigger bear had caught her like prey.

"He's ours now," Taqqiq growled. "He's only a black bear. He's too small and weak to do anything but snuffle out ants and worms."

"Are you going to *eat* him?" Kallik couldn't stop her voice from quavering.

"No, who'd want to eat all that fluff!" Taqqiq huffed scornfully. "Salik says he has to be alive or Kunik and Imik and the rest of the white bears will think we found him dead, and the plan won't work."

"What are you talking about, Taqqiq? What plan?"

"When every bear sees how easily we took this cub from the forest, they will want to return to the forest with us. The black bear territory is ours for the taking, Kallik!"

"He's only a baby!" Kallik exclaimed. "Let him go."

Taqqiq let out a growl of annoyance. "You don't understand."

"I understand that you're hurting him." Kallik dug her claws into the wet ground. "Taqqiq, are you stupid? What about the other black bears? The big ones will be angry."

Taqqiq peeled back his lips, baring his teeth. "They're all hiding in the trees like dumb, scaredy birds."

"Aren't you afraid they'll come looking for this cub?"

"I'm not scared," Taqqiq replied. "The black bears know that they can't fight us. Only one kind of bear can survive now—the strongest and the bravest. And that's us."

"Taqqiq, no! White bears need the ice, with seals and fish. What good is food from the forest to us? Let the black bears have it."

"You don't get it, do you?" Taqqiq's voice was impatient. "The ice melts earlier every year. Nisa told us that back in our BirthDen. What happens when there is no more ice?"

"That will never happen!" Kallik gasped in horror. "The spirits wouldn't allow it."

"I told you, if there are any spirits, then they don't care about us. If white bears are going to survive we must leave the ice and move inland. We have to take the territories of the black bears and brown bears and learn to live there. That's what Salik says, and I believe him."

For a heartbeat Kallik remembered the ice: the vast shining stretches with powdery snow blown across the surface by the wind. She remembered crouching with her mother and Taqqiq beside a seal hole, and the delicious taste of the fat when Nisa had captured her prey. She remembered how safe and warm she had felt in her BirthDen, with the storm winds howling outside. And white bears were supposed to give that up, and live in the dirt and damp of the forest?

"White bears will never do that," she snapped. "Your brain is full of feathers."

As she finished speaking she heard pawsteps splashing through the marshes and looked up to see Taqqiq's three friends bounding along the shore. Her heart sank. She might have been able to convince Taqqiq to let the cub go, but she knew she would never convince Salik.

"Not you again!" Salik growled as he came up. "Didn't I tell you to stay away from us?"

"I'm not afraid of you," Kallik retorted, facing him.

Salik and the two others ignored her. They padded up to Taqqiq, who took his paw off the cub's neck, and let the tiny creature get up. The black bear cub bared his teeth at Salik, and lashed out one paw, but the blow only ruffled Salik's fur. The white bear retaliated by cuffing him over the head.

"That hurt!" the cub snarled. "Let me go!"

Salik gave him a hard jab in the side with one paw, and the cub crouched down, whimpering. Iqaluk padded up to him and gave him a doubtful sniff. "He smells funny."

"Of course he smells funny," Salik growled. "He's not like us."

Manik was eyeing the cub with a mixture of fear and fascination. "I don't like this," he muttered. "I say we let him go. He's going to cause nothing but trouble."

"The white bears need to see him, seal-brain! He's going to help us get *food*." Salik rammed his shoulder into the other bear's side. "Of course, if you don't want any . . ."

"I didn't say that."

"Then shut up and do as you're told."

"You know this is wrong!" Kallik burst out. "Look at him! He's so small and frightened."

Taqqiq and Salik didn't bother arguing with her anymore. Instead, Taqqiq grabbed the whimpering cub by the scruff again, and all four set off to the white bears' territory. The black cub's hind legs trailed along the ground, jarring against stones that poked up from the marsh.

Kallik stumbled after them.

As they approached the gathering of white bears, Kallik bounded ahead, looking around frantically for some bear she knew. Surely the adult bears would be able to stop Taqqiq?

Taqqiq dragged the black cub into the midst of the white bears, with Salik and the others following. A few of them looked up; one old male muttered, "Oh, no! Guess who's back."

Then Kallik heard the voice of Imiq, the young she-bear she had spoken with earlier. "Look! It's a *black* bear!"

She ran up to give the little cub a curious sniff. The cub struggled, flailing his paws as he tried to land a blow on her muzzle. "Leave me alone!" he growled.

Imiq started back, almost bumping into Kunik as the older bear padded up to see what was going on, with yet more bears following him. "A black bear?" he huffed curiously. "What is it doing so far from the forest?"

"Taqqiq brought him!" Kallik cried, but Kunik, intent on examining the black cub, didn't hear her.

A couple of little white cubs bounded up. "Why is he black?" one of them asked his mother, Qanniq.

"The spirits made him that way," she replied.

"But *why?*"

"I want to play with him," the other white cub declared.

"Certainly not." Their mother moved to block them from the struggling black cub. "He looks really mean!"

Kallik tried to push her way through the gathering crowd to reach Kunik. She hoped he would help her; he had spoken out against the raid earlier. But Salik swatted her out of the way with one huge paw, and the curious crowd was growing all the time. Then she spotted Siqiniq dozing on a flat rock with her paws folded over her muzzle. She dashed up to her.

"Please help!" she begged. "Taqqiq has stolen a cub from the black bears."

Siqiniq's head shot up so quickly that Kallik wondered if she had been awake all the time. "Spirits help us! What will these wild young bears do next?"

She heaved herself up with a creak of old bones, then

jumped down from the rock and padded toward the cluster of bears; they parted to let her through, and Kallik thought some of them looked relieved that Siqiniq was here to decide what to do with the strange intruder. Kallik stuck close to her side.

Taqqiq had dumped the cub near the water's edge beside a jutting outcrop of rocks; the little black bear gazed around him, his teeth bared as if he were ready to fight every one of the white bears who surrounded him.

"What is this?" Siqiniq demanded. "Taqqiq, why have you brought this cub here?"

"To show how easy it is to steal from the black bears," Taqqiq growled. "The black bears are fat and lazy from eating all the time. There is food in the forest, food for white bears. We took this cub, we can take the whole forest."

"This is madness," Kunik said.

"No, it's not!" Taqqiq's voice was defiant. "None of you are doing anything to find food, just waiting for the ice to come back. But what if it doesn't?"

"Are you suggesting we eat this cub?" Siqiniq asked, shocked.

"No!" Taqqiq huffed.

"We eat black bear food," Salik explained. "Why should we starve, when they've got a forest full of food?"

"They'll have to give us what we want," Taqqiq added. "They're too weak and stupid to fight."

"That still doesn't make it right!" Kallik snapped. "Take the cub back."

Salik turned on her, snarling, but before he could attack her,

Siqiniq spoke. "This is *wrong*. Haven't we got enough problems with flat-faces, without causing trouble for other bears?"

"This is not the way of the white bears," Kunik agreed.

"You should be ashamed of yourselves, frightening this little cub," a mother bear added.

"But our cubs will die without food," Qanniq pointed out.

"I think Taqqiq and Salik have a point," Imiq growled. He bent his muzzle and prodded Miki.

"Ouch! Get off!" Miki protested.

"Look at his big round belly," Imiq continued. "Why should the black bears fill their bellies when we starve?"

"This is just the start," Salik snarled. "White bears spend their lives staring at the sea, waiting for the ice to return. It's time to stop pretending. The ice is never coming back! We must leave the shore and live in the forest."

"Live in the forest?" Iqaluk snarled. "Never!"

"We need food and the spirits have showed us where to find it," Imiq said. "It can't be a coincidence that the cub came to us on the Longest Day."

"He didn't come to us!" Kallik barked. "He was *stolen*!"

But no bear was listening to her. She saw the little black cub wriggling to avoid the huge feet of the white bears snarling and roaring at one another as they argued about what to do next. Kallik found herself being pushed to the edge of the crowd, and she tried to fight her way back to help the black cub, but a wall of huge furry bodies blocked her way.

After a few moments she spotted Taqqiq thrusting his way out, panting as he padded to the water's edge and thrust his muzzle in to drink. Kallik scrambled over the sharp pebbles to stand beside him.

"Taqqiq, you *can't* do this," she began.

Her brother looked up, water dripping from his snout. "Just leave me alone," he grumbled. "You heard them. Some of the bears agree with me and Salik."

"And some of them don't!" Kallik flashed back at him.

Taqqiq turned on her, snarling; startled, Kallik retreated, and felt lake water washing around her paws.

"Get out of here!" Taqqiq growled, striding forward to push her farther back. "I've had enough of you sticking your muzzle in. Go live with the black bears if you like them so much."

Suddenly afraid of the way he was looking at her, Kallik took another step back and felt the water lap against her belly fur.

"Taqqiq, no . . ." she pleaded.

He advanced another step, and Kallik stumbled into deeper water; now she could barely stand, the waves almost lifting her off her paws. Looking past her brother, she saw that the other bears were still crowding around Salik and the cub. They hadn't noticed what was going on at the edge of the lake. "Siqiniq!" she yelped, but the old bear didn't look around.

"See?" Taqqiq sneered. "None of them want you here, either. You're not a real white bear. White bears will do whatever they have to in order to survive."

"I'm more of a white bear than you are! Real white bears respect the spirits." Kallik tried to make a dash for the shore but her brother stood in her way and pushed her roughly back with his shoulder.

Losing her balance, Kallik toppled over with a huge splash, and when she tried to get to her paws again there was nothing firm to stand on. She paddled frantically toward the beach, but Taqqiq blocked her way with a growl.

"Go, and don't come back!"

Kallik's legs ached and so did her neck as she tried to hold her muzzle above the water. There was something wrong with the lake here: The water didn't flow back and forth against the shore, but around in circles, making it impossible to swim in a straight line. The water didn't seem to hold her up the way it had done in the ocean; it felt too thin, not cold and comfortably thick as she scooped it with her paws. Her fur was heavy and soaked, dragging her down. Wind whipped the waves so that they crashed over her head, and she choked as she breathed in water.

"Nisa!" she wailed. "Nisa, save me!"

But the only answer was the blustering wind and the surging of the water around her ears.

CHAPTER TWENTY-SEVEN

Lusa

Lusa thought she heard a voice on the wind. She stopped swimming and began to tread water, listening. The sun flashed brightly on the lake, hurting her eyes; she couldn't see anything until a wave lifted her up. Then she spotted a white bear cub, only a few bearlengths away. She was trapped in a whirling current that was spinning her around like a twig. Her paws flailed and her head kept dipping under the surface.

"Nisa!" The cry was weaker now, half-choked by water.

"Hold on!" Lusa called. "I'm coming!"

She kicked out, clawing through the water toward the floundering cub. The white bear was sinking again when Lusa reached her; Lusa's legs pumped as she shoved her out of the swirling water. "Don't struggle," she gasped. "I won't let you drown."

She grabbed the white cub's scruff to keep her head above the surface. Out on the lake, so far away from the tree spirits who would have helped her, Lusa wondered if she could keep her promise. It was harder to swim with the white bear's weight dragging her down; the exhausted cub seemed hardly conscious, unable to help herself.

Lusa struck out strongly toward a spit of land stretching out into the lake, its stones glittering in the sinking sun. The currents were fiercer here, threatening to pull her out into the endless lake, but she kept on paddling determinedly. Suddenly her paws thudded against mud and stones, and Lusa managed to stand with water lapping at her shoulders. The white cub couldn't hold herself up, even though she was bigger than Lusa, with longer legs. She slumped down as soon as Lusa let go of her scruff, so Lusa had to half-push, half-carry her until they splashed out of the water onto the stretch of hard, pebbly ground where they collapsed side by side.

Water was streaming from the white cub's pelt. She coughed up a couple of mouthfuls of water and lay still, her chest heaving.

Lusa stood up, shook droplets from her fur, and looked around. They had made it to the end of the spit where it joined the lakeshore. Behind her lay the water; ahead of her and on both sides stretched the bare, treeless land she had seen from her perch in the forest. Just ahead, the ground shelved gently upward to a low hill, where Lusa could see the top of some tall flat-face construction. It wasn't as wide as a flat-face den, but it was much, much taller, as tall as a pine tree, with openings all the way up.

She could hear the grunts and growls of bears many bear-lengths farther along the shore. They were hidden behind a rocky ridge, jutting up like teeth from the marshy ground.

She turned back to the white bear cub, who was huddled on the stones with her eyes shut tight. "Wake up," Lusa urged, nudging her gently.

The white cub woke with a jerk. Blinking, she looked around as if she was trying to remember what had happened. When her gaze fell on Lusa her eyes stretched very wide.

"How did you escape?"

Lusa put her head on one side. "Escape? From what?"

"They were all around you. I thought you were going to be crushed! They should never have stolen you, I'm sorry."

Suddenly Lusa understood. "You think I'm Miki, the cub the white bears took from the forest?"

The white bear sat up, and pulled a piece of water-weed off her head with her paw. "You're not?"

"No, Miki's my friend. I came to rescue him."

The white cub stared at her. "But you're only one cub. The white bears will tear you to pieces. You must get away from here."

Lusa ignored the cold trickle of fear down her spine. "I don't care. Miki is my friend, and I have to save him."

The white cub searched her face for a long moment. "If I can't change your mind, will you let me help?"

"You?" Lusa stared at her in surprise. "Why would you want to help a black bear?"

"Because you helped me," the white cub replied, sitting up. "And . . . and because the bear who stole your friend is my brother, Taqqiq. We were separated when our mother died. I looked and looked for him, and now—" She broke off, swallowed, and began again. "He and his friends took the black bear cub because they want to force the other black bears to give up their food. But that's not the way to feed ourselves. What they did was wrong. Will you let me help?"

Lusa wondered if she could trust this bear she had only just met. And in spite of what she'd told Toklo, she didn't have a plan. Maybe two bears would have a chance when one didn't have a whisker of hope. "Yes, if you want to. Thank you." Later she'd have time to think about how strange this was—how crazy she was, trying to rescue Miki from all the white bears. But it wasn't the right time now. There was a black bear in need of her help.

The white cub stood up, her broad thick-furred paws splayed on the stones. "My name's Kallik," she said shyly. "What's yours?"

"I'm Lusa." *That's enough chatter. We have to help Miki. It's not like this white bear is going to be my friend once Miki and I join the black bears again.* "What we have to do first," Lusa decided, "is find out where Miki is."

"Taqqiq brought him from the forest," Kallik told her, pointing with her muzzle to the dark line of trees on the other side of the lake. "The last time I saw him was over there, where those rocks jut up."

Lusa glanced at the ridge, from where the noises of bears came.

"The bears are arguing about going into the forest," Kallik explained. "I'm afraid that Miki might get hurt. My brother and his friends are stirring up the other white bears, making them angry with the black bears. I don't know what is going to happen."

"Maybe nothing. Maybe they've already sent Miki back," Lusa said hopefully. "But we have to be sure. We need to get closer and look for him. Come on!"

She led Kallik across the marsh to where the ground sloped up to the rocks. As they scrambled to the top, she could see muddy ground spreading out in all directions, the bleak surface broken only by boulders hunched like gray bears, and a few stunted bushes. Here they were closer to the flat-face building she had spotted from the lakeside. A stone path stretched away into the distance; where it started, beside the tower, a firebeast was crouching.

"Be careful," Kallik said nervously. "We don't have to go near that, do we?"

"I think the firebeast is asleep," Lusa said. She tipped her head back and looked up at the top of the building; she remembered how she used to climb the tallest tree in the Bear Bowl, looking down at all the other animals, and beyond. *If I could climb up there,* she thought, *I'd be able to see Miki.*

Looking more closely at the construction, Lusa realized it was too smooth to climb on the outside. But on the inside, visible through the openings all the way up, was a steeply sloping path with ridges. The opening at the bottom was quite small, but Lusa knew that she could squeeze through it.

Yes! That's it!

Turning to Kallik, she asked, "Can Miki still run?"

"I think so. When I last saw him, he was wriggling around quite a lot."

"Good. Then this is what we'll do. If Miki's still down there, I'll find a hiding place not too far away from this building, and—"

"You'll have to hide really well," Kallik warned. "Taqqiq will steal you, too, if he sees you."

"Then I won't let him see me." Lusa's belly clenched with a mixture of fear and determination. "Back in the Bear Bowl, my mother used to say that I could hide in a shadow!"

Kallik still looked worried—but at least she didn't ask what a Bear Bowl was. Lusa was getting tired of explaining.

"What should I do?" Kallik asked

"I need you to tell Miki where I'm hiding, then try to distract Taqqiq and his friends long enough for Miki to find me. Then I'll jump out in his place. The white bears will think I'm Miki and chase me. But I'll run away and climb the building."

Kallik's eyes stretched wide. "But it's a flat-face thing!"

Lusa shrugged. "Flat-faces are okay, mostly."

"What if Taqqiq catches you?"

He'll tear me apart. Lusa could almost feel the sharp claws slashing through her fur. For a moment fear threatened to choke her, but she forced it down. "He won't. He's too big to fit through the opening, and even if he does, black bears can climb faster than any other bear." At least, that's what King had said. But maybe he'd never seen a white bear climb. Her paws tingled. "While Taqqiq is chasing me, Miki can run away, back to the forest."

"I hope it works," Kallik said.

"So do I."

Kallik clambered up onto the ridge and stood on her back legs to see over a boulder.

"He's there." She jerked her head downward.

Lusa's faint hope that Miki had already been returned to the forest vanished. She raced to the boulder and sprang up to Kallik's side.

Down below, she could see a large gathering of huge white bears. Roars and grunts suggested they were arguing about something. Lusa leaned forward and strained her ears to hear what they were saying.

"We're not really going to take over the forest, are we?" asked one white bear, who looked younger than the others.

An old male bear shook his head. "Of course not. Those cubs have blubber in their brains if they think we'd ever do something like that. White bears will starve before they steal food from black bears!"

A couple of bears shot alarmed glances at each other, as if they thought they might really starve, but a she-bear with a small cub by her flank nodded.

"Silaluk loses all his flesh during the hunt, but he still returns each suncircle. We will do the same; we just have to have faith that the ice will come back and there will be enough to eat." Her cub butted her stomach, searching for milk that wasn't there, and she bent her head to hush him.

A broad-shouldered bear with scars on his muzzle stepped

forward. "Even if we are going to leave the black bears in peace, there is still the problem of the cub that they stole. What are we going to do about him?"

There was a murmur of unease among the bears, and a few turned away as though they didn't want Miki to be their problem.

"Siqiniq will know," said the old male bear. "Ask her, Kunik."

"I heard the question," grunted a rasping voice; whoever was speaking was hidden from Lusa behind some larger bears. They shifted apart to reveal an ancient-looking she-bear, her flanks tucked up so that all her bones stuck out through her thin pelt.

"That's Siqiniq, the oldest bear," Kallik whispered in Lusa's ear.

Siqiniq swung her head to look at the bears around her, who were gazing at her hopefully as if she could send Miki back to the forest with a twitch of her nose. "The bears who stole the black cub must take him back. That is their duty. If they appease Silaluk by putting right what they have done wrong, the peace on the Longest Day will be preserved, and the ice will come back."

Kunik shrugged; his fur crumpled into deep folds where it didn't fit his thin body properly. "Your faith humbles us all, Siqiniq," he said. "But I do not share your faith that these young bears will ever do what is right, not for themselves or for every white bear."

Siqiniq moved to the edge of the bears and stared down at

the lake. "Maybe," she commented, so quietly that Lusa hardly heard her over the wind. "But theirs will be the price to pay if they don't. Silaluk sees all, that much I do know."

Lusa followed her gaze toward the shore, where four white bears were sprawled on the ground beside a clump of thorn trees. In the middle of them, trapped by their long legs and massive bodies, was Miki. He scrambled at one of the bears, trying to get past, but the white bear cuffed him and sent him rolling backward. Miki squealed and the four white bears huffed with satisfaction.

"Miki," Lusa whimpered.

"Taqqiq and his new friends." Kallik's sad voice spoke at her shoulder. "Kunik's right: They'll never take Miki back to the forest. Which means we might have to fight them if we want to help him. Lusa, are you sure about this?"

"Quite sure." Lusa squared her shoulders. "There's no one else to help Miki. Let's go."

CHAPTER TWENTY-EIGHT

Toklo

Toklo paced up and down the pebbly beach. The sun was starting to slide down the sky; already shadows were spreading under the trees in the middle of the island. Soon the Longest Day would be over.

Lusa was long disappeared. She had swum away from him toward the shore where the white bears were, determined to rescue her friend. Toklo didn't think he would ever see her again.

She's gone. All that is over.

The black cub had left her home, and gone a long, long way into the wild. She had no idea how to live there or what dangers she would have to face. But she had survived, and in spite of everything, she had found the bear she was looking for.

Me. She did all that for me.

Deep shame swept over Toklo. Because she was small and didn't know the same things he did, he had assumed Lusa was a coward. Instead, she was the bravest bear he had ever met. She had gone alone to the white bears' territory because one of her friends was in trouble. She had gone back into danger, and left Toklo behind.

"I could go look for her . . ." he murmured.

He stopped pacing and looked across the lake at the territory of the white bears. He could see pale shapes on the shore, which could have been bears or rocks, but no sign of the small black bear.

"Then I'd die, too. . . ."

He sat down at the water's edge and sank his nose onto his paws. The shadow of the nearby pine tree lengthened and covered him like soft black fur.

"But I might be able to help her. . . ."

He thought about how Shesh and the other brown bears were relying on him to spend the whole day on the island so that the fish would come back. If he left before sunset, he would be letting them down. "Spirits, help me! I don't know what to do."

A dark flicker in the sky caught his attention. He lifted his head and watched a sleek black bird swoop lower and lower on widespread wings, circling the island as if it was looking for prey. Suddenly, it folded its wings against its body and tipped forward into a dive straight toward the ground. As it descended, it stretched out its claws. When its feet touched the ground, the bird's legs thickened and its body expanded, sprouting brown fur between its feathers, thicker and thicker until the feathers vanished. Its wings stretched into forepaws and its beak swelled and blunted to a snout.

Ujurak!

Shock froze Toklo's paws to the ground. He couldn't move or speak; he just stared at the small brown cub as he approached and gave Toklo's shoulder a friendly poke with his nose. "Hi, Toklo."

Toklo found his voice. "I wish you wouldn't do that."

"Is Lusa here?" Ujurak asked.

"No," Toklo answered.

Ujurak looked around the island, confused. "But I saw her, in my head. She called my name. She was with you, Toklo."

"Lusa *was* here," Toklo admitted. "But she left again. She was upset about a black cub that the white bears took. She thought she could rescue it, the berry-brain!"

Ujurak padded down to the edge of the lake and waded a few pawsteps out into the water. Then he glanced back at Toklo. "We have to find her. Are you coming?"

"Not you, too." A flame of guilt flickered through him. "I'm sorry, Ujurak, but I promised I'd stay here until the end of the Longest Day. You were there! Then Arcturus will send back the fish."

"Now who's the berry-brain? The spirits can't send fish, not even Arcturus. They don't have the power. All they can do is guide bears like us, help us to do the right things. And I bet Arcturus would want us to find Lusa. In fact, I *know* he would."

Toklo stared at him in disbelief. "But I thought—"

"I mean it, Toklo. Lusa is more important than skulking here on your own."

Toklo's claws raked the ground. "Can't I wait till sunset

and then come to help?"

"No." Ujurak had never sounded more certain about anything. "She needs us *now*."

For nearly a whole day, Toklo had felt like a brown bear, alone and fierce and strong. He liked it, but with the choice at his paws he had no doubt what his answer must be.

Lusa, his friend, needed his help.

He nodded, and waded out into the lake after Ujurak.

CHAPTER TWENTY-NINE

Kallik

"See those rocks over there? That might be a good place to hide."

Kallik looked where Lusa was pointing, and spotted an outcrop of broken stones with a thornbush growing over them. They were about halfway from the tower to the thicket where Taqqiq and his friends were guarding Miki.

The sun was sinking down in the sky; a luminous twilight spread over the lake as the Longest Day drew to an end. Kallik's pelt tingled. All the things she had done since her mother died, every part of her long, long journey, even the moment when the blazing metal bird fell from the sky, hadn't seemed as dangerous and terrifying as what she was going to do now.

Just then, she noticed two bears swimming in the lake, heading for the spit of land.

"Lusa," Kallik said, nudging the small black cub beside her.

"Yes, I can definitely hide behind those rocks," Lusa said, staring down.

The two bears in the lake were wading onto the pebbles.

"Lusa!" Kallik repeated.

Lusa glanced at the flat-face tower. "It's going to be tricky getting Taqqiq away from the others," she said anxiously. "Especially with Miki."

Kallik stopped listening. She was staring in disbelief as the two bears walked out of the water. They were *brown*! Siqiniq was right: There were brown bears as well as black ones! How many more kinds of bears were there in the world?

"Lusa! Look!" Kallik squeaked as the brown bears began climbing up the rocky slope toward them.

Lusa spun around. "Toklo! Ujurak!" she cried.

Kallik watched in amazement as the black cub bounded down to the two brown bears and pushed her muzzle into their fur to greet them. "I can't believe you came!"

"You can thank Ujurak for that," the biggest bear said gruffly. "You know what he's like when he gets an idea in his head."

"But how did you know I needed you?" Lusa asked the smaller cub.

"I just did," Ujurak replied. "I heard you calling me, in my head. I knew I had to find you."

"This is Kallik." Lusa led the two brown cubs up to Kallik. "Kallik, this is Toklo and Ujurak. We've traveled a long way together."

"Hi," said Kallik. "Er . . . welcome to the white bears' territory."

Lusa shot her a bemused glance, then pointed out Miki, who had wriggled under the thornbush to get away from Taqqiq and the others. "The white bears stole him," she explained. "But I've got a plan to rescue him." She told the brown bears her idea about luring Taqqiq away to give Miki a chance to escape.

"I think you've got bees in your brain," Toklo said when she had finished. "But I can't think of anything better."

Ujurak stared down at the white bears. "I'll go with Kallik to speak to the white bears," he said. His voice was calm.

"But you can't!" Kallik protested. "You're brown. The white bears will attack you, and—" She broke off. "Your . . . your fur."

Streaks of white had begun to appear on Ujurak's brown pelt. While Kallik stared, the white patches spread and melted into one another. At the same time Ujurak swelled up inside his new pelt, and his body shape altered, his muzzle stretching out and his ears shrinking, so that within a few heartbeats Kallik was gazing at a white bear exactly like herself.

"Spirits help us!" she whispered. "What's happened to you?"

"Don't worry," Lusa huffed, giving Kallik's shoulder a friendly lick. "He does that all the time. Just be grateful he didn't turn into something less useful, like a goat."

"Can we get on with this?" Toklo sounded impatient. "You're not going to stand there all day chattering, are you?"

He led the way down the hill toward the rocks Lusa had pointed out. Kallik followed, keeping a watchful eye out for bears. If any of them spotted Lusa or Toklo, their plan would fail before it had even started. As they reached the rocks, there was a furious roar from more than one bear. They crouched in a dip behind the rocks, half hidden by plants that straggled over the edge and the branches of the thornbush. They peeped out through the screen of stems as one of the bears who had been taunting Miki confronted a full-grown bear who had left the main Gathering.

"That's Imiq," Kallik said, pointing with her muzzle to the younger bear. "He was in favor of invading the forest. The other one's Kunik, who thinks Miki should be returned to the forest and the black bears left in peace. Most of the other bears agree with him," she added for the benefit of Toklo and Ujurak, who hadn't heard the earlier debate.

Kunik leaned forward and cuffed Imiq with his forepaw. "When you're older, maybe you can make decisions that affect all the other white bears," he growled. "But right now, you do as we say. The black bear cub goes back to the forest, *now*."

Imiq reared up on his hind legs, striking the air and snarling. Kallik winced; if he could look this fierce when he was still a cub, she didn't want to make an enemy of him for future Longest Days by the lake.

"Are they going to fight?" Lusa whispered.

"I hope so," muttered Toklo. "If they sort this out by themselves, we might not have to rescue Miki after all. I don't want that white bear clawing my pelt, thank you."

Kallik looked down at her paws. "Imiq won't listen to Kunik. He's too proud. Too *stupid*! Kunik is trying to help Miki, but he's just making things worse."

She looked at her brother and his friends. They were on

their paws, watching Imiq. Salik was saying something, but Kallik was too far away to hear what it was. Suddenly Salik, Iqaluk, and Manik lumbered toward Imiq, their loose pelts rolling on their shoulders, leaving Taqqiq with the black cub.

"Oh, no," Kallik whispered. "Kunik can't fight them all! The other bears won't help him—they know there's supposed to be peace on the Longest Day. If Imiq and his friends win, they'll invade the forest and attack the black bears!"

"Then we have to rescue Miki now," Toklo decided gruffly. "If we get him out of there, Kunik or whatever his name is can sort out the other bears. Let's do it now, while the bears are distracted. I'm going back to the flat-face building. I'll be waiting up there in case you have any trouble."

"Thanks, Toklo," Lusa replied.

"The spirits go with you," Kallik said, fear for Lusa suddenly surging up inside her. She looked so small beside the other bears.

"I'll be fine," Lusa promised, though her voice sounded very small. "When it's over, I'll meet you by the lake."

White-bear-Ujurak nodded as if there was no chance their plan would fail. "Come on," he said to Kallik.

Kallik let him take the lead as they padded down to the thicket where Taqqiq and Miki were. Ujurak even smelled like a white bear. The others wouldn't recognize him, of course, but they would never, ever suspect he wasn't one of them.

"You again!" Taqqiq sprang to his paws as Kallik and Ujurak approached. He gave his sister a hostile glare. "I told you not to come back."

"I can go where I like," Kallik pointed out, feeling less scared of him now that she had Ujurak with her.

Behind Taqqiq she could see the little black cub whimpering as he crouched under the thornbushes, his eyes wide and scared. *Get ready,* she told him silently, wishing there was a way she could warn him what they meant to do. As far as Miki could see, two more of his enemies had just arrived.

Ujurak dipped his head in greeting to the other bears.

"Who are you?" Taqqiq demanded. "I don't know you. What do you want?"

"I've come to tell you to let the black cub go back to the forest."

"And you're going to make me?" Taqqiq sneered. "I'm so scared, I'm shivering in my fur!"

"Oh, stop being such an idiot, Taqqiq!" Kallik dug her claws into the ground. She would have liked to swipe them over her brother's ear, but it was vital not to let a fight break out before Miki had a chance to escape. "It's a question of doing what is right."

"No, this is called *surviving,*" Taqqiq growled.

"White bears don't live in forests," Ujurak told him. "They live by the sea and on the ice, where the spirits of the white bears live."

"My mother respected the spirits, and look where that got her," Taqqiq said scornfully.

"Don't talk about Nisa like that!" Kallik snapped.

"She's dead; she can't hear me."

Kallik could hear the anger and pain in her brother's brutal words. "Don't you remember how scared you were when she died?" she prompted. "When you were left alone?"

"I'm not scared now," Taqqiq grunted. "Not of anything."

"I never said you were," Kallik told him. "Not now. But when you were a little cub . . . when our mother was killed by that orca . . . you were scared then, you know you were." Taqqiq didn't respond, but he dropped his gaze to his paws. "Do you think it's right to make another bear feel like that?" Kallik persisted.

"I miss our mother," Taqqiq admitted quietly. He slashed a claw through the pebbles on the shore, a mixture of grief and confusion in his eyes. "It was all wrong after she died."

"I know." Kallik took a pace forward and touched his shoulder with her muzzle. "I miss her, too. But we've found each other again. That has to be a good thing. It's what she would have wanted, I know."

"Maybe," Taqqiq mumbled. He hesitated, then pushed his muzzle roughly into Kallik's shoulder fur.

"This cub is scared like that now, because you took him away from the forest," Kallik went on, feeling as if she was on the edge of convincing her brother.

"We're not going to hurt him . . ." Taqqiq protested, but he sounded uncertain.

Squinting past her brother, Kallik noticed that Ujurak had padded over to Miki. He looked as though he was just sniffing the cub, but Kallik could see he was really whispering into his ear. Miki had stopped whimpering, and was listening, bright-eyed. Kallik searched for something else to say, to distract

Taqqiq from what Ujurak was doing.

In the moment's silence, Imik's voice carried through the air. "Taqqiq! Are you coming?"

Kallik knew time was running out. "Please, Taqqiq. Don't you remember how Nisa told us that burn-sky is hard, but that we have to believe that the ice will come back? White bears have lived like this forever."

The fur above Taqqiq's eyes furrowed. "But what if the ice doesn't come back? We'll have to find a different way of living."

"But that doesn't mean we have to hurt other bears. Besides, the ice *will* come," Kallik insisted. "And when it does, everything will be all right. . . ."

Taqqiq met her gaze, but before he could speak, Imik's voice came again. "Taqqiq!"

Kallik continued more urgently, "Let this bear go. Stealing from the black bears won't—"

Pounding pawsteps and a roar of rage from Salik interrupted her, and he landed a stinging blow on her ear. Ujurak pushed in front of her, facing the furious white bears. All four of them clustered around; Kallik could see their lips peeled back, baring sharp teeth, and their claws at the ready.

"What are you doing here?" Salik gave Ujurak a hard shove in the chest with his shoulder. "I've not seen you before."

Ujurak tilted his head on one side. "Have you seen every bear on the beach?"

"Don't get clever with me!" Salik gave him another shove. "Why were you messing around with our cub?"

"He's *not* yours," Ujurak said.

Just then, Kallik saw Miki shoot out from under the thornbushes and dash off. *Go, Miki!* One of the other bears followed her gaze.

"The black cub!" Salik roared. "He's escaping!"

He charged off after Miki, with Manik and Iqaluk hard on his paws. Ujurak bounded behind them.

Kallik turned on Taqqiq. "Come on!" she barked.

He didn't answer, just dug his claws into the ground and launched himself after the others. Side by side, they raced up the hill. Kallik ran so fast, the wind made her eyes water and she couldn't see anything but the rock-strewn ground and the white blur of her own paws pounding under her nose. When she reached the top, three white bears were still tearing after Miki. Ujurak had vanished. Kallik saw Miki give a panic-stricken glance behind him, then dive into the dip beside the rocky outcrop where Lusa lay hidden.

Thank the spirits! At least he was safe—for now.

A couple of heartbeats later, another black cub emerged, running hard toward the flat-face building. Her paws sent up a spray of sand over the white bears, spattering their pelts. The bears let out a growl of fury and chased after her. None of them seemed to have noticed that their prey had changed into a she-bear. Kallik's heart thudded; somehow the plan was working. She looked for Ujurak, and spotted a hare running alongside Lusa, keeping pace with her.

Has he changed again?

Lusa was pelting across the ridge toward the building, but

Salik was almost close enough to bite her. Kallik forced her paws to pound over the rough grass, her belly fur brushing the ground, but she wasn't fast enough to catch up. She let out a low whimper of dismay. "Spirits help her!"

Salik was stretching out his neck now, his jaws opened wide as he bore down on the small black cub. He overtook her and swerved into her side, knocking her off her feet. One more stride and his enormous forepaws were planted on her chest; Lusa let out a squeal of terror. Manik and Iqaluk skidded to a halt beside him.

Kallik stopped in horror as Salik loomed over Lusa, ready to sink his teeth into her throat. Desperate, she whirled around to confront her brother, who had followed her up the hill.

"Taqqiq, you've got to help!"

CHAPTER THIRTY

Toklo

Toklo climbed back up the hill and sniffed around the foot of the flat-face construction. The flat-face scents were stale and the firebeast was cold and quiet; he didn't expect any trouble from them. The white bears were another matter, but if Lusa could reach the construction, she'd be safe. The opening at the bottom was too small for white bears to get through.

And I'm ready to hold them off. They won't lay a claw on Lusa.

He found a sheltered spot underneath some bushes that grew up against the smooth white wall. There were a few shriveled berries growing on the branches; Toklo stripped them from their stalks and gulped them down. Then he wriggled underneath.

From his hiding place he could see all the way to the lake. He glanced at the rocky outcrop where Lusa was waiting. As soon as she made a move, he would be ready.

Suddenly a savage roar erupted from below; heartbeats later, Miki came pelting up the hill.

"Here we go!" Toklo braced himself.

Three enormous white bears were racing up the slope; the black cub glanced back and saw that they were gaining on him. He let out a terrified squeal, veered to one side, and dived for cover into the dip in the ground where Lusa was hiding.

A moment later a black cub emerged from the hollow and pelted toward Toklo. *Lusa!* She was faster than Miki, but the white bears were still bounding after her, their powerful strides eating up the distance between them. Toklo spotted a hare keeping pace with Lusa as she fled.

And what good do you think that will do, Ujurak?

Lusa had almost reached Toklo when the leading bear overtook her, crashing into her side and knocking her over. She let out a squeal, her paws batting at her attacker. The big white bear held her down with his paws on her chest, his jaws reaching down to bite her throat.

Toklo hurtled out of his hiding place with a furious roar. From the corner of his eye he spotted the hare, its body swelling and legs thickening as Ujurak returned to his brown bear shape. Together they threw themselves on the white bears.

Knocking Lusa's attacker off balance, Toklo clubbed his broad white head with both front paws. He glimpsed Lusa scrambling away, then turning back with her teeth bared, ready to attack. "Stay out of this!" he growled to her.

He caught a glimpse of Ujurak rolling on the ground in the grip of one of the other white bears. Fear stabbed him; Ujurak was so much smaller! But Toklo had no chance to help him as the biggest white bear turned on him with an angry snarl. *This bear is worse than Shoteka!* A red mist of rage filled Toklo's head, blotting out the fear. He swerved to one side as the white bear attacked him and raked his claws down his opponent's flank.

The white bear spun around with incredible speed; Toklo felt the sting of claws on his rump as he tried to dodge. Skidding into a turn, he hurled himself at his enemy, butting him with his head. The force of his charge carried the white bear off his paws; he and Toklo wrestled together in the dirt, clawing and biting in a snarling bundle of brown and white fur.

Toklo was the first to break away, with a last cuff to the white bear's head. Blood was trickling from the other bear's side and shoulder, staining the white pelt. Toklo felt his own pelt itch and knew he was bleeding, too, but his fury kept the pain at bay. Ujurak was still wrestling with the other white bear, but he looked exhausted. Blood was welling from a gash in his shoulder, while the white bear seemed uninjured. Lusa was circling the third white bear, darting in to give him a nip, then dodging away again. The white bear lumbered after her, roaring with frustration.

She can't keep that up for long, Toklo told himself.

Barking out a challenge, he threw himself at the white bear before the bear could catch Lusa. Savagely Toklo clawed at the bear's chest; blood followed the line of his claws, springing up among the white fur. The bear let out a howl of pain.

But as Toklo followed up his attack with a blow to the head, he felt a heavy weight land on his back. The biggest bear dug his claws into Toklo's shoulders. Toklo wriggled frantically, but the strength of two bears together was too much for him. He glimpsed Lusa tearing at the biggest bear's shoulder; the white bear batted her away as if she were an annoying fly.

Then, through the mountains of white fur that threatened to crush him, Toklo saw two more white bears rushing toward them. *This is the end!* he realized bleakly. *We've got no chance now!*

"Salik, that's enough!" the bear in front barked.

The biggest bear sprang up with a snarl. Relieved of his weight, Toklo landed a blow on the other bear's ear and staggered to his paws. He could feel blood running down his shoulder, but he still braced himself for another attack.

The bear who was wrestling with Ujurak jumped up, too. Ujurak hauled himself out of range and crouched on the grass, shaking his head groggily. Lusa padded over to him and started to rasp her tongue over a wound on his shoulder.

"Taqqiq, are you telling me what to do?" The biggest bear thrust his snout at the newcomer. "I'll claw your ears off."

"No, you won't," Taqqiq replied, facing the other white bear steadily. "You're a bully, Salik. You only face up to bears who are smaller or weaker than you are."

So that's Kallik's brother, Toklo thought, noticing for the first time that the smaller cub with him was Kallik herself.

"You were happy enough to go along with me," Salik snarled.

"I was wrong," Taqqiq growled. "And what you're doing is wrong. White bears don't prey on black bears."

"Oh? Then tell me where we're supposed to find food."

"We wait for the ice to come back." Taqqiq ignored Salik's contemptuous huff. "It *will* come; we just have to wait."

"And starve while we're waiting?" Salik took a pace forward, his muzzle almost touching Taqqiq's. "I'm taking this black cub, and if you try to stop me I'll feed your guts to the fish."

A low snarl came from Taqqiq's throat; Toklo could see his muscles bunching as he braced himself to attack.

"No!" Kallik pushed herself between her brother and Salik. "Too much blood has been spilled already. Food is scarce for *all* the bears, and turning on each other won't help."

Salik backed off a pace or two; Toklo could see that he didn't really want a fight. His glance raked over the brown bears and Lusa.

"Joining with weaker bears won't help, either," he sneered. "Come on, you two." Darting a hostile glance at Lusa, he added, "You watch your step. Steer clear of us in the future if you want to keep your pelt on."

"My pelt's fine, thanks," Lusa retorted; Toklo saw a glimmer of amusement in her eyes as she realized Salik still thought she was Miki.

Salik let out one more snarl and stalked off down the hill; his two friends shambled after him.

"Good riddance," Kallik muttered.

Toklo gave Kallik and her brother a puzzled look. "What's come over him?" he asked, jerking his muzzle at Taqqiq. "I thought he was the bear who stole Miki in the first place?"

"He was," Kallik replied, "but now he realizes that it's wrong to steal black bears."

"Right," Taqqiq mumbled.

Toklo didn't think he looked entirely sorry; just to be on the safe side, he moved closer to Lusa. *Lay one claw on her, and you'll have me to deal with.*

Ujurak had recovered from the struggle, enough to scramble to his paws. Taqqiq gave him an amazed glance.

"There are *two* brown bears here?" he asked.

"That's right," Lusa replied, sharing an amused glance with Kallik. Toklo could see that neither of them was going to tell Taqqiq that Ujurak had been a white bear for a little while.

"Look!" Kallik said. She was staring down at the shore, watching as all the white bears padded over to the lake. "They're getting ready for the ceremony," she said. "To mark the end of the Longest Day."

Toklo imagined the brown bears gathered on the opposite shore, waiting for his return from Pawprint Island.

"Oh, spirits save me!" Lusa exclaimed. "I've forgotten Miki."

Toklo watched her run back toward the rock and plunge into the hollow. He turned to Ujurak. "There's something I need to do, before the end of the day."

"Will I see you again?" Ujurak asked.

Toklo glanced away, unable to look into Ujurak's eyes. All he knew was that he wanted to feel alone and strong again, like he had on Pawprint Island. If his destiny was to continue the journey with Ujurak, he couldn't tell him now. He had to do this first.

Ujurak nodded and pressed his muzzle to Toklo's.

Toklo turned and headed back to the lakeshore.

CHAPTER THIRTY-ONE

Lusa

Lusa ran down the hill toward the outcrop of rocks where she had hidden, and plunged under the thorn branches into the hollow. Miki's eyes, wide and scared, gleamed in the dim light.

"It's okay," she told him breathlessly. "Everything's fine now. You can go home."

Miki blinked at her. "What about all those white bears?"

"They're not a problem anymore. Come on, I'll take you to meet my friends."

Cautiously she pushed her head out into the open and looked around. The sun was low, and it cast the long shadows of the white bears by the water. The flat-face construction was outlined against the blue sky, with Toklo and the other bears clustered together at its base.

"It's safe," Lusa said. "Follow me."

She emerged from the hollow and padded up the hill with Miki a pawstep behind. As they approached the top he stopped dead, his fur bristling with fear as he stared at Taqqiq.

"That's the bear who stole me!" he gasped. "His sister tried to make him let me go, but he wouldn't listen."

"Yes, I know, but he's okay now." Lusa gave Miki an encouraging poke with her muzzle. "Would I lead you into danger?"

Miki didn't reply, but he reluctantly padded the rest of the way up the hill. Kallik and Taqqiq came to meet them.

"Taqqiq has something he wants to say," Kallik announced, giving her brother a shove.

Taqqiq looked at his paws. "Sorry," he grunted.

"I . . . I guess it's okay," Miki replied. He jumped as Ujurak came up, and gave him a nervous glance.

"Er . . . Lusa?" Miki asked. "Is this one of the brown bears you traveled with?"

"That's right," Lusa replied. "This is Ujurak." She wondered where Toklo had gone.

"Hi," Ujurak huffed, bouncing up to sniff Miki.

The little black cub stiffened, his eyes huge; Lusa could see it was hard for him to be brave among so many strange bears who were all much bigger than him. *Does that mean* I'm *brave?* Or was it just that she knew these were her friends? *Kallik, too.*

"It's time for you to go home, Miki," she said. She hoped that Miki would be back in time for Hashi and the others to keep their faith in the spirits, and celebrate the end of the Longest Day.

Miki turned to her with a look of relief. "Thanks, Lusa. It doesn't feel right, out in the open like this, without any trees. Let's go."

Lusa glanced at Ujurak. The smaller brown cub was looking hopeful, as if he knew exactly what she was thinking, and had an answer of his own. But he didn't speak; she knew he wouldn't try to make up her mind for her.

For a heartbeat she was torn. It had been good to live under the trees with the wild black bears and learn how to live like them. Miki had turned out to be a real friend; Chula and Ossi could be, too. But she knew that if she went with him now she would always miss Toklo and Ujurak, and dreams of the place where the spirits danced in the sky would trouble her for the rest of her life.

"No," she said sadly. "I can't come with you, Miki. My place is with Toklo and Ujurak."

Miki gaped at her. "Why?"

"I told you, we're on a journey to the place where the spirits dance above the Endless Ice. You can come with us, if you like."

She wasn't surprised when Miki shook his head. "I'm sorry, Lusa. The forest is where I belong. With other bears like me."

There was an edge in his voice as if he were challenging Lusa to defend herself, to explain why she'd rather be with brown and white bears than black bears. But she didn't blame him for feeling hurt—and she wasn't about to explain why she needed to share Ujurak's journey. Perhaps only the spirits knew why—the same spirits that had helped her to find Toklo in the first place.

"That's okay." Lusa touched his muzzle with hers. "This isn't your journey."

"I'll miss you," Miki said, his eyes dark with sorrow.

"I'll miss you, too. Maybe we'll meet again one day, in a proper forest!"

Kallik stepped forward, touching Miki's shoulder gently with her snout. "We'll take you home," she promised. "You can walk between me and Taqqiq, and we'll skirt around the other white bears, so that no bear sees you."

"Thanks," Miki responded, though he still cast a doubtful look at Taqqiq.

"You can trust me," Taqqiq huffed.

He padded up to stand beside Miki, but before Kallik joined them, she turned to Lusa.

"Your journey . . . to the place of Endless Ice . . . Our mother told us about it, and I know this lake is on the path that leads there." She looked awkward, ducking her head. "Will you let me come with you? I . . . I think my mother might be waiting for me there."

Lusa was startled; then warmth began to spread through her pelt as if the sun were coming out from behind a cloud. She didn't want to say good-bye to Kallik, not yet.

"Of course you can come!" Ujurak gave an excited little bounce.

"Thank you." Kallik's eyes shone. "You'll wait for me until I come back from taking Miki home?"

"We'll be right here," Lusa promised.

Kallik moved over to stand on Miki's other side, screening him from any white bears who might be watching. As they padded off, Miki glanced back over his shoulder at Lusa. "Good luck!" he called.

"And you!" Lusa replied. "Say hi to Ossi and Chula for me!"

The two white bears headed off across the white bear territory, the little black cub invisible between them. Kallik looked back at Lusa and Ujurak.

"Wait for me!" she cried.

CHAPTER THIRTY-TWO

Kallik

As Kallik and Taqqiq approached the edge of the forest with Miki, the sun sank behind the trees, tinging their tops with gold. The lake shone like ice and the breeze dropped to nothing.

Kallik remembered the first time she had been there, and how she had fled in terror from the black bears.

How could I have been so stupid? They're just bears like us.

"Will you be okay now?" Taqqiq asked Miki, halting underneath the outlying trees.

"Fine, thanks." Miki gave them a small nod, stiff with pride now that he was back on his own territory.

"Good-bye, then," Kallik said, touching his shoulder with her muzzle. "May the spirits walk with you."

"And you," Miki said. He was already shuffling backward, ready to vanish into the trees.

Kallik and Taqqiq started to return across the marsh.

"Hey, Miki!" The voice came from above; Kallik looked back and spotted a couple of black bear cubs sitting on the branches.

Miki glanced up. "Chula! Ossi!"

"Are . . . are the white bears coming?" Two sets of bright, scared eyes looked at Kallik and her brother.

"No," Miki told them. "These bears just brought me home. We're safe now. The white bears don't want our food, or our trees."

"We were so worried about you, little one." Kallik saw a full-grown she-bear creep out along a lower branch beneath the cubs.

In another tree, a large male bear peered down at Miki. "Praise to Arcturus! You have brought our cub home," he called. "It's a sign that the forest still belongs to black bears!"

There was a sound of twigs snapping and leaves rustling as the faces of black bears peered down from the edge of the forest. Their eyes gleamed like stars from the shadowy trees.

Taqqiq let out an amused huff. "Black bears are as weird as white bears."

Kallik didn't think it was funny. The black bears were obviously waiting for the white bears to attack, crouched in the trees, scared and convinced they were about to lose the forest, and their only source of food by the lake. If Taqqiq couldn't see that, then he wasn't really sorry. But Kallik wasn't going to give up on him—or give him another chance to cause trouble with the black bears.

"Come on," she said. "The others are waiting for us."

Padding back across the open marshland with Taqqiq at her side, Kallik's thoughts were in a whirl. Nanuk had told her to go to the place where the spirits danced. She longed to travel there with Lusa and the others to see if Nisa appeared in a swirl of light, dancing over the ice. But how could she leave Taqqiq, when she had only just found him?

She halted where a small stream gurgled into the lake and listened to a strange low moaning, like the wind but deeper. She couldn't tell where it came from but it echoed around the lake, and flowed into her mind, washing away her muddled thoughts. Was her mother trying to tell her something? She strained to make out any words, but it was like trying to listen to an echo of the wind. Except that now she knew what she had to do.

"Come with me, Taqqiq," she said.

Taqqiq stared at her. "What?"

"Come with me, to the place where the ice never melts."

For several heartbeats Taqqiq didn't reply. His eyes were wide with shock.

"Please," Kallik insisted. "I don't want to lose you, not after I searched for you for so long."

Her heart sank as Taqqiq shook his head. "I don't think I can. The other bears won't want me."

"You don't know that. Come with me, and we'll ask them."

Then the low moaning stopped and her doubts came back. Perhaps they wouldn't want two white bears with them after all.

CHAPTER THIRTY-THREE

Toklo

Toklo swam back across the lake as the sun dipped behind the forest. He could feel the cool water soothing his cuts and bruises, and the splashes from his pawstrokes sparkled in the fading sunlight. This time, he had no fear of the spirits pulling him under; instead, he longed to feel his mother's pelt brushing beside him, or a playful tug from Tobi on his fur.

"Mother? Tobi?" he called, but a strange silence had spread across the lake. The water was calm, and the only sound was his own splashing.

All of a sudden, the water turned gold, dazzling him. Toklo looked up. As the sun touched the horizon, the sky seemed to be on fire, and on the far shore, the forest looked black against it. He struck out with his legs and headed toward the brown bear territory. Ahead of him, he could see brown bears gathering on the shore. Oogrook was standing on the parley stone, gazing across the lake. Around him, full-grown bears stood singly or in groups, while small cubs bounded among them, splashing through the water and kicking up sand.

Oogrook lifted his muzzle and let out a strange low moaning sound. It echoed around the lake, getting louder as more bears joined in. The sound seemed to be pulling Toklo toward the shore, giving strength to his tired legs. Before he knew it, he was treading in soft mud and looking up at the brown bears.

He stood in the lake for a while, feeling the water lap under his belly. He had done it! He had spent a day and a night on Pawprint Island, and made it back to the brown bears. He felt something bump against his leg and instinctively plunged his paw into the water. His claws sliced through flesh and he pulled up a fat salmon. He held the fish in his jaws as he waded out of the water toward Oogrook. The bears parted to let him through and he dropped the salmon on the parley stone. It flapped a few times, then went still.

Oogrook stopped moaning, and in the quiet Toklo could hear the lapping of the lake and the hissing of the wind in the trees once more. The old bear dug his claws into the salmon and held it up for all the bears to see.

"It's a sign!" a bear called.

"The salmon will return!"

"The cub has done well," Oogrook declared. "Arcturus honors him, and through him, he honors all brown bears."

The bears began barking and huffing. Toklo hoped Shoteka was here to see his triumphant return at the end of the Longest Day.

"Well done, little cub," Oogrook murmured, looking down from the parley stone. "You will be remembered on all the

Longest Days from now until memory fades."

Toklo nodded. He knew he had done well; he knew that most of these bears hadn't expected him to make it back from the island. But there was more to be done. The future of the bears didn't rest on a single salmon.

He looked up at Oogrook, knowing he could never explain what he was about to do. Maybe he didn't need to: The old bear stared into his eyes, then nodded, just once.

Toklo turned and padded through the noisy bears, and slipped quietly back into the water.

CHAPTER THIRTY-FOUR

Lusa

Lusa and Ujurak sat on the ridge, looking down at the white bears gathered by the lake. Some stood with their feet in the water, staring into the setting sun. Others lay on the pebbles, their muzzles touching the ripples at the edge of the lake.

The setting sun turned the water to gold. All the sky seemed to be on fire. Lusa could hear the white bear Siqiniq's voice as the ceremony began.

"Sun, we say farewell to you. . . ."

She glanced at Ujurak. *So what now?* Her paws were itching; was it time to leave the lake and continue with their journey? "Ujurak, are you ready to—"

Ujurak raised a paw to silence her as Siqiniq's voice carried through the air. "Sun, leave us now, so the dark and the ice may return. . . ."

"When I was a white bear, I longed for the ice, too," Ujurak whispered. "Ice is the spirit of the white bear. It feeds them, it gives them shelter, it keeps them safe from flat-faces. But it's melting away, faster and faster, and they fear one day it will be gone. What will the white bears do then?"

Siqiniq's voice came again. This time he was facing the white bears with his back to the lake. "Go now in the protection of the spirits. And may the ice greet you when you arrive home."

There was a stir of movement on the beach as the bears began to separate.

Lusa and Ujurak sat and watched the sky grow dark. The white bears became pale shapes farther down the hill and along the lakeshore. Lusa guessed they were looking for sleeping places, away from the hardest stones on the beach.

There was more movement close by, and Lusa saw Kallik and Taqqiq climbing the slope. She bounded down to meet them.

"Have you come to say good-bye to Kallik?" she asked Taqqiq.

Taqqiq muttered something inaudible, looking at his paws. Lusa gave Kallik a puzzled glance. "Is he okay?"

"He wants to come with us," Kallik explained. "But—"

"I never said that!" Taqqiq interrupted.

Kallik suppressed a sigh.

Lusa looked up the slope and saw Toklo appear beside Ujurak. His pelt was dripping wet and he looked exhausted, but his eyes were bright as ever.

"Let's go talk to the others," Lusa suggested, leading the way back up.

Toklo was licking his wet fur, holding up each paw to dry

the fur between his claws. Ujurak was looking up at the sky. Following his gaze, Lusa saw that the Bear Watcher had appeared, running tirelessly around the Pathway Star.

"Our path is laid out for us," Ujurak said. "It is time to leave. Who will come with me?"

"You know I'm coming!" Lusa replied at once. "I want to see the spirits dancing in the sky, even if I have to go where the trees don't grow."

Ujurak nodded. "What about you, Toklo?"

Toklo stood up, shaking some water off his pelt.

"Come on, Toklo," Lusa urged him. "You know we'll miss you if you stay behind."

"I'll come," said Toklo. "I was always going to come."

Lusa felt a jolt of relief. She wasn't sure that she understood Toklo yet, but he was part of their journey, as important to it as Ujurak was. "Kallik?" she prompted.

"I want to come, but . . ." Kallik turned to her brother. "What do you think?"

"I think you're all crazy," Taqqiq grumbled.

"But think about it!" Kallik pleaded. "There'll be ice. . . . Endless Ice that never melts. We'll have food all the time, and we'll be safe from flat-faces and firebeasts. Don't you want to go find it? And we'll see the spirits in the sky. Oh, Taqqiq, please come!"

Her brother turned his head away. "*They* won't want me."

"Yes, we do," Lusa said at once. She wasn't particularly concerned about Taqqiq coming, but if Kallik refused to be parted from her brother, then Lusa wanted Taqqiq to join them.

"The way is open to any who want to follow it," Ujurak added.

Toklo said nothing, just glared at Taqqiq as if challenging him to make a decision. Lusa could see that he wasn't finding it easy to forgive the white bear for attacking the black bears. Well, she hadn't forgiven Taqqiq for that, either. She just wanted Kallik to come with them.

Please, she begged silently. She knew that if Toklo refused, Kallik would give up her own dream of finding the place of endless ice.

"Come on, Toklo!" Lusa bounded over to the brown bear and gave him a nudge. "Taqqiq is okay."

Toklo let out a disbelieving huff. "All right," he muttered, "but if he lays so much as a claw on any bear, I'll rip his pelt off."

"Way to be welcoming!" Lusa huffed.

"Please, Taqqiq." Kallik locked gazes with her brother. "We'll find the ice." She looked around at the stretch of mud, pebbles, and sparse grass that led down to the waterside. "You can't stay here, and we'd be together."

Taqqiq hesitated. "Okay," he said at last. "I'll come with you." Reluctantly he dipped his head to the others. "Thanks."

Ujurak lifted his head again, sniffing the air. "This is the way," he said, beginning to pad along the lakeshore, away from the territory of the white bears.

"How do you know?" Taqqiq objected, then looked as if he wished he hadn't said anything.

Fear prickled Lusa's pelt as a low growl came from deep in Toklo's throat, and Taqqiq swung around to face the grizzly. Were they going to start fighting *already*?

"Don't get angry," she told Toklo. "Taqqiq doesn't know Ujurak yet." To Taqqiq she added, "We don't know how Ujurak knows what he knows, he just does. He'll get us there, don't worry."

Taqqiq still looked doubtful.

"Come on!" Kallik urged him, giving him a shove in the direction Ujurak had taken. "We're going to find the ice!"

Taqqiq moved off at last, loping after the small brown bear. Toklo followed, still keeping a wary eye on him. Lusa fell in beside Kallik to bring up the rear. As she padded along, she looked up as the sky began to brighten and the Bear Watcher faded in the orange light of dawn.

"Thank you for watching over us," she whispered. "We will see you again soon."

LOOK FOR

Toklo

"I guess the legends about the strength of white bears aren't true, then," Toklo muttered.

"Do you want to find out exactly how strong I am?" Taqqiq snarled.

Toklo bunched his muscles and rooted his hindpaws more firmly on the rock. A fight was just what he needed to show Taqqiq who was really in charge. "I'm not scared of you, fish-breath," Toklo growled.

"You should be, tiny paws!"

"I'll claw your face off!"

"Stop it!" Ujurak barked.

Toklo shuffled his paws on the ground, a growl rumbling in his throat. Taqqiq's fur bristled on his neck.

"He's a stupid badger-face," Toklo huffed.

"Listen," Ujurak said before Taqqiq could snarl a retort, "it does make sense to rest before we go on. Let's go down to the lake." He turned and began padding away down the rocks. "And after we've rested we can keep following the signs," he called.

Toklo couldn't believe what he'd just heard. Ujurak never agreed to leave the path when *he* suggested it. Not even if they'd been traveling for a whole day without stopping.

Taqqiq lifted his head and looked smugly at Toklo. Then he swung around and took off down the hill toward the lake. He was moving a lot faster now that he was getting his own way, Toklo noticed grumpily.

"Come on, Kallik!" Taqqiq called over his shoulder. "Race you there!"

"Not fair!" she cried. "You got a head start!" She took a step forward, then turned and lowered her head at Ujurak. "Thanks," she murmured. With a swish of her stubby tail, she began running down the hill with Lusa close on her heels.

"It won't take long," Ujurak said to Toklo. "It does make sense to eat something while we can. I always forget to look for that kind of thing when I'm figuring out where to go."

"Oh, that's reassuring," Toklo snorted. He followed the other bears down into the shade of the small wood. He could see Lusa with her head stretched up toward the branches, flexing her claws in a little dance. He guessed she was happy to be among trees again. The leaves whispered softly overhead, casting rippling puddles of shade and sunlight on the ground and across their backs.

It was much cooler once they were under the trees. Toklo made sure to check the bark of the trees for signs of any other grizzlies, but there were no claw marks that he could see. No other bears lived here. He wasn't surprised: The wood was too small to feed a full-grown brown bear for more than a half-moon, and there was nothing else around.

Twigs and fallen leaves crunched gently under his paws. The soft sound of water lapping called to him from the lake ahead, so he pushed his way through the undergrowth and padded down to the shore. Compared with Great Bear Lake, it was hardly more than a puddle: He could easily see to the far side, and the surface of the water was flat and shiny, not whipped into waves. Taqqiq and Kallik were already up to their bellies, splashing and rolling in the water. She cuffed a sparkling wave at her brother and he pounced on her.

"Look out, I'm going to get you!" he yelped.

He knocked her backward into the water and she wrapped her paws around him, rolling until she was on top and could pin him down.

"I win!" she cried.

"Never!" he spluttered, surging up out of the water and throwing her off. She landed with a splash, her mouth wide open with amusement.

Toklo watched them playing. He wished his brother Tobi had been strong and that they could have played like this. Then his mother would have loved them both the same, and they would all still be together. For a moment he could see why Kallik had traveled so far and for so long, looking for her brother. If he thought Tobi was still alive, he'd have kept on searching for him, too.

Then Taqqiq noticed Toklo watching them and he abruptly

stood up, shaking his fur so that droplets rained down on the water around him. He pawed at his nose and waded back to shore. Kallik floundered in the lake for a moment, waiting for him to jump on her again. Finally she sat up and noticed he was gone. Blinking as water streamed off her muzzle, she stared after her brother with a confused look.

Lusa barreled up to the lake and leaped in with all paws. "Whee!" she yelped, disappearing in a glittering wave of water. "It's amazing! It's perfect! It's *really cold*! Brrr! I'm getting out!" She charged back onto the shore and shook herself vigorously. Drops of water spattered Ujurak and Toklo.

"Hey," Toklo growled.

Lusa bounced around him like a jackrabbit. "Try it, Toklo! Your paws will feel so much better! And then so much colder! Brrrrr!"

"Are there fish in there?" Toklo called to Kallik. "Or did you great lumbering beasts scare them all off?"

"Oops." Kallik looked worried. "I didn't even think of that. Sorry!" She lifted her front paws one at a time as if there might be a fish hiding under one of them.

"Fish," Taqqiq scoffed. He lay down on a patch of grass under a tree, gazing at them all with narrow eyes. "They're barely a mouthful for a real bear. What we need is a fat seal."

"Why don't you go get one, then?" Toklo snapped. "If you're such a great hunter, surely you can find one?"

Taqqiq bared his teeth at Toklo, but Lusa nudged in between them, trying to draw Toklo's attention back to the lake and Kallik.

"Tell me more about seals," Lusa said to Kallik, who was wading back to the shore. "Do they taste like squirrels?"

"Not really. A seal is like a great big fish, only much better." Kallik padded onto the stones and let the water stream from her fur, which was noticeably whiter. "They're crunchy and chewy and delicious and I could eat nothing but seals for the rest of my life and be perfectly happy. I wish I could catch one for you! I bet you'd love the taste even more than blueberries."

"More than blueberries!" Lusa echoed. "Wow, they must be really tasty. Do you think there will be seals at the Place of Everlasting Ice?"

"Of course," Kallik said. "That's why it'll be the perfect home for us."

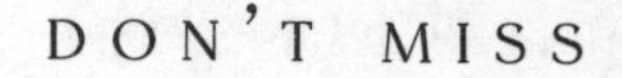

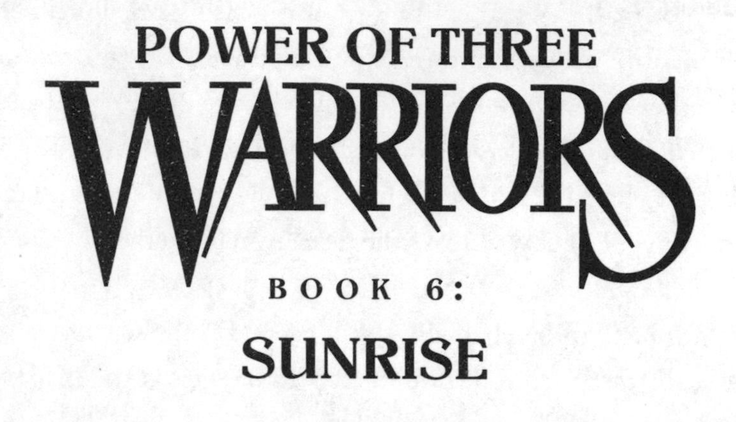

Dead bracken rustled beneath Lionblaze's paws as he stalked through the forest. Above the leafless trees the sky was dark and empty. Horror raised the hairs on the young warrior's neck and he shivered from ears to tail-tip.

This is a place which has never known the light of StarClan.

He padded on, skirting clumps of fern and nosing under bushes, but he found no sight or scent of other cats. *I've had enough of this,* he thought, tugging his tail free from a trailing bramble. Panic sparked in his mind as he stared at the darkness that stretched away between the trees. *What if I never find my way out of here?*

"Looking for me?"

Lionblaze jumped and spun around. "Tigerstar!"

The massive warrior had appeared around the edge of a bramble thicket. His tabby pelt shone in a strange light that did not come from moon or stars. Instead, it reminded Lionblaze of the sickly glow of fungus on dead trees.

"You've missed a lot of training," Tigerstar meowed, padding forward until he stood a tail-length from the ThunderClan warrior. "You should have come back sooner."

"No, I shouldn't!" Lionblaze blurted out. "I shouldn't have come here at all, and you should never have trained me. Brambleclaw isn't my father! You're not my kin!"

Tigerstar blinked once, but he showed no surprise, not even a flick of his ears. His amber eyes narrowed to slits, and he seemed to be waiting for Lionblaze to say more.

"You . . . you knew!" Lionblaze whispered. The trees seemed to spin around him. *Squirrelflight isn't the only cat who kept secrets!*

"Of course I knew." Tigerstar shrugged. "It's not important. You were willing enough to learn from me, weren't you?"

"But—"

"Blood isn't everything," Tigerstar snarled. His lip curled, showing the glint of sharp fangs. "Just ask Firestar."

Lionblaze felt his neck fur begin to bristle as fury coursed through him. "Firestar's a finer warrior than you ever were."

"Don't forget that he's not your kin, either," Tigerstar hissed softly. "There's no point defending him now."

Lionblaze stared at the dusk-lit warrior. *Does he know who my real father is?* "You knew all along that I wasn't Firestar's kin," he growled. "You let me believe a lie!"

Tigerstar twitched one ear. "So?"

Rage and frustration overwhelmed Lionblaze. Leaping into the air, he threw himself at Tigerstar and tried to push him over. He battered at the tabby warrior's head and shoulders, his claws unsheathed, tearing out huge clumps of fur. But the red haze of fury that filled his head made him clumsy, unfocused. His blows landed at random, barely scratching Tigerstar's skin.

The huge tabby tom went limp, letting himself drop to one side and hooking one paw around Lionblaze's leg to unbalance him. Lionblaze landed among the bracken with a jolt that drove the breath out of his body. A heartbeat later he felt a huge paw clamp down on his shoulders, pinning him to the ground.

"I've taught you better than that, little warrior," Tigerstar taunted him. "You're out of practice."

Taking a deep breath, Lionblaze heaved himself upward. Tigerstar leapt back and crouched a fox-length away, his tail lashing and his amber eyes burning.

"I'll show you who's out of practice," Lionblaze panted.

He forced his anger down, summoning a cold determination in which all the fighting moves he had ever learned were at the tips of his claws. When Tigerstar sprang at him, he was prepared; he dived forward and hurled himself underneath his opponent's belly. As soon as Tigerstar's paws hit the ground, Lionblaze whipped around and landed a couple of blows on the tabby tom's hindquarters before leaping away out of range.

Tigerstar spun to face him. "Better," he meowed, mockery still in his voice. "I have mentored you well."